GALLOWS ROAD

GALLOWS ROAD

A NOVEL

by

LISA HALL BROWNELL

Copyright 2022 by Lisa Hall Brownell
Published by Elm Grove Press, Old Mystic, Connecticut
www.elmgrovepress.org

Cover design and photography
by Georgiana Goodwin Design.

Paperback
ISBN – 978-1-940863-16-0
Library of Congress Control Number: 2021952230

Printed in the United States of America

ELM GROVE

CHAPTER I

THE GALLOWS

November 20, 1753
New London
The Colony of Connecticut

> *Mercy Bramble is my name,*
> *England is my nation.*
> *New England is my dwelling place,*
> *And Christ is my salvation.*

THE CHILDISH LINES I used to recite were nonsense to me now, neither truth nor lie, yet they kept repeating in my head as though the words could tether me to this world for another day.

I, Mercy Bramble, had looked ahead to a life of many days, not just one, but because of all of you, this was to be my last night on earth. You'd taken everything from me by then; you'd even taken my name and twisted it into something evil, a bramble weed that chokes other living things. Worst of all, you'd taken away my dream of ever knowing true freedom.

Like a doomed ship striking rocks, a northeast gale slammed the prison walls over and over; the wind had crossed many miles of cold Atlantic waters to reach New England's shores. I used to love the wind when I was a small girl. Now it was hard to believe that I was once such a person—that timid little Mercy who lived as a servant at the Holts' farmhouse and slept in their attic. Hearing the wind rage above her always made that little girl feel so safe from harm.

Now, as I crouched in the dark, without a single candle, I didn't know whether to weep like a child or suffer in silence like a martyr of the scriptures. What was the use in pretending that I was safe anymore?

After living as a prisoner for so many months I'd almost forgotten my former life as a servant. My never-ending duties from those days seemed pointless now, how I kept the hearth fire going from dawn to dusk, even in the blazing heat of summer. It was silly to think of it, but Faith—the sheriff's short, plump wife—had become a sort of servant to me, the actual prisoner. Occasionally she washed my garments and loaned me baggy things of her own while my ragged gown and shift were dried on bushes by the lane. Never had I felt so naked, knowing that all of you—especially you men—could see my clothing spread out on display.

I suspected that my youth and appearance gave Faith more cause to despise me than the crime with which I'd been charged or the sin I'd committed before that.

"It's colder than the devil's heart in here," she'd complained to me earlier that evening. Her tone was reproachful, as if I were a miserly innkeeper who kept my hearth cold and allowed my guests to shiver. When she'd said the same thing to me before, I'd always turned away, rolling my eyes. I always wondered why older people liked to repeat themselves. Did they think that we younger ones weren't really listening?

In months past I would have answered her with a touch of impudence, "So just let me out of here, you silly old hag. You won't have to wait on me anymore or mind this hearth." Or better yet, "Why don't you open a window so I don't have to smell your rotten stench anymore?"

There were no windows, of course, and I couldn't have summoned any strength to crawl through one anymore.

My life had been short, but I'd learned one lesson well: people were not always as they seemed to be and could change from day to night. That proved true again when Faith returned much later than usual one evening, carrying an armload of dry kindling to light my fire and, as always, a bowl of boiled potatoes.

"My husband's fast asleep already. Even a sheriff has to close his eyes sometime, but who knows what a prisoner could do when no one is looking?"

She lifted her apron and showed me a set of keys tucked into her bulging waistband.

"And look, the door is wide open. How careless of me!" She laughed like a nervous young girl, her small eyes darting away.

Yet I hadn't been able to walk through the door that night, suspecting that her offer had only been a kind of trick.

Once I'd been such a strong young woman, but I'd been fasting for days now; my strength was gone from both my body and mind. All earthly matters were fading, slipping away inch by inch, like a dry snakeskin.

Hope was growing thin and slipping away as well. I saw no way that I could escape into the darkness of the woodlands. The pathways leading away from New London and across rivers to the east and west were for others to travel, not for Mercy Bramble.

All of you had determined my route and chosen my destination. I would begin my journey the next morning, but I still had one long night ahead of me to reflect and to remember. And so, I did.

❧

I knew where they would set up the gallows because I'd been to that crossroads once before, only eight years earlier. Just outside the town's Common properties was a rugged pathway called Gallows Road; it branched to the west from a wider road that stretched north to Norwich. When I was nine, my first master, Mr. Holt, had taken me to a hanging with all of his family. Mrs. Holt was not yet sickly, so she came along that day as well.

The gallows were far enough away from the meetinghouse so as not to pollute its consecrated ground, yet near enough that townspeople wouldn't have to travel far to watch a hanging. Nothing drew so many people together as an execution did, far more than just a public whipping or branding. It wasn't uncommon to travel twenty or thirty miles to see such a spectacle.

For weeks afterward, whenever men or women could seize an idle moment at the tavern or mill, they'd talk of the most recent hanging. Then they'd exchange tales of executions many years past, saying things like "Were you there at the hanging of Indian Kate? So was I! Killed her baby, that one did."

I was a small girl, then, but I listened to everything. I hoarded any knowledge that I might need later for my own betterment or even my survival, should I ever be free and on my own.

Rocky ledges, rolling hills, and steaming swamps surrounded the gallows. The land had frustrated at least one man who'd tried to farm it. He later signed on a ship engaged in trading of slaves and was never seen again in the colony of Connecticut. No doubt he died of fever on a faraway shore, leaving his bitter and penniless widow to scrape by on the town dole.

Folks claimed they heard strange cries and laughter there at night. They saw lanterns that glowed and disappeared, leading wayfarers astray. Even during bright days of summer, the path to the gallows always lay in shadow. Over the swamps and pools, sullen mists lingered late into afternoon, long after any coastal fog had disappeared. Here black vines enslaved the trees, bending their lower branches to earth. Huge ravens built their nests in rocky ledges. Crying hoarsely to one another, they would sail out over the trees, seeking something recently dead.

A decade earlier, New Londoners might have met a wolf in a place such as this. Now hunters, hungry for a bounty, had driven most of those desperate creatures into wooded hills to the north.

On the day of the hanging, we children weren't allowed to leave my master Mr. Holt's wagon. I stayed on the wooden seat, because Mrs. Holt said that my shoes would be ruined in such deep mud. I'd surely be punished since they were my only pair.

From my perch above the rowdy throng, I had a clear view of the prisoner; they'd made him stand alone in a small wagon drawn by a huge horse. The wagon stopped under a long, thick branch that extended over the road.

All eyes were on the man.

He was a slave, owned by one of the colony's wealthiest men. To meet his Maker that day, the condemned man wore a muslin shirt, whiter than sails of ships cresting the horizon in Long Island Sound. His feet were bare, and in my childish mind, I wondered if he were being punished for losing his shoes.

No one tried to explain to me why he was condemned to die; all I heard was something about a stolen hog. They didn't hold trials in the meetinghouse for slaves or Indians. Nor did anyone preach a lengthy sermon or beg for salvation of the condemned man or woman.

The minister had barely uttered a few brief words when someone whipped the horse savagely. As horse and wagon surged ahead, a rope hoisted the man up as though he were weightless.

The crowd cheered but I was silent. According to those who

had bragged of seeing many hangings, it took an unusually long time for this man to die. To me—that small girl watching his final moments—it felt like an eternity before he grew still.

Mrs. Holt leaned over and put her mouth close to my ear. "That's what becomes of sinners, Mercy. They die in the hands of an angry God."

Eight years later, in my cell, I heard Mrs. Holt whisper those words to me once again, although she was long dead and buried.

※

"I've committed no crime, at least not knowingly."

That's what I'd told the judge and jury just two months before, and I repeated it aloud to myself that last night in jail.

Some of you might have found it curious or amusing that I sometimes spoke aloud to myself—even addressing myself by name at times—but that is what happens after being a prisoner for so long. To be honest, I would have laughed at such a person myself not too long ago.

A fortnight earlier I'd tried in vain to explain my situation to a scribe with slipping spectacles; the young man who was hired to record my so-called final statement. Many of you believed that an account of a wayward servant girl—one who had sinned against the laws of God and man—would serve as a warning to all who read it in the future.

"This is going to Timothy Greene's press to be printed, along with the Reverend's sermon," the scribe had mumbled, his eyes averted. "Perhaps Mr. Greene will give you a copy when the pages are bound."

He'd tried to impress me with his own importance, but I soon learned that he was just an apprentice like me. We were even the same age: seventeen years old. He'd written steadily, his forefinger growing black with ink, until he finally finished the job by candlelight.

I watched a title emerge word by word, like a slender serpent gliding behind the nib of his quill pen. Although I recognized my own name, it was hard to read the rest from where I sat; his paper was upside down and the words were long.

"Tell me what it says," I finally demanded.

"An Extraordinary Account of Several Occurrences and Remarks Concerning a Certain Mercy Bramble."

Then, to my great surprise, the apprentice handed me his pen. He pointed to the bottom of his page.

"Sign here to swear this is the truth."

Not knowing how to write, I made my mark: a bold X, larger than anything on his paper. Not long ago, I might have felt a wave of shame at such a moment, but not on that night.

Shame was something that all of you must live with not I. Shame was *your* inheritance.

"Save room for the signatures of the witnesses," the scribe had admonished. Then he went to fetch the sheriff and reverend from next door. They all came in together.

Before he'd signed, the sheriff had leaned in closer and squinted at the title.

"An extraordinary account, eh? I don't know what makes you so extraordinary if you don't even know how to write," he snickered.

But no one else dared to laugh at such a somber moment. Then the ledger snapped shut, and the men were gone, taking the candle as well.

No doubt they believed that they were taking my story with them, but I knew better. What the scribe had written was a useless exercise, as meaningless as the X that I'd signed to it. My story—Mercy Bramble's story—did not belong to the sheriff, scribe, reverend, judge, or jury. Nor did any of you own it. The story only belonged to *me*.

On the next Sunday, a member of the congregation had read my so-called final statement from the pulpit. Although I'd been invited to attend the service, I'd chosen to remain in my cell. Nor had I wanted to hear a sermon preached by my old enemy, that awful Reverend Jewett. He'd claimed it was for my benefit and for other "sinners and infidels."

At least that was what Faith had reported back to me that evening when she brought me a supper of cold codfish and potatoes. My statement had begun with rambling prayers, she said. Yet the congregation had hung on every word, even when those words became "nothing but gibberish."

That was how I knew that none of you had ever wished to hear the truth at my trial, only what would justify your actions.

That same night, Faith had told me, with a certain excitement, "You'll be the *first*, Mercy. The first woman in New London!"

I had to question her several times, because she too could speak gibberish. Then at last I understood: Mercy Bramble would be the first *white* woman to be executed in New London. Faith took a kind of ghoulish glee in telling me this fact, and it filled me with horror. How many other women—of black or red skin—had been brought to the gallows before me? What crimes had they committed? I wondered whether they were dumped in unmarked, paupers' graves or if loving family members had returned to the gallows tree after dark to retrieve their bodies for proper burial.

I doubted that I'd be laid to rest among the fine men and women in the town burial ground. Many of their tombstones were carved with round-eyed angels, heavenly beings who would carry them, clean of any sin, into their next life.

But who would cut me down from the tree? What would happen to my body?

My mother was unlikely to take on such a responsibility.

She'd left me at age seven, and though I'd begged her several times to take me back, she'd always refused.

Perhaps my first master, Mr. Holt, would come with his slow oxen and return me to a field where his wife and dead children lay under plain stones.

Or maybe it would be the kind Reverend Graves who collected my remains. After all, he was the man who'd finally baptized me and told me that he pitied me for "falling an early and easy prey to lust."

Then, after a silence, he'd added in barely a whisper, "Perhaps if you had not been so fair to look upon…"

He'd let his voice trail away, but I'd heard sufficient love and kindness there.

Had I viewed myself through the reverend's eyes that day, would I have seen a ruddy young farm girl, a hardened criminal, or a pale, delicate saint? He told me that my wide-set blue eyes, with their flax-colored lashes, were as innocent as a child's. But I knew there was nothing childlike about my round breasts and narrow waist, features that drew looks from even the most pious of men.

The Reverend Graves was a man as well. In our long hours together, he'd taught me many things about the Good Book, yet I'd learned far more than that from him. We kept a secret between us, a secret as deep as one that still bound me to my second master.

Now I conjured another scene in my mind. A man in a hooded cloak silently approached my lifeless body, still swaying beneath the tree. He cut me down, put me in a coffin of smooth white pine, and took me away in a carriage drawn by two fine black horses with silky manes. But where did he take me? I couldn't see beyond that part of my dream. It was as though the mist from the river had closed around my vision.

The cell door banged, and for an instant, fear seized my breath.

"Everyone's coming to see you tomorrow," announced Faith, whose sudden reappearance had interrupted my reveries. "There won't be a soul in the streets or fields."

"How many, do you think?"

"You'll just have to count them tomorrow."

That was such an ordinary word she'd used—tomorrow— but soon I would never speak it again.

Realizing I had no need for sleep, I lay awake all night. At last, a new day finally dawned: the twenty-first of November, 1753.

I heard the rain coming down. Through a crack in the wall, I could see that the wind had finally torn any remaining leaves from the huge oaks surrounding the Commons.

A few nights ago, I'd dreamed that the wind would do my bidding, as if by ancient witchcraft. It snatched up my five accusers, tore away their black shawls and prayer books, and carried the women far out to sea to be drowned.

It was a terrible thought, but one that I allowed myself, since none of those women had shown any mercy for me. Nor had any of you.

Now I had nothing to do but brush out my long hair. As a final act of defiance, I'd decided not to wear my white linen cap that morning. Custom always had dictated that it must hide my locks, keeping them cleaner but without any fancy style. How often I'd cursed that cap, feeling choked by its button at my throat.

Perhaps I'd always known that I should protect my own neck.

Washing my face with water from a wooden bowl, I remembered my baptism day on an afternoon not long ago. Many of you had promised that receiving the sacrament and learning

God's laws would save me; I'd fought so long and hard to make that happen. Before that battle to be baptized, my only weapon had been *endurance*—my friend and fellow servant, Cate had taught me all about that—but now she was a free woman and I was not.

The washbowl water was cool. As it ran down my neck and under my gown, I shivered as though a lover's hands had passed over me.

Soon Sheriff Christophers would be coming with two reverends and a wagon driver. Rain thundered down as if it would never stop, as if it would rain for all eternity.

I heard my own voice ask, "Is it too late?"

CHAPTER II
APPRENTICESHIP

"Come when you are called, and do what you are bidden."
—THE MINISTER COTTON
MATHER'S ADVICE TO SERVANTS

MY CHILDHOOD WAS hard, but I never had enough hardness of spirit to accept its deprivations. Whenever I heard adults talk of children who had been "spoiled" by too much affection and indulgence, I yearned to be spoiled myself.

Time and time again, my elders told me, "You're very fortunate, Mercy. Very blessed." Had they known what a great sinner I would turn out to be, they might have treated me differently, even then.

My mother, Mary Bramble, worked as a seamstress to feed the two of us. She told everyone we met that she was a widow, her husband having died on shipboard when they crossed the Atlantic from England.

I spent the first seven years of my life on cold, wooden floors clinging to my mother's rough gowns and aprons as she worked. Her skirts always smelled of other people's fireplaces, other people's warm dinners, but as long as I could be near her, then that was my home. Although some might have called her a plain woman—her face wore the cares of someone twice her age—to me she was very beautiful.

For whatever reason, my mother never was inclined to show affection, but she made an exception one time when I fell ill with a fever. That night she allowed me lie in her lap while she stroked my hair and repeated, "Poor Mercy, poor little Mercy. You never asked to be born."

Because we lived from day to day, seldom staying more than a week in one place, my mother said she had no time to take me to church services or to educate me. She did teach me one lesson by her example, however: "Work hard or marry well."

All of those masters and mistresses who hired her might as well have been nameless; they seldom spoke to the small girl carrying a sewing bag or parts of a spinning wheel. I was expected to be useful and could knit a fairly good stocking by the time I was five.

The kitchens were always cold in winter—a bowl of water could freeze over, only a few yards from the fire—and stifling in the summer. Great cooking fires burned no matter how hot the day, while flies swarmed on food and droned against the oilcloth or diamond panes of the windows. Even a very scrupulous house-keeper couldn't get rid of the stink of rancid grease, unwashed bodies, and soiled babies.

After the master and mistress of the house had eaten, we often would share a meager meal with the servants. My mother sometimes whispered to me, "We are better than them, Mercy, but we must eat too."

If I were lucky, the mistress of the house would grant me a precious hour with her own children, allowing us to play with simple toys like hoops or dolls. Kites were my favorite playthings;

entrusting themselves to the winds, they rose above the bonds of earth and sometimes broke free. I liked to imagine that I could sail through the sky with them and land safe and sound in a better place.

Courage like that comes naturally to a child, but time itself can steal it away. All too soon the games ended, the toys were taken away, and my mother decided to sign me as an apprentice to Mr. William Holt for seven years.

I didn't cry on that winter morning when my mother left me with Mr. Holt and his family in a dark, drafty farmhouse two miles outside town. Of course, I longed to cry, to stand on that doorstep and howl until my face was red, but at seven years old, I already knew that tears would bring a whipping and an empty bowl that evening.

The evening before she left me, my mother had tried to make me believe that my apprenticeship was a great privilege.

"We're so blessed to receive the charity of Mr. Holt. He's a highly respected member of the Church."

I was too young to ask her why I'd never been to church services . Nor did I know what it meant to be baptized or why it was of such importance to a person's lot in life.

Mr. Holt would be like the father I'd never had, my mother explained. He would take complete control of my physical and spiritual welfare, my body and soul.

"As his apprentice you will obey all of his lawful commands; in return, he will give you food, lodging, clothing and proper schooling so that you can learn to read and write."

All I understood was that I was being left among strangers.

Looking back across the distance of many years, I would see what really happened on that morning. On the day that my mother had left me, the soft, sweet Mercy had left as well. Like someone playing hide-and-seek, that innocent little girl never came back again. Perhaps a new Mercy had already begun to form deep inside me, someone who did not hide in silence but who stood her ground and raised her own voice to be heard. Such a great change takes time and knowledge, however, and I had very little time to myself or any proper schooling.

The Holts expected me to work fourteen hours a day, six days a week and sometimes seven. In all seasons I was a scullery maid, laundress, cook, cowherd, and sometimes a farmhand as well. Like all children, I was taught to obey, but as a servant I was expected to live and breathe obedience.

"When will my mother return?" I asked Mrs. Holt after several weeks had passed.

"That should not be your concern," she'd reply. "Your mother cannot take care of you, Mercy."

"But she always cared for me when I was small."

"That doesn't matter now. Every child must to learn to bend her will, whether or not she is a servant. To indulge you would be cruel."

Sometimes I dreamed about running away to find my mother, but the sheriff would have tracked me down and returned me to Mr. Holt. That was not so different from how they hunted down runaway Negroes and Indians, some of who were slaves or servants hereabouts. Knowing what I learned later in life, I doubt that I would have received much kinder treatment than they did.

After that winter day when my mother abandoned me on the kitchen step, I'd see her only once or twice a year. The Holts would pay her a few shillings to come and sew plain gowns for Mrs. Holt and her daughters or to spin wool after the sheep were sheared in spring.

When it came time to send her off by oxcart or sleigh to the next household wanting her services, I would grab her gown or coat and plead with her.

"Please, *please* mother, take me with you so we can be together! I promise I'll work hard and do whatever you tell me. I won't even eat much."

She would tug her skirt away from me.

"I'm sorry, Mercy, but I'm a poor widow and cannot afford to keep you. In six months, I may see you again or whenever the Holts need me. Now let go of me and get back to your chores."

As months turned to years, I had no choice but to accustom myself to my new household, even though I would never be a family member.

The Holts had five living children and four more buried on the hillside. When I arrived, the oldest, William Jr., was twenty, the youngest, an infant girl only three months old. In the evening, the family gathered around a long table board in their front room while Mr. Holt read scriptures. Another apprentice, red-haired Hannah, always sat with me on milking stools in the corner; I would pretend that she was my sister.

Every Sunday, before first light was breaking, the family dressed in their best clothes and rode in their wagon to the meetinghouse. They didn't return until evening time, after sitting through two long services and Reverend Adams's sermon. Back then I didn't know that their attendance was decreed by law. Had it been in the olden days, the church doors would have been locked from the outside to keep them all in there.

"You must stay behind because you've never been baptized, Mercy," Mrs. Holt explained. "Only those of us who are members of the Church can attend services."

Even if labor was forbidden on the Sabbath, someone still needed to feed and water the animals on the Lord's Day. The Holts owned many creatures: six cows, three pigs and many piglets, ten sheep, and a large flock of chickens. My favorite was an old mare, Rosie, and I loved to gaze into her huge, dark eyes, stroke her dappled nose, and feel her moist breath upon my hand. I fancied that Rosie loved me in return.

At first, Hannah worked alongside me, but one day she fell ill and was sent away to the smallpox house at the mouth of the river. No one told me that she had died there until many months later. Maybe I would have grieved for her more had I seen her final days.

Without Hannah, I found myself all alone on Sundays. On those days, the farm became my vast kingdom of solitude.

Made bold by the stillness of the deserted farm, deer grazed by the woods. Sea gulls, blown inland from the coast, wheeled overhead with strident cries. At even greater heights, hawks glided through the heavens, far above the lowly, quarreling gulls and supremely free of all earthly ties. I tried to imagine how they would have viewed our miniature world below.

Sometimes, silence roared like the surf of the sea. Then a reckless spirit would fill my small body, but I was uncertain how far I would go to test the limits of my courage. The seacoast was only two miles away, but it might as well have been two hundred. I'd never been allowed to go there, to feel soft sand and cool water on my feet. Some days, if the wind was from the south, and I could smell the salt air, I'd start to walk towards the beach. About halfway there, however, I always turned back, not wishing to be caught out wandering alone.

Often, I'd take a branch and scratch my mark in dust or in snow on the frozen pasture pond, simply because I liked the look of it. I always signed my name with a simple cross—the same mark that Mr. Holt notched into his cows' ears so that he could tell them apart from others grazing on the Commons.

❧

Not going to church may have marked me as an outsider, but it didn't bother me as much as not learning how to read or write like other children did. There were no schools nearby, of course, and only the wealthy had private tutors.

According to the terms of my apprenticeship, Mr. Holt was supposed to teach me my lessons; he was slow to fulfill that duty, however. About six months after joining the household, I asked my master if I could join his children in their lessons so I could learn to read and write.

He was only half willing to comply.

"Women must learn to read their Maker's book so that they can live in a godly manner, but they have no need of writing," he had told me.

"Why not, sir?" I asked, but he waved his hand to dismiss me.

"They don't need to sign contracts as men do or write important books or sermons."

"And don't forget Eve," Mrs. Holt chimed in from her seat at her spinning wheel. "Eve went seeking knowledge and what a terrible mess that made for everyone else."

I didn't like the restrictions Mr. Holt was imposing but was ready to accept them if I had to for now.

"So just teach me to read, then," I conceded.

Secretly, I vowed to learn to write as well as any boy or man, perhaps better, but I knew I'd have to pursue that desire on my own.

Eventually my master sat me down for my first reading lesson. For an hour he left me waiting in a dark corner while his own children made use of their precious books and writing slates.

"I don't want to share with a *servant*," they often complained.

Because I had to wait my turn, it took me a full year to

learn the alphabet, but I memorized it well, both forward and backward.

What little I knew of the greater world I learned from strangers: the wayfarers who stopped by in all seasons, often for a pint from the Holts' cider mill. When a traveler brought a newspaper from faraway Boston or New York, William Jr. would read the news aloud. I hung on every word about shipwrecks, drowning, suicides, and robberies. William Jr. also read reports of births, deaths, marriages, and notices seeking the return of runaway slaves.

Soon I began saving those old newspapers so they wouldn't be burned. I'd hide them under my straw bedding and try to decipher words by myself late at night. The letters of the alphabet were like old friends to me by that time. Each had its own peculiar character—from the sturdy A, with its practical little shelf, to the writhing, impractical Z—but I couldn't make sense of whole words and sentences without someone's help.

It frustrated me that my reading lessons had ended so soon and that neither Mr. Holt nor William Jr. would make more time for me. They said that they were far too busy; I couldn't argue with them about that. The year-round farmwork was more than even a large family like the Holts could handle. Many other neighbors—and sometimes their servants or slaves—came to help harvest flax in June or pick apples in September.

Every autumn, without fail, Mrs. Holt's two sisters arrived for several days to make candles for the winter. For me, candle making was a hateful chore, even worse than the monthly laundry day with its burning lye soap. Mrs. Holt's quilting bees went on for a week or more; to make room for the visiting women, I'd give up my bed and sleep in the barn close to the mare, Rosie. It was more of an adventure for me than a hardship.

Peddlers came by the farm in those days as well. The sun-burned Hugo Moreaux was dressed head-to-toe in patched leather, even in summer's heat. He traveled a circuit of hundreds of miles with tin trunks full of spices, medicines, and other stuff.

The sound of bells on Hugo's wagon would bring me hurrying to the roadside, trying not to spill a drop from a tankard of beer I had for him. He'd drain it all in one long gulp, telling me he had to fill his hollow leg. As soon as he'd handed me the empty mug, I'd beg him for any news of my mother. All he could tell me was what she'd bought from him—lengths of calico cloth and other such things—and that she'd bartered hard for every penny.

Hugo always remembered anyone who'd ever bought his wares, but he never revealed much about himself.

"I'm half Yankee, half Indian, and half French," the old man had told me once. He always had a gift for each of the Holt children—some marbles or a top for spinning.

The peddler never gave me anything from his cart in those days—that would come many years later—but he taught me to sing all the words to "Billy Boy." For years it was the only song I knew; I loved a certain part about a young girl who could bake a cherry pie and wouldn't leave her mother. How wonderful it would be to live with my own mother again, I thought.

"You'll meet your "Charming Billy" someday," old Hugo had promised me one afternoon. "What a lucky lad he'll be to have the likes of you."

Would my suitor be as kind as he was handsome? Would he take me away from servitude and be "the joy of my life?"

I'd even tried to imagine what it would feel like to be kissed by a young man, but affection was something missing in my world. Every night my mistress gave each of her children a goodnight kiss and an embrace; in all those years, no one ever had an embrace for me.

Looking back to that time, I swore that this had left a hollow place inside of me.

When I was eleven, Mrs. Holt told me surprising news: my mother had just been married.

"Her new husband's a shipwright named Elisha Bunce. What a fine new home he's built for her a few miles north on the Great River. Mr. Holt said it took a dozen men to raise the roof."

"So, does she have room for me, now?" I asked eagerly.

"Don't be *selfish*, child. You should rejoice for your mother and thank God for His blessings."

"I'm glad for her, but I wish to join her now."

"You are still bound to us, Mercy."

After that, I didn't see my mother for nearly two years; I almost forgot what she looked like, having nothing to remind me, not even a lock of hair. Yet every single day I still hoped that she would return for me and bring me to her new home. I even dreamed of having a real bed, my own bed, and perhaps even my own room with a little window through which to look out through lace curtains.

For many years I'd made my bed on the lid of a narrow wood box by the Holts' kitchen door, curling up under a sheepskin every night. When I was thirteen and no longer childish in form or size, Mrs. Holt saw that I'd outgrown that wood box and allowed me to sleep under the eaves in their attic. Late at night I'd prepare a bed warmer to heat all of the beds in the household, pushing a heavy copper pan of hot coals in circles beneath each quilt. Afterward I was too tired to reheat the pan and carry it up the ladder to warm my own cold bed.

In spring, I loved the sound of rain as it streamed over the roof, but I dreaded thunder and lightning storms. I imagined that hideous goblins and demons from hell were dancing with delight while fireballs rolled off the roof.

My demons may have been imaginary, but the fireballs were all too real.

One night in front of the hearth, Mrs. Holt told me about The Awful Thunderclap that had struck the first meetinghouse in the middle of a service.

"The lightning knocked forty parishioners senseless to the floor," she said. "It killed a man in mid-prayer."

"Why didn't God save him?" I wanted to know. "If the man was praying for forgiveness and salvation, why didn't he receive any?"

Mrs. Holt hadn't even lifted her eyes from her stitching.

"All catastrophes such as that are God's way of punishing the wicked," she explained. "That's what brings about great storms and plagues, and in my grandmother's time, attacks by Indian savages. The Indians had to be punished too, because they were infidels, worshippers of Satan, whom God would never save."

It sounded as if my mistress was done with the subject, but I persisted with my questions.

"But was it truly their fault if they didn't even know who God was?"

Before she could answer, Mr. Holt had the final word as he lit a lantern for his evening watch in town.

"Don't be impudent, Mercy. Only the chosen few receive God's gift of salvation, but we all must strive ceaselessly to be worthy of that gift," Mr. Holt declared. "He is the light of the world. He sees *all* that we do."

Then my master disappeared into the night to make his rounds.

I wasn't comforted to think that God was watching us all so closely; I also feared that my lack of absolute faith might draw His anger, bringing on another catastrophe like The Awful Thunderclap.

Sure enough, only two nights later, it looked as though my fears might come true. Shaking the dome of heaven, a ferocious storm bore down on the farm just after midnight. A lightning bolt struck so near to me that I couldn't tell if it were inside or outside of the attic; my hair almost stood upright, and my body trembled as though all my bones were melting.

There was a long silence. I wondered, was it over? Then, all of a sudden, a single explosion shook the house to its foundation, ending with a long, shuddering groan.

William Jr. shouted to wake the household, but everyone had already jumped out of their beds. Tumbling downstairs and rushing outside, they were almost blinded by a roaring inferno.

A lone tree by the well was ablaze, like a torch ignited by an unseen hand.

Its thick trunk and short limbs had always reminded me of a portly old man, angrily waving his arms at me. Now, engulfed in flames, the dead tree was the most beautiful sight I'd ever seen. Sizzling, red sparks shot out against the sky, even as the rain fell.

The next morning, as I examined a scorched circle of ashes on the ground, I picked up all that was left of the tree: just one smooth, black splinter, no larger than a man's forefinger. A shiver went through me, as though I were holding the very power of heaven in my hand. I hurried to hide my relic in a secret place in the attic; whenever I looked at it, I was convinced that the burning tree had been a sign. Perhaps my life might hold something else in store for me, something not ordinary at all but quite extraordinary.

Such thoughts were just idle daydreams, because I had neither power nor free will at that point in my life.

Then unexpectedly, when I was about to turn fourteen years old, Mr. Holt told me something that took my breath away.

"Your mother has sent word she is coming tomorrow."

My spirits soared so high that I could scarcely breathe, let alone speak.

"She has business to attend to, now that your seven years of service are almost done," he continued.

I didn't fully understand what he meant, but nothing could tarnish the shining joy that his news gave to me.

"Am I to go home with her? May I pack my things?"

"I don't know, Mercy. That will be her choice, not yours. You must be patient."

The next morning, I heard hooves against stones on the pathway, followed by a distinctive clang of iron against stone: someone had just tied his mount at the granite hitching post. I was stunned to see my mother astride a beautiful dappled grey horse—I did not know she could ride in that manner. She looked older and somewhat heavier, perhaps more well fed. She was well dressed in a fashionable riding habit with silk shoes.

Escorting her was her husband, Elisha, who stood by the horses. I could tell from one glance at his face that he wished to be elsewhere.

"Let us be quick about it, Mary," he ordered. "I have other matters to attend to in the shipyard this morning."

Forgetting that Mrs. Holt had told me to stay in the house, I raced outside, my feet barely touching the ground.

"Mother! You've come! And is this my new father?"

I bent my knees and lowered my head in curtsy to him.

She did not answer but looked right past me to Mr. Holt who was summoning his two visitors into the house.

"Fetch Mr. Bunce a mug of beer," he ordered me.

Trembling with excitement, I went to the kitchen to pour beer into a pewter mug, then carried it to the front room where all three had seated themselves.

"Set it down on the table and leave us alone, Mercy," my master said.

"But I wish to stay, sir."

"I apologize for this outburst," Mr. Holt said quickly to his guests, who both sat ramrod straight in their chairs. "As you see, the girl can be obstinate and stubborn. She needs a heavy hand to rule her."

Mr. Holt stood up and pointed to the door. I'd never heard him so angry.

"You will go out to the barn, Mercy, and stay there until Mrs. Holt comes to fetch you. Is that understood?"

I backed away, left through the kitchen door, and retreated to the barn. Hours must have passed, but I had no way to mark time; it was dark when Mrs. Holt came to fetch me back to the house.

She told me that my mother had signed a new contract of indenture for me, and I was to remain their servant until I was twenty-one. Until that age, I wouldn't be permitted to marry. Had I known then what would happen a few years later, reaching the age of twenty-one would have been seemed like the promise of a ripe old age.

All I could think of to say to Mrs. Holt was: "Perhaps I might be dead."

Seeing my distress, my mistress tried to calm me by showing me a paper my mother had just signed.

"See, that X is her legal signature."

The terrible letter X dripped excess ink like a wound drips blood; it would haunt my dreams for many nights afterwards. My mother couldn't read or write either.

※

When I was fifteen, something else happened that changed the course of my life; Mrs. Holt went up to her bed one mid-day and didn't come down again. We heard her uncontrolled coughing fits throughout the house. After a week with no improvement,

Mr. Holt sent for the doctor. The physician came at last to examine her.

"She has lung fever," he pronounced. "No one has a cure."

Death was in no hurry to claim my mistress, however; I came to accept the sight of her sunken cheeks, her ribs clearly visible when we washed her body. Perhaps she could endure forever in such a state, I thought, clinging to her life's ragged remains.

Then, suddenly, and without a sign, poor Mrs. Holt just slipped away.

It's strange how, years later, I could still remember every detail of that day. It was autumn, and I'd gone to pick a pumpkin to mash for bread when I heard Mr. Holt calling the children into the house. I found them all seated together, heads bowed in prayer, faces streaked with tears.

Their father read in a clear voice from the Scripture.

"God's will is done. Praise be to God," Mr. Holt intoned as he closed the Bible.

An hour later my master rode into town alone and hired a man to carve his wife's headstone and footstone. When he returned, he found the family at their evening meal, the food untouched and cold on their plates.

"He only knows how to carve two images—either a skull or a cherub. I chose the angel for your mother."

They buried her the next day with her head to the west and her feet to the east, so that when Judgment Day dawned, as it must for all of us, Mrs. Holt could stand up from her grave and face the rising sun.

Bad things happen in threes, or so my mother used to say. Three days later, my darling horse, Rosie, stepped into a rabbit hole and broke her front leg. Within minutes, ravens had gathered in the trees—waiting.

William Jr. was a gentle lad, but that afternoon he had to act as quickly as a cold-blooded killer. After slitting Rosie's dappled grey throat, he hurled a large stone against her head with all his force, breaking her skull.

For days, I tried not to look at a wide stain from her blood on the ground where I had to walk to reach the garden. I'm ashamed to say it, but it was far easier for me to grieve for the mare than it was for Mrs. Holt; perhaps some of the tears I shed for Rosie were really for my mistress.

Time did not stand still after these deaths in the family, however, and I wondered what would be the third misfortune. Mr. Holt needed another draft horse to pull the plow; he'd recently heard that his half-crippled neighbor, Mr. Bryan Palmes, had a fine black mare he was willing to sell.

"I've decided to trade you to another household," my master told me one morning as he finished a bowl of ale with his bread.

"But am I not supposed to be here seven years?" I asked in disbelief.

He shook his head.

"That is a matter to be handled between Mr. Palmes and myself. Pack your things, Mercy. The girls will help you get ready."

The next morning, I was loaded in the family wagon. I'd tied up all of my belongings in a shawl: a few garments, my precious scraps of newspaper, and the burned piece of the lightning tree.

The Palmes lived in a stone house on a steep, grassy hilltop a mile to the east. The first thing that I noticed was how their roof sagged between two chimneys; a barn behind it sagged in exactly the same way. The sight reminded me of two swayback nags whose heads were lowered in deep grass to graze. A strange odor lingered around the property. It probably came from a rubbish heap behind the barn, but on that day, I thought that it must have been the smell of hopelessness itself.

Before he went to collect the mare, Mr. Holt told me to step off the wagon on a footpath leading to the house.

"There's the way in," he said, nodding to a heavy door that had been painted red with ox blood. It was ajar just a few inches.

I hesitated, stalling for a little time.

"I'd be thankful if you'd tell my mother where I've gone to, so she won't fret the next time she comes out your way."

"She no longer works as a seamstress now that she is married," he replied. He touched his hat brim, however, and promised to send word to her through a man at the sawmill who knew her husband.

I wondered if that would ever happen.

"We all wish you well, Mercy. But my children will be better off with the big, strong Irishwoman I've hired. She can take on more of a load around the house than you and work our fields as well."

I searched for any words.

"Well, I'm much indebted to you and to Mrs. Holt, God rest her soul," I managed to respond.

Although I was grateful to the Holts, I was more terrified about what might await me beyond that ox-blood door—and equally determined not to show it. How was I to know that one day I'd be called upon to show that same fearlessness as I faced the unknown? But that day was still years away.

I'd heard that my new master was part cripple and was curious to see if that was true. Mr. Bryan Palmes didn't ask me to enter his house right away, however. He met with Mr. Holt who handed over my certificate of bondage, the paper that would keep me in his service until I was twenty-one; I could not read its contents, but I knew that it forbade me from selling or damaging any of my master's property, from committing fornication, or entering into a contract of marriage while in his service.

Close by, on the other side of the window, I saw Mr. Palmes writing; he crossed out Mr. Holt's signature on the document and added his own with a great flourish.

Observing my new master seated at his desk, I saw no defect in his frame, nor any sign that he had a bad leg. He was a well-made man with raven-black hair, fine white teeth, and dark eyes. Most women would have stolen a second glance at him, but this was the first time any man had aroused my curiosity in such a way.

I strained to hear what the two masters were saying, but a thick glass windowpane muted their words.

Soon Mr. Holt was steering the wagon back down the stony hill, the black mare following behind on a rope. Her belly was great with foal and swung from side to side as she walked among the stones.

"At least Mr. Holt has made a good bargain. He's traded me for two creatures, not just one," I consoled myself. I did not know my own worth back then.

As soon as I turned around, I saw that a servant was gesturing silently, beckoning me to enter. She placed her hand on her ample bosom and patted it twice.

"I'm Cate. You are Mercy?"

She was dressed plainly, just as I was. Only the long braid down her back—and her beaded moccasins—hinted to me that her ancestors had been those Mrs. Holt called "savages." There was nothing savage about Cate, however.

"I know how to read and write," she told me right away. "I've been baptized too. A good Christian woman."

I had an impression that two different women lived in her body. Wiry strands of an old woman's grey hair escaped her braid—pulled so tight that I wondered if it hurt her—but her skin was as plump and smooth as a child's. Her face held another contradiction: her mouth was frowning deeply while her eyes appeared to be laughing about something.

Within a few short weeks she would be combing my hair each night, teasing me, and calling me names like "Little Sister" and "Pretty Girl," but on that morning she was still a stranger in a strange house. I did not fully trust her yet.

Cate made sure that I knew what that needed to be done. Speaking as little as possible—saying only "look here"—she showed me the hearth, broom closet, linen shelf, and rubbish heap. Next came the animal pens and barn. Then she told me how old Mrs. Palmes, Bryan's mother, liked her bread and tea served, and where extra stores of food were hidden, including a few jars of wild honey. I would steal a taste of it just as soon as an opportunity arose.

Even with Cate's help, it took a while for me to find my bearings in this new household. My elderly mistress appeared more dead than alive under her lace cap. Her son, the widower Bryan Palmes, usually kept to himself at his desk; sometimes he disappeared for days on mysterious errands. Had anyone asked me about my master's character, I would have said that I knew almost nothing about the man.

Looking back, how I wished that my ignorance on the subject of Bryan Palmes had continued; but that knowledge would come later in my story.

I missed the large, noisy household kept by the Holts. No one appeared to be in charge at the Palmeses but Cate and her husband, the Negro slave Coffey. He was nearly twice her height and had to duck his head to move beneath the low ceiling beams. Even when he had room to stretch up tall, he seemed bent down by an invisible burden, anticipating that he would have to bend down again soon.

Cate warned me that he was blind in the left eye, and never

to approach him on his bad side, but I'd already noticed that flaw in him. A white scar appeared to float in the center of his eye like a piece of boiled egg in water.

I was accustomed to taking my orders from Mrs. Holt a dozen times a day. Now I had to seek Cate and Coffey's instruction on everything, at every hour; if I didn't ask for direction, then I had nothing to do. And to do nothing was the greatest sin of all. In truth, it felt as though we servants were masters of the farm, while its true owners—mother and son—were phantom tenants who drifted through their days in silence.

I soon realized that I was adrift in this Purgatory as well, no longer a girl and not yet fully a woman.

Seven long years awaited me like a prison sentence. If I couldn't escape, perhaps I would find something to make my life more endurable.

❦

Bryan Palmes had been part-crippled all of his life, some twenty-eight years in all, or nearly twice the span of my own lifetime. As months rolled past, I learned parts of his story from different people: Cate, servants on neighboring farms, and even my new mistress. The old Mrs. Palmes spoke without knowing what she was saying one night when she had a fever.

Still, there were many missing pieces to Bryan's tale. Several years later, as I sat in my jail cell, I tried to piece it all together in my mind like small scraps sewn into a single quilt. How I wanted to understand this man who had so much power over me, who drew me to him from the first day that I was left on his doorstep.

Some claimed that Mrs. Palmes had dropped her infant son from a wagon when a wheel fell off its axle. Others said that Bryan was a bastard child of a servant woman who had thrown him on the rocky banks of a stream when he wasn't an hour old, leaving him for dead. A day later, the elder Mr. Palmes and his wife were passing over a bridge on their way home from the meetinghouse when they heard Bryan's cries, and found him still alive.

The second story had more of a ring of truth to it, though no one, not even talkative Cate, would tell me the name of the baby's real mother or where she went.

The elder Palmes, who were childless and no longer young, lived in the small stone farmhouse on a hillside crossed by tumbledown stonewalls. Mr. Palmes had inherited the property from his older brother, who had outlived all his own children. Their cows were close to starving, mainly because old Mr. Palmes kept them in a small pasture instead of putting them out to graze on the wide, grassy Commons with his neighbors' cattle. I figured that he hadn't trusted man or beast—neither his dishonest neighbors nor his own wandering cows.

The couple found a servant who was already nursing a child for another family—the mother had died in her labor—and hired her as a wet nurse until the baby was old enough to drink goat's milk. Mrs. Palmes, who thought the baby was a gift from the Lord, named him Bryan.

As she told me in her delirium years later, "Not a week went by that someone hereabouts wasn't burying an infant, and yet this one was alive. God must have a plan for him, I told my husband."

She said that her spouse argued long and hard for giving Bryan away or binding him out as a servant.

"He even looked at the baby's jet-black hair and wondered if he was a Spaniard or an Indian child," she confided in a hushed voice. "But I would always point to Bryan's blue eyes and that would settle any doubts," she declared with a small smile of satisfaction.

"Then his eyes turned a deep brown, but I never mentioned it again."

When at last the baby tried to take his first steps, he stumbled, then stumbled again; his parents saw that he would be lame in his left leg and could never perform hard labor. Finally, he'd learned to walk on his own, doing so with a graceless, uneven gait. But no defect is small in the eyes of the able-bodied. Neighbors would forever call him the Cripple Bryan Palmes. That was how the Holts had described him; before I'd met the man, I'd always pictured a deformed old man with a hunchback.

Although Bryan couldn't stand for very long without a wooden walking stick for support, he was otherwise well formed. His shoulders were broad and muscled, his waist narrow, and his hips slim. Ringlets of long, raven-black hair framed handsome features that were free of any smallpox scars. Unlike so many men, who suffered from loss of teeth, Bryan's shone pure white when he laughed.

Any observer—man or woman—might have found a certain beauty in that face. I even fancied that our Creator had taken extra time with him, making only one of his kind, then adding one imperfection to make him humble. But I dare say that the Creator failed in that respect, for my new master had far more pride than humility, even as a young boy.

On Sunday mornings, Mrs. Palmes liked to make a single braid at her son's neck and tie it with a black silk ribbon. He held his head with the haughty bearing of a young prince and scorned anyone who dared to pity him.

In the saddle, Bryan was the equal of any horseman. He could ride any horse, even bareback, as a savage might do. Neighbors would see him grinning like a madman astride his mount as it tore over the meadows, flinging clods of turf behind its hooves, and frightening their livestock. Often, he would accompany his father on rides as far as Norwich or Saybrook where they would hear a sermon or watch a ship launching, a whipping, or even a hanging.

Although he was a good marksman, Bryan couldn't serve in the militia like all young men were required to do, so at first, he devoted himself to the needs of the family farm. Later he began breeding and selling some of the finest horses in the colony, sending them to Barbados and Surinam by ship. He was continuing to profit in that way at the time when I came to live at the farm.

"Why do they need so many horses in the West Indies?" I asked Coffey one day, after he and my master had taken four fine horses to the town docks. "What purpose do they serve there?"

"They be worked to death turning wheels at the sugar plantations," Coffey told me mournfully.

After that, I was always sad to see the horses led away but shed my tears in secret.

My master also profited by his mastery with a quill pen— how I envied that precious gift of writing when I came to live under his roof. He would draw up wills, deeds of sale, and other legal documents for those who needed them. The lines that issued from his pen were beautiful and extravagant; he loved curls and flourishes, and men would pay him more just for the look of it. Nor was there any better mapmaker to be found. The demand for his skills brought him far afield in Connecticut and Rhode Island and put money in a strongbox beneath the floorboards of his solitary bedchamber.

The more he cultivated these other interests, the less love he had for farming.

"The soil is ungrateful," he often complained to Cate and Coffey, or to any inquiring neighbor who asked about his crops.

But the land wouldn't let him go.

When Bryan was twenty-four, old Mr. Palmes died of ague and bloody flux, leaving his bachelor son to care for the hundred-acre farm, its orchard, and, of course, Mrs. Palmes. By that time, she was in her sixties and seldom left her chamber except to attend Sunday services.

Although not a very pious man, Bryan would read to the old woman from the scriptures for several hours every evening. When she dozed off, he sometimes put aside the Bible and read to himself in silence from a few other smaller volumes that he kept in a strongbox.

He didn't pray to God for help with his house and farm, but help came to him unbidden one day. Early one morning, about three months after his father died, Bryan heard a knock at the door and found an Indian woman standing on his doorstep. Cate was a familiar face, and he knew that she and her husband Coffey, a slave, were working for an elderly neighbor who could no longer afford to feed them.

"We will help you," Cate told him. Then she pushed by him into the kitchen.

Cate knew how to drive a deal. She persuaded Bryan to buy Coffey from their current master, sign Cate on as an indentured servant, and bring these two to his farm.

She had offered to work for seven years to buy Coffey's freedom with her own labor. Bryan readily agreed, drew up a contract stating these terms, and went to his neighbor with an offer to pay thirty pounds for Coffey.

Cate did not know the exact date of her birth but guessed that she was almost thirty when she had come to the Palmes' farm; Coffey was a few years younger. Their new master gave the couple a back room under a sloping roof adjoining a chicken shed. He let them run his property from that day on. He and his mother would share meals with them at their table each evening. A year later, the servants' family doubled in size when twin boys, Jonathan and Joseph, came into this world .

Although she was an indentured servant like me, Cate always called herself a free woman. I never once heard Bryan refer to her husband as his slave. He always spoke of Coffey simply as his "man."

When her son was twenty-five, Mrs. Palmes gave Bryan a command that could not be disobeyed: "It's time to take a wife."

He obliged, setting his sights on a neighbor's spinster daughter. For many years, Abigail Smith had been sitting in her family's pew across from him in services, but she had never let him see her face, piously lowered under her cap. Then, one day, she must have felt his dark gaze going right through her. They had no courtship, but after publishing their intent to marry with the magistrate, the two were made husband and wife, just eight days later.

For a time, Bryan Palmes knew life as other men do, not as a cripple. That's because the pleasures of the marriage bed were sweet for him. I would come to that secret knowledge firsthand, though I would be ashamed to say it so plainly.

As Cate once told me behind his back—nodding in his direction with laughing eyes—"You'd never believe it, but that master of yours liked to take his bride to his bedchamber at all hours of the day. Never even waited 'til nighttime!"

Cate said she was glad that Bryan's mother was half deaf and never heard the shouts and screams coming from that bedchamber. When I worked up enough courage to ask Cate to tell me more, she shook her head. Her eyes weren't laughing anymore.

"One year to the day after they married, his Abigail was dead. Died in childbirth."

Under an apple tree, at the highest point of the hillside behind his house, Bryan buried both bodies in a single grave. Then he dragged a flat stone over their resting place. No man could lift so large a stone by himself, let alone someone with a bad leg, but in his grief, he'd done this without ever considering that it was impossible.

One night when she'd been combing the tangles from my hair and telling me stories, Cate described how Bryan would sit for hours in the orchard alongside that stone, his Bible open on his lap, his eyes closed.

"You wouldn't believe this, Pretty Girl, but sometimes he just sat there all night like a *madman* in the moonlight."

I wondered if he'd heard his wife's screams again, her pleas for help in her final hours. Perhaps he would ask himself if he were not a wretched sinner, responsible for her suffering and death. Eventually he may have believed that God was punishing him for his lustful thoughts and for the unquenchable desire that he'd felt for Abigail from the first time he lay with her. He should have known that it was never in God's plan for a cripple to father children; Cate had heard a minister tell him that very thing only one day after his wife's death.

"That's how his heart became crippled too," Cate whispered to me. Then she spread her hand across her heart as if to measure it.

"His heart never grew to the full size a man needs to love someone."

I wondered if my own heart had been damaged too, watching the Holt children collect their embraces and kisses all of those years while I went unloved by a mother or father.

"But no one can say he's not a handsome man, Cate."

She pressed her fingertips to my lips.

"You listen. He's a broken man. He can't love another woman, so he's not good for husband. Worse than that, Mercy, he doesn't know where he comes from or why he is here."

As we worked side by side, week after week, I began to wonder how Cate seemed to know so much about Mr. Bryan Palmes, as though he were a part of her family. But then again, she knew a lot about all the neighbors around us, even their most private affairs. She never made quilts like white women did, but she certainly knew what went on underneath them every night.

It was Cate who finally told me, in crude words, what happens between a man and wife in their bed.

Afterwards, she could see by my silence that her descriptions had shocked me to the very core of my being.

"I didn't want to talk to you like this, but your mother's gone off and left you, Pretty Girl, and no other woman ever going to tell you what a man wants."

The more I knew about human nature, though, the more I wondered how Bryan could keep to his own company without a woman. I would guess that more than once, while riding, he'd been accosted by women returning from the tents of militiamen out on Great Neck. The "hedge whores" walked out there all the time. I'd sometimes see disheveled, bareheaded women by the side of the road, slyly lifting their skirts to their thighs or pulling down their necklines to expose pale, plump breasts as a man passed by.

No doubt many men were tempted to follow those women; it was just as tempting for me to imagine those unlawful encounters. What drove these women to sell themselves in such a way? And did they, perhaps, have more money and more freedom than I had? As a servant, I certainly had neither.

One day, in jest, I voiced my thoughts to Cate.

"Do you think that such women offer apprenticeships to a girl like me? Perhaps I'd fare better in that occupation than this one."

Cate's eyes laughed, but her mouth didn't.

"I'll be praying long and hard for you tonight, Mercy."

She told me that any man who was caught with a whore would face one of two punishments: stand for long hours at the pillory while his neighbors leered at him, or take a public whipping on the Sheriff's fence. While such a man might get forty lashes, a knave accused of raping a young maid could meet a worse fate.

The constable once punished a rapist by nailing his ear to a post, then cutting it off in a bloody stroke. But the man's torture didn't end at that point. He endured a brutal whipping before a crowd ran him out of the colony. Who knows what had happened to his poor victim?

The more I learned about my master from Cate's late-night stories and Mrs. Palmes' delirious ranting, the more I yearned to know. If Bryan Palmes were really a servant's child, abandoned by his mother, then he was just like me, I mused. He was probably a bastard by birth; in my heart I was beginning to wonder if I might be one too, though my mother always said that my father died on their voyage from England. Perhaps she'd made up that tale to avoid a fine or punishment from her new master.

Was that why she'd shown so little love for me and didn't come to claim me after she remarried? After sailing to the colonies, perhaps she just wanted to keep sailing through life without me.

I swore to myself that I would never abandon a child of my own. Mercy Bramble would never do such a thing. No, I promised, she would rather die herself.

※

Life followed a pattern at the Palmes' farm. As a young woman of sixteen years, I found it a dull pattern at best, lacking in any diversions or joy except my growing friendship with Cate. I even found myself looking forward to visits from Hugo Moreaux, welcoming the peddler as a dear old friend.

There was no time for idleness, but that didn't mean that my mind was always contented or occupied. Above all, I couldn't forget my greatest desire: to learn to read.

For days I planned how I would approach my master and ask for an important favor. Over and over, I rehearsed the exact words that I would speak to him. Then, one night, after I'd cleared the evening meal, I approached him at his writing desk.

"I wish to beg a favor of you, sir."

"Speak it then," he replied crisply, not looking at me directly.

"I wish to take up my studies of the scriptures, just as Mr. Holt had begun to instruct me. The law says a master must teach his servant to read and write so that she can know the Lord's teachings. It says so in my papers from Mr. Holt, does it not, sir?"

A look of mock surprise came over his face.

"A roof over your head, meat on your plate, clothes on your back, and wood in our fire, is all that not payment enough? And how can you be so sure it is in your papers if you cannot read them?"

I had no answer for him. Although I bid him good night and left the room, I promised myself that I'd find another way to get what I wanted.

Bryan Palmes was gone for days at a time, riding north to Norwich and east to Westerly on errands that were often a mystery to me. Coffey claimed that our master had been betting on horse races in Rhode Island,—the practice was unlawful in our colony—and that he'd sometimes wager all he had on a single fast Narragansett pacer.

"These honest church folk don't know there's a sinner in their midst," Coffey would whisper. "You wait and see. Master will lose this here farm, and we'll all go hungry, maybe even *starve* to death in winter."

Bryan Palmes would return in a state of exhaustion, almost sliding off his foam-flecked horse. He'd order me to serve his supper at midnight and then fall asleep in a straight-backed chair by the fire. As dawn was breaking, he might call for me to fetch his staff, which often had fallen out of reach during the night. I don't think that he really needed me to help him, but I liked feeling useful.

When called to his chamber, I saw him in many states of undress and sometimes even fully naked. In my experience, bathing was something people did in private with most of their garments on, employing a rag and a little water in a basin every now and then. But my master liked to strip down at the well, empty the bucket over his head and shake his dripping hair. I'd even seen him bathing in the stream sometimes; then he would lay on a rock so that the sun or wind could dry his body before he dressed.

As a servant, I knew how to be discreet, to look the other way, but I was not blind. Besides, to whom could I complain of his immodesty? Certainly not to his elderly mother who was almost deaf and blind.

In truth, I did not mind the sight of him.

Although it happened in such an unstable climate, my great downfall did not begin with fire and brimstone or an Awful Thunderclap. No, it started with the smallest of comments and actions hardly worthy of notice, like the brush of a feather.

On a rare occasion, after old Mrs. Palmes had fallen asleep in her chair, Mr. Palmes would set aside his Bible and read to his servants from a few volumes like Poor Richard's Almanack, The Pilgrim's Progress, or Mr. Gulliver's Travels. Even as we listened, we all stayed busy: I would weave, Cate would sew, and Coffey would whittle spoons with a barlow knife.

Mr. Palmes seemed most to enjoy the last part of Mr. Gulliver's account. That book told how the traveler came to live among a race of intelligent horses, soon finding them to be superior to humans. I thought it was a rather weird chapter of the book.

After he concluded a reading, Mr. Palmes would ask me eagerly, "Did you like that tale, Mercy?"

"Yes, I did, Sir."

"I thought it would please you," he would say in a lowered voice so that only I would hear. This was a strange new situation: the master wished to please me, just as I was supposed to please him. It felt like a kind of growing conspiracy between us.

Still, I could not forgive his failure to teach me to read or write; my entreaties on that subject were always met with silence. Cate was right—he was not a very kind man—yet it mattered so little when he began to treat me differently.

Once or twice when I was assisting Mr. Palmes—such as when I handed him the reins to his horse—he would suddenly favor me with a smile as bright as the sun. His eyes would sparkle and I couldn't look away.

At other times, without saying a word, perhaps absentmindedly, he'd grab my hand and press his lips against my palm. Late one evening, while still seated after dinner, he'd gently, playfully taken my hand between his white teeth as though to finish his meal with a taste of me. Then he'd simply stared into my eyes, like a hungry cat toying with its prey.

My face had flushed, and my skin prickled; yet I confess that it wasn't a wholly unpleasant sensation. Then suddenly he pulled away.

"They say 'never bite the hand that feeds you,' but I had to give it a try," he said with a self-mocking air.

One day, as I bent to stir the fire, and Cate was nowhere around, I recognized the sound of his footsteps. He came up behind me and drew one hand very slowly from my breast to my thigh, tracing the outline of my body as a sculptor might. Then he sat down on a bench by the fire, slipped both hands around my hips, turned me around to face him, and kissed my gown between my thighs.

It would have been easy to cry out in protest, but whatever he was doing had taken my breath away, and I couldn't make a sound.

Removing myself from his grasp, I said nothing and pretended that nothing had happened. But something *had* happened; I was still burning where he'd touched me.

While performing my daily chores, I'd sort through possible explanations for his behavior; several threads had become tangled in my thoughts. Perhaps he couldn't control his actions; some are known to have fits, to do strange things in a trance, or walk in their sleep. If he were suffering from a touch of madness, that also might explain his shocking immodesty when he bathed, I thought.

Then again, maybe Bryan Palmes was just playing a lecherous game with me, assuming that I was too timid to object. I didn't wish to think of him as sly, or cowardly, or even half mad, however. I wanted to believe that he was wooing me in a gentler manner, helping me to overcome my fear of him.

With my simple ways and lack of schooling, perhaps I'd been too childish to know the true nature of a grown man. Nor did I realize there was still some measure of a wild beast in all descendants of Adam. Wasn't that why Cate had been trying to instruct me with her crude lessons and warnings?

Now that I'd become a woman, perhaps I was expected to learn those ways in order to survive, even if it tested my virtue, I told myself. Yes, that was the answer, I decided; I was being tested to see if Mercy Bramble were fit to be the future wife—and lover—of Bryan Palmes.

A year later, as I looked back on that time, I would laugh at how ignorant I'd been, but it was a bitter kind of laughter, not a joyful kind. Had I known how to write at that time, I would have recorded all of this on paper and made a careful study of it, but that wasn't yet possible.

Amid such great uncertainty, one fact was perfectly clear, however: my master was occupying a great deal of my thoughts in almost every waking hour. Much less clear were the strange sensations in my body whenever he came near me. Nature herself had designed this feeling, and like the tightly wound spiral of a fiddlehead fern, it was unfolding without my control.

And so, I waited for his next move, unsure what mine would be.

Then, late one evening, when my master returned from a long ride, he'd addressed me brusquely as he dismounted.

"Come to the barn. I have something to show you."

I had sworn to obey my master and to do it gladly, to come when I was called, and to do his bidding, but this time I feared his intentions. We would be all alone together in the dark barn.

Slowly I followed, my heart beating very fast.

He rarely spoke my name if he didn't have to, but that evening he did so in a hushed tone.

"Come closer, Mercy. Come to me over here."

Frowning intently, he took something from his saddlebag: a burlap sack he'd found while riding through the salt marsh. Inside were four half-drowned kittens.

"Maybe at least one will live," he said thoughtfully. "The rats have been in the corn, again, and we need a cat here."

As he passed me a warm, squirming handful of kittens, he smiled boyishly, showing perfect teeth like two rows of ivory.

His prediction was correct: all but one of the kittens died within two days. Coffey tossed their remains into a heap of chicken bones, corncobs, broken pottery, and other rubbish behind the barn. The survivor, a male calico, had a great appetite for a few drops of cow's milk that I gave him in a saucer. I named him Captain and loved him deeply, perhaps more because he'd been a gift from Mr. Palmes.

Captain grew strong quickly and in time was the sole fighter in a relentless war against the rats in both the barn and the kitchen. I noticed how Bryan often paused to scratch him gently behind the ears and say a few kind words; the two seemed to respect each other. Perhaps that was the best that my master had to offer another living creature, having something of the wounded animal about his own character.

Yes, I saw that my master was sometimes kind, but he was changeable and didn't have a steady habit of kindness.

After he'd denied me lessons in the scriptures, I was determined to seek out the Holy Writ on my own. Soon I would find knowledge that was wholly unwritten, unprinted in any text, and unspoken by any decent, church-going soul.

When Bryan Palmes was playing cards at the tavern some afternoons, I'd secretly go into his chamber and slip his Bible from its wooden box on his bedside table. In the dim light, I would strain to see letters of the alphabet that I'd learned years before and to remember their sounds. No matter how hard I wished the words would speak to me from each page, they often remained a mystery, indecipherable, and mute.

The room was sparsely furnished: an oaken chest of drawers, a washstand, a row of iron hooks for Bryan's coat and hats, and a rack that he had devised to keep his staff ready at his bedside.

A large, canopied four-poster bed dominated the room. The bed's dark green velvet drapes were always drawn, and its bottom sagged with fraying rope-work beneath a feather mattress. To me, however, that bed was suitable for a king and queen. I may never understand why it tempted me so. Perhaps the untamed desire that Bryan once had for his wife Abigail still lingered behind those velvet curtains.

Against the far wall stood a chest of drawers that the late Mr. Palmes had brought by ship from England; this held Bryan's gloves, hose, shirts, cravats, and a small moneybox. I also found his well-worn copy of The New England Primer, a little book from which Bryan had learned his alphabet and the Commandments as a boy. I loved to look at its tiny illustrations, which helped me speak aloud the words beneath it. One showed a butterfly in flight, another, a crocodile weeping below a palm tree.

But his Bible and primer weren't the only treasures to examine as I stretched my limbs across my master's forbidden bed.

In a bottom drawer of the chest was a hinged silver box wrapped in a silk handkerchief; nestled in its black velvet lining was a miniature portrait of Bryan Palmes. A decade earlier, a French artist had roamed from one town to another, painting each congregation's most important members. Bryan's mother had insisted that her son sit for a portrait. The likeness had never been displayed though; instead, it was hidden away like a family secret.

For a young woman who lived without a looking glass, it was a marvel to hold this image of a man in my hand.

And he was such a very handsome man—even more so than I'd ever pictured Charming Billy. In my imagination, the fairhaired youth in my favorite song had been like some kind of angel. My master, on the other hand, had a touch of the devil; somehow that made him all the more irresistible.

With vivid colors and delicate strokes, the artist had added every hair, every eyelash. He'd given his model a somewhat prim smile, perhaps to suggest a refined gentleman. Oddly, Bryan's image had a complexion like ivory, whereas the living Bryan was quite swarthy.

In each other's company, I would never have met his gaze in the bold manner with which I studied his likeness. Those painted eyes—their deep chestnut hue faithfully rendered—seemed to stare right through me, trying to seduce me.

Holding the frame in one hand, I'd slowly trace the line of his face with my fingertip or gently kiss his image. Then, very carefully, I'd clean its glass surface against my gown's bodice so as not to leave marks from my hand or lips. Whenever I did so, I thought of how his hands had recently brushed mine or how he'd stroked me from breast to thigh without my giving him license to do so.

The memory made my entire body blush and my heart pound. Once I even wondered if I had a fever or had taken leave of my senses. At other times I would press myself so passionately against the place where he slept that my body burned within.

That is how, in the course of a year, I began to long for Bryan's attentions as if he were the only man for miles around. Indeed, in my secluded world, he may as well have been the only man on earth.

I was all but blind to the fact that my master could be less than kind to me. I should *never* have excused that fault in him, nor in any man, but learning such a lesson takes time, and the devil himself must have been hurrying me toward sin.

They say that lust always springs from idleness, and yet I found that was not true. I worked as hard as any other servant, from dawn to long after dark; yet still lust awakened on its own.

※

In mid-November, Bryan had been gone for several days to conduct business of some kind; he hadn't even told Cate or Coffey when to expect him back. Old Mrs. Palmes was complaining of a fever that night, but when I offered her a drink of cider in the household's best pewter cup, she had refused to take even one drop.

"Maybe Coffey should ride for the doctor, Miss Mercy," said Cate. She had long ago despaired of Mrs. Palmes accepting any of her own herbal medicines and charms that she gathered in the warmer seasons.

Doctors charged by the number of miles they had to travel to tend a patient, and we were far from town. I wasn't hard-hearted but didn't want to make the decision to summon a physician; my master might reprimand me for any fee I'd incurred him. I also remembered my mistress's tenacity when facing worse maladies that year.

"Let's just leave her to her sleep for a little longer, I said firmly.

I closed the old woman's chamber door as if to end the discussion.

After Cate and Coffey had retired to their quarters, I slipped into the master's bedchamber, eager to look at his Bible verses and miniature portrait. Lately I'd begun dreaming of having my own portrait painted, perhaps as Bryan Palmes' future wife.

As I lay in the hollow that my master's body had made in his bed, I opened his Bible and found something I'd never seen before: a note written in my master's hand. It only had three words, which I spelled out letter by letter:

W-a-i-t f-o-r m-e.

Surely this message had only just been written. Although my heart was racing, I decided to stay a while more. The sound of the rain on the roof began to lull me to sleep, however, just as it had in my attic room at the Holts' when I was a child.

The harder the rain fell, the heavier my eyelids became.

Using the open Bible as a pillow, I lay my head on its pages, enjoying the smooth paper against my cheek. Then I slipped into a dreamless sleep, deep and dark as a night with no moon.

That was the night that Bryan Palmes found me asleep in his own bed and lay down with me in the darkness without a word or even a sigh.

I won't compound my sin by telling anything but the truth about what happened. Had I known what great misfortunes my action would set in motion, I would have been seized by a terror beyond words. Even dulled by sleep, I could have rolled out of that bed in the blink of an eye and hurried down the hall. No one either entrapped me or blocked my way, certainly not Bryan Palmes, nor had I suddenly forgotten the Commandments and other teachings I'd learned with the Holt children.

Looking back on that night, I would wonder what exactly had happened to that timid little Mercy Bramble.

I'd come up with only one answer—someone or something must have bewitched her. The man who practiced that dark magic was none other than my master who should have protected me.

In the canopied bed, a sweet smell of rum and tobacco hung all around us, changing the atmosphere to one that I'd never breathed before. It was as if I'd sailed as a stowaway to a foreign port in a country with no laws, no rules, no orders except one: "Thou shall seek pleasure." And because there seemed to be no way of going back without exposing my guilt, I chose to stay where I'd landed and to see what fate had in store.

But I was no stowaway, and this was no sea captain or lawless pirate. This was my master, Bryan Palmes, and he was alone with me in the dark.

Without speaking a word, he unbuttoned my gown—I had to assist him—and began to give me slow, gentle caresses along the full length of my body. Surely, he must have known that no one had ever touched or caressed this body before him, yet he took astonishing liberties, seeking out my most secret places.

I didn't wish him to stop.

Starting with my hands, which were rough as any servant's, he kissed me as though he owned every inch of Mercy Bramble. Then, pressing his entire weight upon me, he finally kissed my mouth as if he'd just discovered it, hungering, no, starving for more of whatever he was seeking. His hair, untied, fell like black silk curtains on either side of our faces.

Just when I thought that he could do nothing more to shock

me, he went over my body yet another time, gently biting and then kissing each place again. Surely, he'd become a madman, but I was already halfway to madness myself by then.

Then we both stopped. As if we'd gained possession of our faculties, we seemed to know that something was wrong: I was fully naked then, and he fully clothed.

He drew himself to his knees, and even in the dark I could feel his eyes assessing our situation, deciding what action must be taken.

I thought I understood as well. Wondering if this would be my habit as the future Mrs. Palmes, I helped him from his shirt and breeches. No, "helped" is too civilized a word: I almost tore them from his straining body—a body I already knew from his immodest behavior in the past. He gasped for air, as though he'd been choked by his clothing and could finally breathe freely.

Suddenly there was no Bryan Palmes, nor was there any Mercy Bramble. There was only one of us.

A quick, efficient pain marked my surrender. That pain was quickly drowned by astonishment, waves of pleasure, and kisses so deep that they had no beginning or end. I had a sensation that my master was lifting me up from the center of my being.

Whenever he caught his breath, he took the Lord's name in vain again and again.

During our dark, secret hour in that feather bed, there were no orders to follow, no cares, and no shame. No shame at all. If that sweet illusion was the Devil's work, then I confess I'd gained new respect for the Prince of Darkness and his powers of deception that night. Satan showed me a multitude of revelations: Heaven and Hell, my birth, my life, my final prayer, and my death.

So here was the reason that men built great churches and wrote their sermons, all in hopes of holding such powers in check. I thought that my heart would surely explode from this knowledge I thought I'd just gained.

But when Bryan Palmes was finished with me, he started to fall asleep. I heard him murmur just one word: "Abigail."

Then all I heard was his breathing.

The room grew cold.

That's when I fully awoke to my situation and was conscious of what I'd just done, knowing that I could not undo it. There had been no voyage to a magical land ruled by pleasure. Nor was it all a dream from which I'd awaken.

Clutching my garments, I stole away from the bed, and having no candle, felt my way with outstretched hands down the hallway. The familiar passageway seemed decidedly unfamiliar and at least twice as long as it should be.

In the middle of the hall, I stepped over what I believed were Bryan's boots and saddlebags; the weary traveler had dropped them when he'd come home, knowing that I would pick them up later that morning. Men could be so careless, so heedless of others, I thought. Yet that is what made them so free of the burdens that Cate and I were asked to carry. That is what made them so free to come and go in this world like kings and to put their wants and needs first. I, on the other hand, was held by the bonds of a mere slip of paper.

Then I knew that I—Mercy Bramble—had just made a terrible mistake and could not undo it.

Passing the cold, extinguished fireplace, I dragged myself up the steep ladder to my sleeping place in the attic.

CHAPTER III

DROUGHT

"When the well is dry, we know the worth of water."

—Benjamin Franklin

It was still raining the next morning, but even torrents of water couldn't wash away my memories of what had happened a few hours before.

I'd risen earlier than usual, before Cate and Coffey. Hastily filling a washbasin, I cleaned myself with a rag as best I could under my homespun shift and woolen gown.

"No one saw us. No one will ever know," I told myself, but why did my heart feel like it was beating in my throat?

Others might never learn what the two of us had done in my master's dark bedchamber, but what about the all-seeing God? I prayed that a servant girl, one never even baptized, was too far beneath heaven to deserve His attention let alone His wrath. Then I realized the very sinfulness of such a prayer. No matter how I looked at it, I was doomed; not wanting to further multiply my sins, I even refrained from cursing.

Shortly after dawn, as if waking a second time, I remembered that old Mrs. Palmes had been ailing and scolded myself for not looking in on her. Hastening to her chamber, I almost fell over a dark object on the hallway floor.

There on the cold, muddy planks, was my mistress.

She lay in her nightdress, mouth agape, eyes wide open. One hand was outstretched as if she'd been seeking help when she fell. Her lace cap had slipped back, exposing her ashen gray skull and a few wisps of white hair. A scarlet ribbon of blood curved around her lifeless head on the floor.

I covered my mouth, but my scream was already ringing throughout the house.

Suddenly I remembered my blind flight a few hours before and how carefully I'd stepped over what I'd thought to be boots and a saddlebag. My stomach turned.

What had my mistress been doing in the hallway before she fell? Had she been seeking help in her last moments or trying to investigate strange noises from her son's bedchamber? I didn't know which would have been more damning.

Quickly, I mopped up the blood stain with a rag so that no one else would see it. It had been an accident, after all, not a murder, I told myself, trying to stay calm.

"Call Master Palmes!" shouted Cate, running up behind me with her husband.

"Lord have mercy on us poor sinners!" Coffey groaned. Not wanting to get near the corpse, he told his wife to knock on their master's bedchamber door.

"Master Palmes, Mrs. Palmes is dead, sir!" Cate cried from the doorway, pouncing on the word "dead" like a barn cat on a mouse. But no response came from within. Finally, all three of us entered unbidden, and Coffey started roughly shaking the master. I turned away, not wanting to see Bryan still naked, the quilt twisted on the floor as if thrown aside in a fit of passion.

To my horror, I saw the Bible that I'd been reading; it was cast upside down and splayed wide open on the floor beside the bed. I grabbed it and returned it to its table, pretending that I was just tidying up, as servants must do.

It was Coffey who finally handed Bryan his shirt from the foot of the bed, then gave him his staff. Seeing that his master was only half awake, he also guided him down the hall. The master stood a minute, gazing down at what remained of the woman who'd saved him from death on the riverbanks so many years ago.

He had been lucky, I thought. Lucky to be so wanted.

After a silence of only a few heartbeats, Bryan told us to bow our heads while he recited a solemn Lord's Prayer. I'd never heard him pray aloud before that morning. Then, without bothering to put on his breeches, he pulled on his enormous greatcoat that came down to the top of his boots. Taking a hat off a hook, he ordered Coffey to bring his horse and wagon to the front of the house.

"I'll speak with the minister. The gravedigger too," he told us.

It was strange to see Mrs. Palmes' body without life at last: a few times in the past year I'd mistaken her for dead because she often slept with her eyes open. More than once I'd peered into those rheumy eyes and thought how faraway I was from my own mother and how remote a being God had seemed.

Now, in vain, I tried to fold Mrs. Palmes' hands in prayer, but they were as dry and stiff as a turkey's claws and wouldn't bend in any natural way.

Death was no stranger to me. Once, when I lived at the Holt's, another servant and I had been called to a nearby farm to prepare a body for burial. The magistrates would pay each of us a few shillings from the town treasury.

The deceased was an old woman of nearly four score years

who had fallen down a well, broken both legs, and died there half submerged. I would never forget the stench of her bloated corpse on that hot, summer day as we loaded it in her coffin. It was a miracle that she'd lived so long, they said, no matter how her life had ended. The victim received more blame than pity, however. Her neighbors said that the accident must have been punishment for a terrible sin she had committed earlier in life or a misdeed by one of her children.

Now, as I sat by Mrs. Palmes' body, the memory of what I'd done in the four-poster bed began to fester and rot in my conscience. Would God punish me at any moment in a fiery explosion like the Awful Thunderclap? Or would He wait—and wait, and wait—until I least expected some hideous retribution? Either way, I was certain to rot in Hell or burn forever with other sinners in a lake of fire.

For the first time in many years, I began to weep, letting huge sobs shake my body. Through my tears I was dimly aware that Cate kept peeking in the doorway; she seemed puzzled that I was so awash with grief for my mistress. Finally, she took off her apron and mopped my face as though she were cleaning a teakettle, managing to coax a weak smile from me.

"Crying's no good, Pretty Mercy Girl. It won't bring our mistress back."

Late that afternoon, Bryan Palmes returned with a carpenter who set to work building a coffin—Cate called it an eternity box—in the front room. The man had arms as huge as gnarled tree branches; he drove in each hand-cut nail with a single blow.

In such a dank house, the fresh-cut pine smelled good to me, like a forest on a summer afternoon. Cate wrapped Mrs. Palmes in a sheet of linen that I'd woven earlier that fall, never guessing that my creation would clothe my mistress on a journey to her eternal rest.

After the carpenter nailed my elderly mistress into her coffin, Coffey lifted the load onto the wagon bed. It would rest there until it was brought to town at dawn. Most families carried their own dead relations to the burial ground—men and boys would shoulder a coffin for several miles—but no one expected that of Bryan Palmes. Everyone knew that the Lord had already given him a sufficient burden.

"No wolf can get in that coffin tonight, I suppose," said Coffey uneasily.

The next morning, all three of us servants accompanied our master to the burial ground on Stony Hill. Mrs. Palmes had wanted to be buried next to her husband.

"The shadow of the meetinghouse steeple will fall right across our resting place," she once had told me. Now she would get her wish.

A fresh grave was waiting for her. The gravedigger, old Benja Fargo, had finished his work early that day. I remembered that he'd dug a grave for that old woman who'd fallen in the well and also for Mrs. Holt.

For more than twenty years Benja had been carrying out many duties that no one else wanted. In addition to digging graves, he also carried the bodies of those who had died of smallpox to separate burial grounds outside town lines. He dragged them behind his oxen cart, since no one else would touch them. Several times a year he even cleaned the smallpox house itself, a cottage near the mouth of the river that sheltered those who were dying.

I had a strange notion that Old Fargo would be digging a grave for me, Mercy Bramble, one day.

While Coffey went to collect Reverend Jewett from his home nearby, we servants waited for him in silence.

The muddy graveyard was deserted that morning except for

two women. Both were strangers to me. They wore black capes over black widows' weeds and large black bonnets that made them look like owls.

"Those ladies are kin to Mrs. Palmes, daughters of her cousin," Cate explained to me. As usual, she knew everything about these strangers. Both were widows, their husbands having died years before. One man perished of yellow fever in Barbados and was buried on the coast there. The other was swept off a schooner's deck by a rogue wave within sight of New London Light.

"Couldn't swim a stroke," said Cate, shaking her head.

While the minister started his sermon, beseeching God to show divine mercy for us all and deliver swift punishment for sinners, Cate and I stood at a respectful distance near the graveyard gate. I studied the two women closely, especially their fashionable capes, black gloves, and tortoiseshell hair combs, though I wondered if they were wearing wigs.

"Aren't they like two angels of death, those two?" I whispered to Cate.

A dark glance from the minister warned her that we should be quiet. She raised a finger to her lips to silence me, but I was feeling reckless and persisted.

"Maybe after the burial they'll be hearing news about a wedding day soon."

With her mouth pressed firmly shut, Cate continued to stare at her deerskin moccasins peeking out from her skirt hem.

"Don't you want to hear some gossip, Cate?"

When she still didn't answer, I couldn't contain my secret any longer.

"Our master shared his bed with me the other night. He must want someone young and pretty to warm his bed again."

I poked her gently in her ribs.

"Maybe *I'll* be the new Mrs. Palmes and give all the orders.

What do you think, Cate? Will I make a good mistress or will you secretly hate me?"

At first, I thought that she hadn't heard me, but finally her response came like a cat's low, warning hiss.

"That's a very bad thing you told me. Will bring you nothing but trouble."

"But Cate, you were the one who told me all about what a man wants…"

She cut me off again.

"And to think you sinned while his poor mother lay dying on the floor."

"The master's a good man, and he's all alone now, part-cripple as he is," I went on. I did my best to sound like my elders did when explaining why they were right and I was always wrong.

"Don't you know? A man will be punished for lying with his servant, and a maid will be too. The magistrates deal a harsh blow to a servant who has a bastard. It's a bad crime, Mercy Girl. Not a hanging crime but very bad."

I swallowed hard.

"And what do they do to such a servant, Cate?"

"She'll have to pay a fine to her master, out of her own pocket! And if she hasn't any money, they make her bond longer by a year or more."

"Well, I won't be bearing any bastards." Suddenly my voice had dried in my throat. "Not if the master makes me his wife soon."

"Lord help you! He was drunk on rum and won't remember what he did to you, Little Mercy. I know things about Master Palmes you will never know, things that I cannot speak now. He likes his drink and his women too."

"So does every man, master or servant," I murmured, and at last Cate seemed to agree.

"Ugly or handsome," she said. "Cripple or blind, makes no difference."

For a moment I wondered whether it was my master's defect that had drawn me to him, not his handsome face. What else would have given me the notion that he would marry a girl of my lowly class? After all, I'd be a bride with neither money nor land. Neither horses nor cattle. Not even a chicken, for heaven's sake. The truth stung like a nettle.

"Please don't call the master a cripple, Cate. That isn't right."

"Isn't *right*? You don't seem to know what's right or wrong now do you, Mercy? Didn't your mother warn you that lust is like a serpent?"

"But Cate, I was only seven when she gave me up. She wasn't talking to me about lust and serpents and all that nonsense."

"A girl's never too young to learn. Lord knows I had to."

Suddenly she reached for my hand and spoke far more softly. "Better start to pray right now, Mercy. Your soul is in bad, bad danger."

Cate knew plenty about souls, as well as sin and salvation. Sometimes she and her husband walked for miles to hear the Christian preaching of Samson Occom, a Mohegan. Every Sunday morning, without fail, the couple could be found among a group of Negro slaves and Indians in the highest loft of the meetinghouse. In winter, the loft was the meetinghouse's coldest part; in summer, the hottest. But Cate and her husband endured long sermons without complaint.

"We're closer to God up there than any of those folks below," she'd boast to me when they returned.

Now, in this graveyard, Cate squeezed my hand and spoke to me in a tone that struck fear in my heart.

"Master will *not* be marrying you," she whispered slowly. "And he'll never grant permission for you to marry another while you're bound to him. That's the law, plain and simple, Mercy Girl."

"But what about you and Coffey…"

"I told you, we were *already* married when I was bonded as a servant."

She clicked her tongue impatiently and continued her own hushed sermon.

"Listen, you gave in to temptation, now beg God for mercy. If you don't, you'll be wandering the highways with a swollen belly and heart full of shame, begging for a crust of bread or even stealing it."

If I'd ever believed that I was somehow better than Cate, that belief now lay in tatters at my feet. I stood there as if naked, fully exposed as a sinner in Cate's eyes.

The Reverend Jewett looked up and called all the way across the graveyard: "Silence!" His massive brows were knit together in anger.

Stones and clods of earth began to hit the coffin lid in a volley of dull thuds. As any trace of pinewood disappeared, Mrs. Palmes disappeared as well, ceasing to exist as a resident of this earth. Her headstone, yet to be cut or carved, would be erected soon, but for now her grave was unmarked, like that of any pauper or transient.

In my mind's eye I could see the dead, gathered in a restless mob beneath our feet. Angry that their days above were over, and unwilling to bear the burden of our joys and sorrows, they clawed the earth from below.

"From dust God created us and to dust we shall return!" Reverend Jewett bellowed, enjoying his oratory duties to the fullest. His words echoed off the meetinghouse.

Behind his wagon, we three servants waited silently as Bryan Palmes conversed in low tones with his female cousins. Their carriage was waiting outside the gate with a team of black horses; they were magnificent animals, the kind that Bryan so loved to possess. His hand slid down one of the horses' dark, shining flanks but didn't linger there. It was like that secret caress he'd once given me by the fire.

Now I burned with shame to recognize it.

Finally, he offered his hand to one lady to help her into their carriage. His gesture was that of a gentleman, not a country farmer. He was more accustomed to receiving assistance than giving it to others, but that day I saw a different Bryan Palmes: a man who could possess just as much charm as Charming Billy did.

※

The following week was a somber one, and winter's first snow arrived before the ground was frozen.

I swept a thin layer of dust out of the dead woman's chamber with one of Cate's freshly made birch brooms, then scrubbed the walls and floor. Our master had instructed Cate to throw away whatever we found under his mother's bed. Although we were always very thrifty and wasted nothing, we did as we were told.

The two of us found many odds and ends hidden under her bed, but nothing of much worth: slippers with missing heels, parts of broken spinning wheels, and the like. The last object I pulled out from the dust was a curious thing, however: an old wooden cradleboard with strange painted designs and strips of deerskin.

"Shall I break this up and burn it?" I asked Cate, trying to be helpful.

"Give me that," she said sharply. She grabbed the strange board away from me took it to her quarters without another word.

I'd hoped that my master would offer me a few of his mother's finer possessions—how I coveted her fancy gloves, combs, lace-edged handkerchiefs, and prayer books—but all of those things stayed exactly where the old woman had left them in her room. Having no money of my own, I was tempted to steal just one small treasure, should I ever need to trade it for something.

Meanwhile, Bryan had not spoken to me at all that week.

Perhaps Cate was right; he simply didn't remember anything about the time that I spent in his bed. On the other hand, I feared that he might remember it all too well but chose not to acknowledge me.

Somehow that thought was far, far worse for me to bear.

One afternoon, when Bryan was away, my housekeeping chores brought me to his chamber again. I eagerly lifted his Bible from its wooden box, hoping to decipher a few words on my own. When I tried to open its cover, however, I saw that the clasp was not only closed, it was securely locked.

There was a note alongside it, penned in Bryan's hand.

Hurrying to the kitchen, I showed Cate this paper and she read it to me: "Not for Servants."

"Why doesn't the master trust me?" I begged Cate miserably.

As always, she did not spare her words.

"Too late now, my foolish Little Sister. It was never meant to be."

"But why not?"

Cate grimaced and looked away.

"Your master will be bound in marriage tomorrow. Taking his vows with his mother's cousin, Widow Way. Elizabeth Way she's called."

Never taking her eyes from a freshly killed chicken in her hands, Cate continued.

"The Church tells its men—single men and widowers—to

marry the town's widows, to take care of them. And like the Bible says, 'tis 'better to marry than to burn.'"

At first, I couldn't fathom what she'd told me; I was too dumbfounded by her mysterious power to know everything going on for miles around her.

"How do you do it Cate? Do birds speak to you in some secret language? Does the wind carry secret messages only for your ears?"

She chuckled, plucking one last, almost invisible feather from the chicken, and impaling its body on a spit for the fireplace.

"Yes, Cate hears it all. Nothing's hidden from me, least of all under this roof."

She stopped laughing and heaved a sigh.

"My Coffey has no chance to stray or cheat, 'cause I'd know before it happens. Someday I'll buy that man's freedom, but he'll never be free of this eagle eye."

Then, perhaps to soften the blow of the news she'd delivered, Cate began speaking of other matters, but I was no longer listening.

I raced out into the snow-dusted yard, scattering hens from their resting place. My thoughts fought one another in a struggle for comprehension, but I was too shocked to begin crying.

Should I run away? How far would I get in hostile regions beyond the town limits? More drastic courses of action raced through my mind, wicked things that would break our Lord's sixth commandment. I'd heard stories of other servants, desperate for release from bondage, who'd made a final escape to freedom: they'd taken their own lives.

One woman had made a rope of all her mistress' silk handkerchiefs while the family was away at meeting on Sunday; then she'd hung herself in their attic. A young man had drowned himself in his master's millpond. Yet another, a slave woman, had sharpened a knife and slit her own stomach, shouting to her keepers, "I'm going home at last!"

The violence of my thoughts caught me off guard, like a gentle horse that turns and knocks down its own master for no reason. Bryan's betrayal struck me with no less force.

Soon I decided what to do: I must speak to him right away.

The next night, when Bryan was writing in his ledger by the light of a whale oil lamp, I came up behind him in the doorway of the keeping room. He turned to look at me as I twisted my hands in my apron. When something was this hard to say, I knew I had to say it very quickly.

"Master Palmes, have I done something to cause ill favor?"

He glanced warily around before he answered, accustomed no doubt to seeing his mother in a chair nearby. When he realized that no one would hear him, he cleared his throat.

"You came to my bed of your own free will, to satisfy your *curiosity*, did you not?"

"Perhaps I did, but..."

"Ah ha, so you freely admit to your sin. Therefore, I hold you responsible for what happened, Mercy. You must know that I have to cut you off now."

"What do you mean, sir?"

"We must never be alone again, and you must never set foot in my bedchamber. Cate can change the linens."

"I thought you had true affection for me," I said quietly, but he had no reply. "If it is your wish, I will never mention that night again, sir," I faltered.

We stood there without speaking for what seemed an eternity; then I surprised myself by breaking the silence with my own demand.

"I will never ask anything more of you, Master, but I happen to know it is my right to learn to read and..."

Angrily, he interrupted me.

"If you want to go elsewhere, I'll bind you to another master.

Perhaps a more elderly gentleman with no desires of the flesh, one who cannot be tempted. Such a man might be more inclined to teach you to read than I am."

"But I wish to stay here in this house for now."

"Well, if that is your choice, you must be completely obedient to your new mistress when she arrives."

"Are, are, are you to take a wife, so, so suddenly?" I stammered.

"That is solely my concern. Not yours. Am I making myself clear? Do you understand what I'm saying to you?"

"Yes, sir."

My voice was only a whisper but inside my head I was shouting at him, "How can I possibly understand? Nothing makes any sense anymore!"

He calmly returned to his writing, but as I withdrew from the room, he suddenly called back to me. His voice was strangely cheerful, and his lips showed a trace of a smile, just like in his miniature portrait.

"You really should know that some good has come from our encounter," he said, tapping his pen against the inkwell. "You made me realize how much I needed a good wife."

Whenever I looked back on that moment, even years later, I knew that I should have detested him. But did I? No, I was sixteen years old and thought anything was possible. I still loved Bryan Palmes and believed that he would come around to loving me.

That was my curse.

❧

Three days later, as evening was falling, the same carriage and team of black horses that I'd seen at the burial ground pulled up to the farmhouse. Bryan Palmes was at the reins, and at his side was Widow Way, the new Mrs. Palmes.

They were quiet, sober, and fresh from their vows before the magistrate. Her gloved hand rested on his arm ever so lightly.

After the newlyweds had come inside, I remained on the doorstep. My heart was slamming and a strange dizziness prevented me from walking. It was as though I were having a nightmare and my feet had turned to stone.

Bryan's bride walked right past Cate and myself just as though we were invisible.

"I'll give you your orders in the morning," was all she said.

After Coffey unhitched her two horses and led them to the barn, he dragged two large trunks across the threshold and straight into Bryan's bedchamber. Through an open door I could see her already sitting on my master's bed, her gown's skirt spread out around her in an enormous black circle.

If she only knew how I'd surrendered my body to my master behind those green curtains only a week before.

How quickly my life had changed. Another woman had replaced me in Bryan's favor, dashing any hopes I may have had of being his bride. That truth was hard enough to bear, but there was more. Whatever privileges or freedoms I'd earned at the farm would now be surrendered to my new mistress.

On her second day as Mrs. Palmes, she sent Coffey back to town to retrieve her most treasured possession: a harpsichord that her late husband had given her. It was a beautiful instrument, with fine, inlayed ornaments in a wooden case. All other household furnishings now appeared plain, even crude by comparison.

Coffey also delivered something else—someone else— who belonged to our new mistress. After the harpsichord was unloaded, he helped a small, pale figure emerge from the back of the carriage.

Seeing a thin, wide-eyed girl no older than twelve gave me a start. She reminded me of myself not so long ago, clutching a small bundle to my chest when Mr. Holt had left me at the Palmes' household.

"And who might you be, little one?" Cate asked her kindly.

"I'm Madam's servant, Zenobia Turner."

Zeno—for that's what she answered to—told us that she'd been indentured to our new mistress soon after her own mother had died from smallpox. Her father had no use for his daughter on his farm, judging her to be too small and weak. Cate later said to me that she believed Zeno was feebleminded, like her two idiot brothers who worked the land with their father. Neither must have worked very hard, because everyone said that old man Turner's farm had fallen into ruin in recent years.

That morning, I had scant interest in Zeno, however. I was only concerned with two things: my new mistress and my own misery. I would have believed I was having a nightmare, but I was awake and the day was clear and bright.

As soon as she was satisfied that her beloved harpsichord hadn't been damaged, the new Mrs. Palmes gathered all four of us—myself, Cate, Coffey and little Zeno—in the kitchen. Then she called for silence, although none of us had spoken a word.

"You should be grateful that I've brought Zeno to help you out, but there's much to be done here. It will take a stronger hand to make this an *orderly* household."

"Cate and I already keep a tidy house for Mr. Palmes," I ventured.

"Servants don't talk back to their betters," she snapped, "not if they want to avoid a sound beating. You'll thank me for this one day."

As soon as my new mistress had left the kitchen, Cate advised me to keep my mouth shut.

"Get on her good side now, Mercy," she urged. "For heaven's

sake, don't provoke her. Keep your eyes lowered like I do. Just watch me, girl. You'll learn."

But I was too stubborn to listen to Cate's well-meaning advice.

"I refuse to go through life with my eyes cast down. Maybe she's broken poor Zeno, but *she won't break me.*"

But winter was coming so I had very little time to ponder my sudden change in circumstances. Late November was what they called the killing time; we servants had to slaughter, butcher, salt, smoke, and pickle any fattened ox and swine chosen for winter stock. We worked from sunrise until after sundown. My fingers were numb with cold, my arms soaked in blood.

Each hour seemed twice as long, now that I now had Elizabeth Palmes as my overseer. My new mistress insisted that I always address her as "Madam," and her husband as "Sir." Although that was very hard for me to remember, I did make an effort to do so.

"Madam" said that we servants had been much "too familiar" with her new family. I prayed that she never discovered exactly how familiar I'd really been.

My mistress was distressed to learn that Cate and Coffey often joined their master at the same table for their evening meal.

"Why do you indulge your servants by letting them eat with you?" she demanded of her new husband. "This abomination must stop immediately!"

"But most farmers I know share a table with their help, if only for the sake of efficiency," Bryan replied in an even tone. "The table need only be cleared once, not twice."

His answer made her face flush red with anger.

She decreed that Cate and Coffey would eat their evening meal only after their master and mistress had finished their food and left the table.

"You, Mercy, can continue to eat with us," she informed me

grudgingly. "And Zeno too if she wishes, though the child eats hardly anything."

My mistress offered no further explanation, but I knew why she was making an exception for me. I was an Englishwoman, and my skin was white like hers. She certainly wasn't expecting my reply however.

"No, I will eat with Cate and Coffey at a later hour, then. But thank you, Madam."

A look of sly amusement stole across Bryan's face, and I had to turn away. My mistress must not see how my expression mirrored her husband's.

"So, this is quite the little mutiny, isn't it, my dear Elizabeth? Our servants are rebelling," he observed.

His words had pleased me—he'd seen that I could stand up for myself—but his new bride didn't find anything humorous in what he'd said.

"And you will keep that mangy cat, Captain or whatever you call it, out of my house! No more feeding him scraps from our table!"

And so, the long days of a very long winter had begun.

The bride of Bryan Palmes was thirty-eight years old, several years older than my own mother. Every morning she arose from bed and promptly dropped to her knees, saying her prayers out loud. With Zeno's help, she tightened her corset stays until her waist was just as small as mine. Her garments were austere; although her time of grieving was long past, she continued to wear black mourning clothes.

"Black suits me," she told me. "Why waste a perfectly good gown?"

More handsome than pretty, she had a shock of iron-grey hair under her cap and unblinking blue eyes that held your gaze in a curious manner.

It was hard to overlook her greatest flaw, however: a large, sharp nose gave the unfortunate impression of a beak. Cate and Coffey wasted no time in assigning her a secret name: The Hawk.

Had I been older and wiser, I would have seen that Elizabeth was a pious woman who struggled like any daughter of Eve. Nor did she lack certain virtues. She was a good cook; I couldn't resist her stew or meat pie, even the last portion that no one else wanted. In the evening she liked to play a few hymns on her harpsichord, but only if Bryan were there to listen and praise her. She brought more practical possessions for us to use, including a good spinning wheel that she allowed me to use late at night.

Having managed a household for years on her own when her first husband was at sea—never knowing if he would return—the Hawk was no stranger to adversity. I knew she was likely to face more years of hardship; no doubt Bryan Palmes would gamble away any money that she had saved so scrupulously.

I didn't want to be at sixes and sevens with this woman, but my broken heart had already tipped the scales, and I was a loser several times over. I'd lost my chastity, I'd lost Bryan Palmes, and now I'd lost any small freedoms I had.

I simply couldn't afford to lose any more.

My master saw me every day. He took his bread and drink from my hands and often passed me as I worked at the hearthside. Sometimes he spoke to me, but he'd become miserly with his words. As he had decreed, I never entered his bedchamber again, but I still hoped for a sign from him or one of his secret smiles. We were in such close quarters that he could have made such a gesture quite easily, seeming almost by chance, yet he allowed a hundred opportunities to go untried.

Every day of that hard winter, I longed for just one soft word from him.

Even as he avoided me, however, I often felt a desire for him that defied all reason. I imagined, again and again, all of the ways that he had touched me that night. Sometimes I feared that it might be the sinful act itself that I longed for, not just my master. I'd given myself to him only once, yet I could still close my eyes and feel the warm imprint of his flesh against mine.

No amount of shame could extinguish this sensation. It was like the tree that I'd seen years before, consumed by fire from a bolt of lightning even as heavy rain fell. Were there others who lived on earth in this condition, burning to be touched by one whom they desired? Or was I the only one so damned?

I'd recall a single passage from Genesis, when God sent Adam and Eve forth from the Garden: "… in pain you shall bring forth children, yet your desire shall be for your husband…"

Your desire. The words were from God Himself! Wasn't it clearly God's fault then, that I'd desired this man and had wanted to be his wife? Perhaps He had made me so, condemning me by my very nature as a daughter of Eve. Maybe He would forgive my single, flaming fall from grace.

Now Zeno was my only bed partner. Young and simple-minded, she still slept clutching a cornhusk doll. I noticed that she'd sewn the doll's eyes herself, using little crossed stitches on its cloth face, but her doll had neither a nose nor mouth.

Our cramped attic was reached by ladder-like stairs from the kitchen. It was the coldest room in the house that winter.

When the last notes of a harpsichord died away, I envisioned Bryan Palmes taking that woman in his arms in his bedchamber downstairs. Perhaps he would tell her to remove her gown, knowing that he alone was allowed to stare at her nakedness. I wondered if he fully possessed her body as he had mine—with equal parts sweetness and savagery—and if he found any true pleasure in his marital duties to a woman ten years his senior.

Poor Zeno had no idea why I would groan aloud or cry

myself to sleep whenever I heard sounds from the conjugal bed below us. More often, though, I just kicked the wall in anger, not caring if Bryan would hear me. I *wanted* him to hear me.

"What's wrong with you, Mercy?" she asked timidly one night.

I couldn't tell her what I was really thinking.

"I'm trying to scare off these wretched mice in our wall! If the Hawk hadn't sent Captain out of the house, these vermin wouldn't be everywhere."

Without a cat to chase them, mice had taken over the kitchen. They scampered through our attic all night, attracted by old corncobs that stuffed our bedding. One disgusting creature even chewed a hole in the face of Zeno's cornhusk doll, but she patiently sewed a new one.

Only Cate knew the depth of my unhappiness at that time.

Ever since that day I'd sided with my fellow servants when the Hawk had banished Cate and Coffey from her table—Bryan Palmes still referred to it as Mercy's Great Rebellion—Cate was always there when I needed her.

When winter storms raged in the night, she'd come up the ladder to our sleeping place, bringing thick woolen blankets that she'd traded for her handmade baskets and brooms. Sometimes she'd rub my chapped hands and sore feet with her special potions or braid my hair to make me look like a chief's daughter. Although I'd always hidden those braids under my cap the next day, I'd felt like a princess.

Cate even conspired with me when I'd started taking a terrible risk. In secret, I'd been removing a few pages from Bryan's books, taking out one at a time with a sharp knife. She would help me read them late at night, and later, would hide the loose pages in her own quarters. Although she prayed that no one would discover them, she was prepared to take all the blame if they did.

"Don't it say in Poor Richard's Almanac that God helps those who help themselves?" she assured me. "So, God knows we're just helping ourselves to a few pages of Mr. Palmes' books."

Ever so slowly, I'd begun making progress with my reading. Like pieces of a torn treasure map that I was assembling in my mind, each new lesson pointed the way to understanding more words, sentences, and whole stories. With great difficulty, I also began reading aloud.

Zeno had known enough of her letters to stitch a verse on a cloth. Thanks to my lessons from Cate, I could now read it to her:

Zeno Turner is my name
England is my nation,
New London is my dwelling place and
Christ is my salvation.

Sometimes Cate asked me to memorize a few lines at random, usually from Mr. Swift's Gulliver's Travels, and repeat it back to her as we worked the next day.

Those bits and pieces would amuse us as we toiled.

"A wife should always be a reasonable and agreeable companion because she cannot always be young," I recited. Cate would laugh so hard she had to wipe away the tears.

"What Mr. Swift needs is a swift kick in the arse, if you ask me," she said.

※

By March the Hawk announced to me that she was three months with child. Before I could say, "What a blessing, Madam!" she advised me that I'd have to improve my housekeeping chores to relieve her of any additional burden.

Then, for no apparent reason, she delivered her harshest edict yet.

"You and Zeno will have to give up your attic and make your beds here in the kitchen."

I didn't even try to hide my horror.

"The kitchen!" I exclaimed.

"There's room for you to put your bedding right here," she said, pointing to the top of the great chest that held firewood.

Then, as if offering us some new privilege, she continued: "Zeno is smaller so she can sleep on this deacon's bench. That way you can stoke the fire all night long and keep the house warmer for all of us."

This was only a skirmish in what would be a long war between us, but I took a shot at her with my words that morning.

"I'm quite certain that the terms of my indenture say your household must provide me with lodging. The animals have better lodging than that!"

"What do you want, Mercy? A four-poster bed?" she fired back at me. "What an ungrateful girl! And you must call me *Madam*!"

"I think we deserve to know the reason we must move."

Raising her hands at her sides and waving them like a goose flapping its wings, she abruptly left the kitchen.

That morning Zeno and I swept out our sleeping quarters in the attic, sending dust swirling through the air and billowing downstairs.

"I hope she chokes on it," I said to Zeno, but we were the only ones coughing from the filth.

When our mistress came to inspect our progress, she drew a half circle in the dust with her shoe.

"Look at this grime! I want this floor to be as clean as the table we eat on!"

She ordered us down on our knees and stood over us for the next half hour to be certain the job was done.

Zeno and I were still crouching on the floor, cleaning rags in hand, when we heard men shouting nearby. Their voices were unfamiliar. I ran to peek out the window, but the Hawk got there before me and pushed me aside. Suddenly a horrendous explosion shook the entire house.

Zeno let out a scream as though she were being murdered. I threw my arms around her, not knowing if we were about to perish in some kind of attack, but she kept on screaming.

In the midst of this confusion, the Hawk had stood paralyzed, her mouth agape. Then she'd flung open the front door and run straight out into clouds of white smoke.

At first, I couldn't see anything in the swirling haze, but I finally discerned the shape of two young men who had just fired their flintlock muskets repeatedly into the air.

They wore the same outfits and three-cornered hats that I'd seen on men who were drilling for the militia on the village green several times a year.

The Hawk flung her arms around one youth who was stockier and more disheveled than his companion.

"Oh, thank God for my brave, darling boys!"

Even as she clutched him to her bosom, the homely newcomer made an awful face at me over her shoulder, baring his teeth like a snarling dog. Then the other, thinner youth took his turn in his mother's arms, but she didn't hold him quite so tightly as his brother.

That was when I'd learned that the Hawk had two grown sons—Timothy and Nat. Both had been serving in the Connecticut militia and were returning home between musters.

Bryan Palmes, their new stepfather, would not meet them

until the evening meal. Although he was reserved at first, he welcomed them with his most courteous tone.

"It is good that you've come in the spring. You're just in time to start breaking up the fields for plowing," he told them. "And you can work alongside my man, Coffey."

Having two hungry men around created more work for all of us servants—more food to prepare and serve, more clothes to mend and to boil on laundry day, and more dried mud to sweep. No sooner had I cleaned a floor to the Hawk's satisfaction than her sons brought more mud back inside, caked on their hob-nailed boots. Sometimes I suspected that they deliberately tromped through every mud puddle or swamp that they could find.

Timothy, the younger one, was a sickly youth of sixteen. Already scarred from smallpox, his face was prone to erupt in pimples and hives; his mother even made him sleep with rags soaked in salve on his face. Timothy often fretted that his wheezing cough would prevent him from rejoining the militia when his regiment was called back to duty again. On some mornings I'd pretend not to see him stop on his way to the privy to spit blood in the garden.

For a few weeks after his arrival, Tim was quite kind to me. I was overjoyed when he even promised that he'd help me learn to read. But that would never happen.

The very first time that the Hawk saw her son sitting close to me in the kitchen, writing words on a slate, she told him in a loud voice, "You mustn't have such close association with a *servant*."

He didn't need to be told twice.

Nat was as robust as Tim was sickly. His eyes were gray slits under a mat of uncombed hair that reminded me of wet hay after it turned moldy. At eighteen, he was already a brute of a man with a fondness for ale and chewing tobacco.

Although he was a lazy farmer, Nat was a good marksman and sometimes set off before first light to shoot deer in nearby clearings. After months of eating potatoes, I was grateful to have a taste of roasted venison, and the Hawk was never stingy with leftover meat after her family had eaten their fill. Once she even made a dozen meat pies for Cate and Coffey and their boys; they thanked her for days afterwards. Even I had to admit that a good meal could make the most miserable of situations a little more bearable.

Nat's mother had raised him without a father to discipline him; he'd never felt the rod's sting and had no fear of punishment. Nevertheless, she'd tried to instill the values of the Congregation in his character. After only six months in the militia, however, most of that strict upbringing and hours of studying scripture had been undone as quickly as a knotted rope by a saber.

Having consorted with men of rougher breeding, including thieves and convicts, Nat had lost any fear of retribution for cursing and drinking. Nor had he any respect for women of the servant class. He did what he pleased and said what he pleased, heeding no one but his own mother. He even started calling Bryan "the Cripple" behind his stepfather's back.

"My mother picked a poor excuse for a man, didn't she? He thinks he can control her, but she's the one who can lead him by the nose," he boasted to me and to Cate.

As for Coffey, Nat steered clear of him. Perhaps he feared the older man's sheer size and the strength that he was always holding back. Coffey held his words in check too. He knew that a slave who spoke against his master—or his master's child—would earn a lashing.

When his new stepfather wasn't looking, Nat devoted his

time and energy to seizing my attention. He had no strategy other than to try to grab any part of me. As I bent over to pull weeds, he'd reach for my waist. When I went to gather eggs, he'd push me into a corner of the barn. Most of the time however, his bulky form and slow, lumbering gait allowed me to dodge his advances.

Nat was a natural born hunter and must have figured that I was fair game, but I was determined to outfox him.

One morning when Nat approached me, his eyes told me right away that he was about to say something lewd.

"Did you hear the Cripple rogering the old woman again last night?"

He snickered and added in a hoarse whisper, "It's disgusting, isn't it? He just can't stop, the filthy old goat."

Even as I told him to shut his mouth, I was grateful for one thing, however. Nat didn't seem to suspect that my relation to Bryan Palmes had gone beyond that of a servant and her master. But he had no shortage of other taunts. Although poorly educated, Nat was well schooled in the art of humiliation; he practiced those lessons to perfection whenever he could.

"What's the matter, Mercy *Bramble*? Why are you so prickly? Why does such a pretty wench have such an ugly weed of a name?"

Sometimes he'd recite an old nursery rhyme that made no sense to me:

There was a man in our town
And he was wondrous wise;
He jumped into a bramble bush
And scratched out both his eyes!

Then he'd grab me, shoving his lower body against mine.

"Want to stick to *this* Bramble?"

I would always wrench myself away, but one day I felt the

hardening in his groin and knew this was no longer a game for him. One of Cate's warnings came back to me: "Be careful, Mercy. Sometimes a man cannot be stopped. He'll hurt a girl bad, even rape or kill her."

Remembering what I'd shared with Bryan Palmes, I still believed that I'd done nothing sinful, that I had a right to a few hours of secret pleasure if no one else had to suffer for it but me. On the other hand, Nat's advances felt very different, very wrong.

After that day I vowed to keep my distance. That was easy enough to say, but very hard to do, since he dogged my footsteps everywhere, and I had to shoo him off.

One morning, as I was returning from our root cellar with the last shriveled apples we stored last fall, he lunged to grab away my basket. Although I saved my precious load, I had a sudden urge to fight my antagonist, at least with words, and let fly with choice insults.

"Are you trying to have your *way* with me, Master Way? Or don't you know how? Why should I bother with a boy who's nothing more than a *gnat*? Someone should have swatted you and finished you off on that evil day when you were born, miserable *Nat*."

But he retaliated with words that stung me even more deeply.

"Call me any names you want, Mercy. You're a bastard, aren't you? Didn't I hear that your mother's a whore? Paid her own way from England, flat on her back!"

He started to laugh.

I grabbed a rotten apple from my basket and shook it in his face.

"Shove this in your lying mouth! Then you'll look like the pig you really are!"

As Nat rolled on the ground squealing and snorting, I made a run for the kitchen door. My basket was intact, but tears streaked my face.

When I was small, my mother often had told me that my father had died on shipboard when we all came from England. Now, under Nat's taunting gaze, I'd just lost my most cherished illusion: that I'd had a kind-hearted father who only wanted a better life for his family.

In my mind, my loving father was gone forever; in his place was a brutal, faceless stranger, lying with my mother belowdecks. For all I knew, that scoundrel still walked the same earth as me, yet had no interest in his daughter.

Nat also knew the reason I could not attend church service on Sunday: I hadn't been baptized and was mostly unschooled in holy matters. He was fascinated by anything forbidden. If I were a heathen sinner, doomed to burn in hell, then he wanted to see how close he could come to the flames as I descended. But first he had to elude his mother's watchful eye and that of the Cripple as well. It was the perfect sport.

Hateful as he was, Nat always had the latest news of the wider world, and when he sang some ditty or sea chantey coming home late at night, I couldn't help lingering by the window. That spring I heard "The Handsome Cabin Boy" time and time again.

His cheeks they were like roses
And his hair rolled in a curl.
The sailors often smiled and said
He looked just like a girl!
But eating of the captain's biscuit
Her color did destroy
And the waist did swell of Pretty Nell,
The Handsome Cabin Boy.

How I pitied that poor girl in the song. Although she'd only wanted to see the world, she'd ended up groaning in labor as sailors made sport of her. It was such a terrible song, so unlike the carefree world of Charming Billy, where young girls baked cherry pies and lived so happily with their mothers for years and years.

And yet Nat's song wouldn't leave my mind.

※

When milder weather finally arrived, I was overjoyed to be relieved of my nighttime duties at the hearth, but I still had to rise well before sunrise to start a fire for cooking. In the dark, Zeno and I could roll up our quilts and dress with some modesty before family members started walking through the kitchen.

June unfolded like a wild lily in the sun. In a flood of pink blossoms, mountain laurel spilled out of the woods and tumbled extravagantly over stonewalls. Nature was giving us a most wanton display of her gifts, I thought.

The hard work of plowing and planting was over. I marveled at delicate green rows of tiny corn plants; it gave me such joy to see them inching upward where my own hand had planted them during the dark of the moon. At one point, we all feared that a flooding rain had drowned the crop, but miraculously, all the roots had held.

In late June, something terrible happened, or rather, something failed to happen: the rains stopped coming. After a week of reveling in the sunshine, I began to worry when each day dawned as bright and cloudless as the one before it. The sun burned any tender shoots in the fields and gardens, scorching the soil until it became dust.

Days turned to weeks, and then an entire month passed without rain. A little pond where cattle waded became no more than a puddle, exposing a muddy bottom. Soon, that too dried up and split with giant cracks. Suffering from thirst, our cows barely gave any milk, and we servants drew water to fill their trough several times a day. I'd send the wooden bucket on its rope lower and lower into the well, until I feared that I might only be imagining a glint of water below.

After several weeks, my heart would sink as low as that empty bucket.

The Congregation prayed long and hard for rain each Sunday and fasted for days to win back God's favor. But the skies stayed cloudless, and each July day stretched to an eternity. I was told that the sermons and prayers were becoming longer every Sunday, and Reverend Jewett's call for repentance still more urgent. Surely all men and women were being punished for the misdeeds of a few, he said. Perhaps it was the sin of only one or two among them.

Cate told me how the reverend would shout at them from his pulpit: "Search deep in your souls and the souls of all those around you! *Find the sinner!*"

I had to beg her to stop, because my own conscience had begun to chafe at me so.

Finally, one morning I lowered the bucket down the well and drew it back, empty save for a handful of mud and pebbles. Coffey shook his head when I showed him.

"Master Palmes never did have that well dug deep enough," he said, rubbing a massive hand over his close-cropped hair. "Was dug just enough to get us by, and now it's gone dry on us."

He too needed someone to blame.

"I got no choice, so we have to stay, but when my Cate buys me free, it won't be a day too soon. Old Coffey will be just a memory around this farm. I'll go dig us the finest, deepest well in the world."

"And build a higher roof, too, so you can stand up straight?" I teased him.

Coffey didn't laugh. He just walked away, still shaking his head.

Of course, no one in the household ever drank the well water except for Cate and Coffey's little boys. Not many people judged "Adam's Ale" to be fit to drink; we always drank warm beer or cider with our meals. Water was for farm animals, and for laundry, boiling vegetables, making tea, and taking an occasional bath.

Nonetheless, I was troubled that the well had failed. The Hawk ordered us servants to carry water from a neighboring farm owned by the Browns'. Only Zeno was excused, seeing as she was too frail to lift any buckets when they were full.

"She can stay and wash chamber pots instead," the Hawk decreed.

Hauling water was not as hateful as emptying or cleaning those vile pots, but it was still a shameful chore. I hated the strain of carrying two buckets of water hung from a pole across my shoulders, feeling every inch as though I were an ox in its yoke. Worse yet, I was humiliated to depend on others when my master's own resources had failed.

Never had my state of servitude seemed a greater curse. I wondered if it were time for another Mercy's Rebellion and if I could stand the consequences of disobeying my mistress.

The Hawk certainly wasn't going to trudge a mile out and a mile back with that miserable yoke across her shoulders. Suddenly it seemed that she needed far more water than ever before, sending me out several times a day. Sweat soaked through my shift, my linen gown, and the apron I always wore for propriety's sake. Strands of hair slipped out of my damp cap, and maddeningly, I couldn't put down my load to tuck them back in without prolonging my discomfort. And so, the buckets grew heavier and heavier each day, leaving dark bruises on my shoulders.

"It's as though the devil himself were in these pails," muttered Cate, who seldom complained aloud of any hardship and never shirked any chore.

Nat, who was still enjoying the comforts of home before heading back to join his regiment, noticed my growing discontent and recognized an opportunity.

"I don't know why you're walking out so far, Bramble. You could get clean water much closer to home," he said one day, exhaling smoke from his long-stemmed clay pipe. It was a rare interlude between plugs of chewing tobacco.

"There's a fine deep well in the field out where new recruits are camping out. No shortage of water there."

At first, I met Nat's suggestion with silence, but he could see me mulling it over.

Of course, I knew enough to steer clear of the encampment, having seen shameless women who went out that way. Cate had told me plainly what debauchery went on in the secrecy of the tents at any hour; I pictured myself trapped in a frenzied struggle, almost suffocating beneath a tent's moldy canvas as some blackguard had his way with me.

"It's no place for innocent young maids," she'd warned both Zeno and me.

In my heart I knew that I was no longer an innocent child, nor was I without sin. Those facts pressed on me more relentlessly than the yoke's weight.

Finally, I'd made up my mind: I'd fetch the water that was closer at hand. Three days after Nat had told me about the other well, I urged Cate and Coffey to go to the Browns' without me.

Then I set off alone and soon turned down a footpath that led to the militia's campground.

Sprays of tiny violets lined the path; they were so pretty that I tried not to trample them. Even though I still carried the yoke, I felt a lightness in my steps, feeling glad that I'd made my own choice for once. The Hawk would never know that I wasn't obeying her directions, I told myself.

After I'd gone just a short way, however, I thought I heard another set of footsteps behind my own. When a twig snapped, I froze, then spun around to look behind me.

A man stood in the path, not a stone's throw away from me. Sweat glistened on his reddened face and soaked his open shirt and the waistband of his breeches.

It was Nat, and he carried his hunting gun.

The woods were very still, as though all of nature were holding her breath; even the birds had stopped singing. Heat pressed around me as fiercely as if I were inside a cast-iron oven.

My eyes darted around to find a means of escape. On one side was a rocky cliff; on the other, a stonewall. The wall bordered an old burial ground where smallpox victims had been laid to rest. Never touched by pallbearers, their coffins were dragged far from town with ropes behind wagons.

Dropping my yoke and buckets into the deep ferns, I felt for a fleeting instant that I was free of an ignominious burden. I wanted to run, but my feet couldn't move.

Nat took a few steps forward, his eyes narrowed. One look at his face told me that he was not about to waste any time teasing or insulting me.

Carefully he propped his rife against a tree trunk and started to unbutton his breeches.

"No one will hear you scream out here, Bramble."

Then he lunged at me.

Although I opened my mouth to cry for help, it was just like a nightmare: I couldn't make a sound.

"Keep your mouth shut or I'll shut it for you!" he snarled.

Then he pushed me roughly off the pathway into the graveyard, his hands around my throat. My voice dried up and I could no longer speak, let alone shout.

I started kicking him, but the harder I fought, the more his hands tightened. He pushed me down, and as I fell, the back of my head struck a gravestone, but I scarcely felt it.

By then he had me fully pinned, forcing my legs apart.

As I sank deeper into a mossy gravesite, he began to tear at the skirt of my gown.

"You were born to be a whore, so why don't you act like one?"

His words alone almost paralyzed me, but something about his awful weight brought me to my senses; I would fight him off even if it cost me my life. Filled with hatred for the beast that lay on top of me, I tried to strike him, but he was far stronger than I'd ever imagined.

My attacker was trying to push his way between my legs when we both heard a noise close by.

He stopped his grunting, lifted his head, and listened.

A small but distinct voice cried out only a few feet away from where we struggled together.

"Mercy! Mercy! Are you all right?"

Through the headstones, I saw Zeno's doll-like face. Pale with fear, she stood paralyzed inside the graveyard wall. For some reason she was clutching a bunch of violets to her chest.

"Zeno!" I cried. "Thank God!"

Never in my life had I so loved the sight of someone's face as I did at that moment. Even in her state of terror, she was more beautiful than any angel sent from heaven could possibly have been.

My attacker—an enraged bull only seconds before—suddenly became an awkward calf. Nat was tripping over himself in embarrassment that someone should see parts of him so exposed below his flabby, fish-white belly.

"Huh?" was all he said, fumbling to button his breeches as he staggered to his feet. "What are *you* doing here for Christ's sake?"

Zeno couldn't answer.

"Did my mother send you after me, you little bitch?"

He took her silence as consent.

"That spying old hag," he muttered, but a look of fear had crossed his face.

Nat swatted at a few ants that were crawling up his forearm, grabbed his rifle, and spat on the ground near my foot. Walking away cursing, he didn't even look back at us.

Still stunned, I managed to sit upright and pull down my skirts. With one hand I rubbed my throbbing head, grateful that I had no blood in my hair. As I sat there still dazed, I traced the gravestone's inscription with my fingertips.

In a clear voice, Zeno read aloud:

Here lies Ann Turner.

Death is a debt

To Nature due

That I have paid

And so will You.

Suddenly I understood.

"Oh, Zeno," I cried. "Is your mother buried here?"

She dropped her violets below the gravestone and reached for my hand.

"Let's go home now," was all she said.

❧

Nat had no trouble finding a way to punish me, for cruelty was simply in his nature. After the day he'd attacked me in the burial ground, he turned his lustful eyes to Zeno, even though she still had the body of a child.

Whenever she was alone—carrying eggs to the house or returning from the privy—Nat would sneak up behind her, untie her apron or grab her cap.

It made my blood seethe with anger to see him do to her what he'd lately done to me.

"Leave her alone!" I screamed when I caught him in the act one day

As Zeno dashed back into the house, I struck Nat with a broom, but the lout just wrestled it away from me. He snapped its wooden handle in half, dropped the bristles upon the ground, and brandished a long section of the broomstick like a sword.

Then he declared his intentions as though they were the most reasonable consequences in the world.

"Since you wouldn't give in to me, then I'll have to settle for Zeno. There's not much meat on her bones, but she'll do nicely."

"Don't you dare go near her, you filthy scum," I hissed.

"I'll slice her in two like a little chicken. You know how I'm going to do it, don't you?" He thrust the broomstick up from between his legs.

"Just say the word and I'll settle for you instead," he taunted me. "Let me finish what I started and your little friend can stay in one piece. It's up to you, Bramble."

"That's blackmail. I'll tell the master and mistress what you're doing, and you'll be whipped."

"By the Cripple? That's a good laugh."

But I didn't tell either the Hawk or Bryan Palmes, fearing that neither one had reason to believe me. Nat would simply deny his intentions, which could only make matters far worse for me.

The next day Nat came back from the woods with a pair of pheasants that he'd shot. Bursting through the kitchen door, he flung the birds' limp bodies at Zeno, their blood spraying her face and apron. The girl dropped a porcelain bowl that she'd been clutching to her chest; it smashed to pieces on the stone hearth.

"It's fresh meat I want! There's enough spoiled meat in this house," Nat sneered, with a jerk of his head towards me.

Turning abruptly, he went back outside, just in time to avoid his mother. The sound of a bowl breaking had brought the Hawk rushing to the kitchen, skirts flying.

"It was broken by accident," I told her right away, trying to keep my voice level.

But it was too late. Our mistress had seen the fear on Zeno's face; she moved in on her as fast as a panther. Never questioning why the girl was already spattered with blood, she struck her twice, aiming sharp blows on either side of her head. As I tried to block the beating, the Hawk shoved me aside. She felt as strong as her son; I knew then where he had gotten such sinewy muscle.

"You have wantonly destroyed property in this house! That bowl is from *England*. Did you think you could get away with this?"

"It was an accident, Madam. You shouldn't blame Zeno," I repeated, standing up straight to look her in the eye.

"You'll both be whipped if I catch you breaking something again!"

After our mistress had stormed out, we took any broken shards to the trash heap and finished plucking the pheasants in silence. The heat was stifling, and the flies so numerous we couldn't swat them all.

"Don't worry, Zeno. I'll always protect you," I promised.

"But who will protect *you*, Mercy?"

How I wished that I could have replied, "My beloved mother will protect me," or "My good friend Cate will always stand by me."

Such answers would have sounded like foolish hopes or outright lies. Nor could I claim that God would protect me, since He already knew about my sins.

Only three days later, Zeno went missing.

On Sunday morning I'd been fetching water from the Browns' farm and had left Zeno behind for no more than an hour. My master, mistress, Tim, Cate, and Coffey had all taken the family's best carriage to the meetinghouse. Nat had gone too, on horseback, but he never showed up for the service.

Late that evening I heard his mother question her son before she went to bed. The Hawk looked less formidable at that hour, especially without her maid to attend to her. Disheveled and uncombed, her grey hair hung below the shoulders of her dressing gown.

"Did you see Zeno on your way to the meetinghouse?" she asked Nat.

"Yes, I'd met your servant girl on the road. She begged me for permission to go and tend her sick father for a week."

"And why hadn't she asked me or the master?"

"Said she was too scared to ask you. Guess she decided to take advantage of our empty house and return home. Of course, I tried to forbid her," he'd said sulkily, "but the little sneak just ran away from me."

Mrs. Palmes believed her son's story, but she was most displeased with the runaway.

"Well, she'll have to come back, or we'll notify the sheriff," she told her husband. "I suppose her father might die, and then she'll return sooner. She owes us seven years, no matter what her circumstances are."

She turned to her husband for a resolution.

"You must go to speak with her family, Bryan."

He looked up briefly from his desk.

"There's no one else in her family but two brothers, and I've heard they're halfwits like she is," said my master, who seldom discussed his neighbors' business.

At that point he opened a book; it was his way of closing the subject.

I knew that Zeno's sudden departure was more than just strange behavior. Her bed gown was still in the chest where she always kept it, as well as her cherished cornhusk doll, and sewing sampler.

Weeks passed and no news arrived from my fellow servant. Cate asked everyone she knew within five miles whether they'd seen Zeno. For once, my resourceful friend came up empty-handed.

August came to a burning close, and as katydids screeched like a shrill chorus, I harvested the last of the corn alongside Coffey. Our bushel baskets were both full to the rim that afternoon—for the fifth or sixth time.

The sun was low—a jewel in a crown of blood-red clouds. Coffey said that it reminded him of sunsets he'd seen as a young man, when he was cutting cane in the West Indies. That was before a slave trader chained him belowdecks of a coastal schooner and brought him to New England. There Coffey was sold as a "seasoned" slave—one who'd survived years of hard labor in the tropics when so many had died. It made me think how terrible it would be to be on the auction block, hands bound.

As we gathered the last of the corn, I told him how much I missed Zeno.

"Your little sister won't never be coming back," he said.

The lines etched on his face grew deeper; perhaps it was just the light of the sinking sun that changed his appearance, but it looked to me like true sorrow.

"And what do you know about her?" I demanded.

I gave Coffey's arm a hard push, as I'd seen Cate do many times, but it was like trying to move a stone wall.

"I know when something's wrong," Coffey replied.

Although he wouldn't give out another word on the subject, his face was a testament to the awful truth.

That week, Bryan began to question his stepson's tale about Zeno, but he didn't confront him directly. Instead, he did what his wife had asked him to do on the day Zeno disappeared; he and Coffey finally rode over to the Turner's farm to question her sick father.

The neighbors said that Mr. Turner was afflicted with barrel fever—they didn't come right out and call him a drunkard. He couldn't manage even his few miserable acres; last winter some of his poor hogs froze to death in the deep mud because he was too lazy to build the creatures a shelter.

When Bryan and Coffey returned, I overheard my master telling his wife about their visit. He described how the yard of the farmhouse was littered with broken wagon wheels, a rusty plow, and even skulls and bones from slaughtered cattle. The fences were so broken down that they no longer served any purpose.

Two half-wild dogs had kept Bryan and Coffey at bay until Mr. Turner finally called them off and bid the two men enter.

Inside the house, smoke from an unclean chimney had charred all the walls. Brown stains under the rafters and black mold also belied a leaky roof. In Bryan Palmes' opinion, the walls looked unlikely to stand through another winter.

Mr. Turner wasn't pleased to receive company but removed his pipe and answered their two questions with a shake of his head.

No, he hadn't been ill lately. And no, he hadn't seen his daughter in four or five months and had believed her to be still at the Palmes' household.

"We had a most peculiar conversation," Bryan mused.

"Well, that's all very interesting, but where *is* she, then?" his wife demanded. "A person doesn't vanish in thin air like a ghost."

Bryan didn't answer her, but in his silence, I could read his first inkling of suspicion: Nat was an outright liar, if not a murderer.

⁂

A few days later, Coffey and I had been working together in the barn, loading corn to take to the town mill. That was when Coffey saw something white deep inside the corncrib.

"Looks like a hand," he said, his voice low and solemn.

"A hand? How could that be?"

As I watched in disbelief, he started pushing aside the corn, digging deeper to see what was hidden there.

Then he groaned and staggered backwards.

Rats or other creatures—possums maybe—had eaten whatever flesh that Zeno still had on her bones. They'd left only her delicate face and hands untouched. As if to block out whatever or whomever she'd seen in her final moments, her eyes were squeezed shut.

I ran outside and fell to my knees to be sick.

Doubled over and choking, I gasped for fresh air. I thought of all the times that Nat had tried to push me into that same corner where we found Zeno, and I was sick again.

Coffey already had hurried into the house to share his awful news.

"God help us!" Cate cried. She dropped to her knees and buried her face in her hands.

Bryan ordered Coffey to ride into town for Sheriff Christophers. Without delay, Coffey slung a saddle on one of the mares and headed off.

A few hours later, the stocky constable rode out to the farm with two other men. I'd never met Sheriff Christophers before that day. He was a short man, and his eyes were very close to the level of my breast. He quickly looked me over in a manner that felt indecent, given the somber circumstances of his visit.

At first the sheriff spoke sternly to Cate and Coffey, asking if there had been some kind of argument among any of the servants.

Then, to my surprise, he questioned Mr. and Mrs. Palmes, but the Hawk did all the talking. No one asked us servants to leave, so we stayed and listened.

In her plainspoken manner, my mistress admitted that she'd struck Zeno in the head because the girl had been both careless and insolent. But the girl hadn't been seriously injured, and that incident had taken place several days before she disappeared.

"She must have gone off to sulk a while, then she fainted, Sheriff Christophers," said Mrs. Palmes calmly. "Of course, she was such a sickly thing. Some days I wondered how she could even hold her own head up."

She sighed deeply and rolled her eyes.

"There's just no other explanation, Sheriff. The corn must have piled up in the corncrib and no one saw her asleep inside."

"So, she must have died of suffocation," the Sheriff said gruffly.

He asked Bryan how the name Zenobia should be spelled, then made a note of her death for the town records. No one asked further questions or examined any evidence of how my friend had died.

Bryan told Coffey to put the girl's remains in an old wooden cask, nail it shut, and load it on the sheriff's wagon. The men would bring Zeno's body and her belongings back to her father's farm.

That night, when Bryan and the Hawk were in bed, Cate and I stayed up late. She sat on a stool before the hearth until long after midnight, her hands clasped in prayer. I'd never seen Cate cry before—I'd even wondered if she was so strong that she didn't show pain as others do—but tears flowed over her round cheeks in streams that night.

As I stared into the dying flames, my own eyes remained bone dry. If another had been there to observe me, that person might have believed that I didn't feel any grief. In truth, the raw horror of Zeno's death had not yet softened into sorrow, which was something more familiar, more bearable. All I could think of was that terrible proposal Nat had made to me—either I gave myself to him, or he would take Zeno instead.

When at last I turned to tell Cate my story, I found I was alone. She must have slipped away to her quarters; I'd never heard the soft footfall of her moccasins crossing the floor.

I tried to whisper Zeno's name into the darkness, but I could not do it. My tongue was paralyzed.

I'd lost my voice and could not speak, not a single word.

CHAPTER IV

MY TROUBLES INCREASE

"Oh sinner! Consider the fearful danger you are in: it
is a great furnace of wrath, a wide and bottomless pit,
full of the fire of wrath… You hang by a slender thread,
with the flames of divine wrath flashing about it…
nothing to lay hold of to save yourself… nothing that
you can do to induce God to spare you one moment."

—Jonathan Edwards,
"Sinners in the Hands of an Angry God"

CATE AND COFFEY both knew that I'd lost my power of speech, but they only partly understood the reason why. Discovering Zeno's body was a terrible thing to bear; fearing that I might have played a role in her death was far worse.

Cate did everything she could to hide my affliction. She stayed at my side whenever the Hawk gave orders and asked any necessary questions of our mistress. All I had to do was nod in reply. This worked for a few days, but we both knew I was heading for trouble if I couldn't answer my mistress or fulfill my household duties.

Coffey decided that his small sons were big enough to carry a single bucket, so Jonathan and Joseph followed him back and forth to the Browns' well, bringing back water I should have carried myself. As for working in the barn, I would no longer go anywhere near it, so Cate had to milk all four cows twice a day. She even left some milk in a saucer for the cat, Captain, as she had seen me do many times.

As soon as the Hawk had left us to our labors, I'd steal away to hide in the dark root cellar or lie down in a field to weep.

One morning Cate tried to pull me to my feet in the garden.

"Come on Mercy Girl, I need your help. You got to come back to the living!" she begged. "Don't you get sent away and leave me alone."

All I could do was shake my head. When I closed my eyes, I could still see Zeno's hand in the bottom of the corncrib.

I wanted to cry out, "Just let me die and be buried!" But no matter how hard I tried, I still remained completely mute.

My loss of speech continued for another seven days, and so did the drought. For everyone who'd been praying so fervently for rain, it probably felt more like seven years.

Coffey killed a black snake, as long as a man was tall, that had slithered out of a stone pile to find water. After that day I was beside myself with fear, knowing that such serpents were living close at hand; I imagined that they were crawling everywhere. At night, when I was alone in the kitchen, I could almost see them ready to drop from the rafters onto my shoulders. No matter how scared I was, however, I couldn't even whisper, let alone scream.

One morning in late July, when the air was already baking hot before noon, Cate simply couldn't tolerate my condition anymore.

"I'm going to help you," was all she said.

She told the Hawk that a cow had gone missing. Two of us

could cover more territory to find it than one alone could do, Cate explained to her. We would walk in opposite directions in a giant circle until we met.

"It's an old Indian practice," she assured the Hawk sagely.

To my surprise our mistress didn't challenge her.

"Then you must take Mercy with you," she ordered Cate, as though it had been her idea in the first place.

Earlier that day, before sunrise, Cate had led the cow to an overgrown pasture, half-hidden by dense forest. Then she'd tied the animal to a split-rail fence with a long rope and circled back home.

While the cow grazed in a shady spot, far from any path, the two of us set out on foot toward the Great Neck. Still mystified where we were going, I could only silently raise my hands and look searchingly at my companion.

"I promised Coffey I'd cook him some clams," Cate said with a smug look. "We're going to the beach."

My friend saw me trying to smile. At last, I was going to see the coast, a place I'd longed to visit throughout my childhood! I imagined I could already smell sweet salt air and feel the breezes.

After crossing shallow streams and swamps for an hour or more, we finally reached the White Beach. She scouted the low dunes and sparkling sands for any fishermen or wanderers, but saw no one under the cloudless skies.

I filled my lungs with the freshest air I'd ever breathed.

Cate first took off her shoes and stockings. Next, she started to remove her gown and shift, motioning to me to do so as well.

At first, I balked at her suggestion. Then I realized that Cate knew everything about me; I was already naked in her eyes. Our aprons, light gowns, and shifts had felt like woolen blankets in the heat, but now we simply stripped them off, along with our caps.

Soon we were standing at the sea's foaming edge, just as our Creator had made us.

Cate appeared even rounder without her garments than she did when fully dressed. She looked me over from head to toe in a manner that made me feel doubly naked in broad daylight. Then she started to chuckle and gave my waist a sharp pinch before I could slap her hand away.

"I always say you're a pretty woman, Little Mercy. No man since Adam could resist that temptation," she said, shaking her head. "No wonder he took what he wanted."

I shook my head vigorously and tried to shape the word, "No."

"But he took your precious chastity, didn't he?"

I turned away and covered my face.

"You tell me now, or I pinch you again!" she threatened.

Splashing me with seawater, my companion dragged me straight into the frothing waves.

Without thinking, I let out a hearty scream: "*I can't swim!*"

We stared at each other and burst out laughing.

"Oh, but you can talk, Mercy Girl! Praise the Almighty, you can talk!"

At first, I covered my mouth with both hands, trying to stop any more words that might spill out. It suddenly seemed pointless when the rest of me was so exposed.

Just like that, Cate had given me back the power of speech. After that day, I was convinced she had other magical powers, as well, ones that I might never understand. Some people might have thought she knew witchcraft to float like a cork the way she did. Having spent her earliest years in a village on the Nehantick River, Cate had learned to swim as soon as she could walk.

Now, without thinking, I surrendered myself to the sea's salty, fulsome embrace. Never in my life had I felt so free.

Hundreds of small, sparkling fish darted all around us. As the tide lifted me, I thought how easy it would be to slip under its surface and be forgotten. How else would I ever drown my sinful thoughts of Bryan Palmes, my hatred of Nat, or my memories of Zeno?

Just for a moment, however, I pushed those torments far from my mind.

Kneeling in the sea floor's rippled sand, I dropped my hair forward and let it swirl like a sea creature. I could have lost myself in its motion for hours, but Cate, ever watchful, had spotted a small skiff approaching with two men at the oars. She called out a warning and yanked me by the hand.

Running behind the dunes, we tugged our clothes back onto our wet, salty bodies as seagulls scolded us from above.

Cate had planned to fill our apron pockets with clams and make a feast for Coffey, but now that would be too risky. The men might be smugglers, she said, bringing in goods to avoid the customhouse in New London. Perhaps they were scoundrels or blackguards. I understood why it was dangerous to be alone so far from the farm.

Even though we left in such great haste, I managed to grab a single shell—a tiny marvel of pink and white curved like a baby's ear—and slip it in my pocket.

As we trudged back to find the Palmes' cow, we talked of many things, just like I imagined that sisters must do. She even urged me to forget what happened with my master.

"But he made me feel *bewitched*, Cate. How does a mortal man learn something like that unless he knows some kind of magic spell?"

My friend howled with laughter. "It's very old medicine, that spell. Not learned from the Scriptures!"

"Nor from The New England Primer!"

Cate stopped in her tracks. She faced me with a somber look.

"Promise me that's all over, Mercy. It's time to pray for forgiveness."

Now that she'd given me back my voice, I wanted to tell her everything: how Nat had tried to rape me in the graveyard; how Zeno had come along by chance and saved me; and how Nat had threatened Zeno if I didn't submit to him. But something made me hold my tongue that afternoon. After all, Cate already knew about my downfall with Bryan Palmes. She might think of me as an immoral woman if she suspected that I'd been consorting with another man, even against my will.

I also had a more selfish reason for staying silent at that moment: I didn't want to ruin what had been the best day of my life. The sea had washed me clean, and now I wanted a clean start with my friend too.

Even though Cate had a wild, stubborn streak, she was, above all, a God-fearing woman who obeyed the Commandments. Although she may have had an occasional lapse, she honored the laws of the church, and worked every day to buy her husband's freedom. No matter what we were discussing, Cate was likely to clasp her hands together and passionately declare her gratitude to God. She did so again that afternoon.

"Thank the Lord my little Jonathan and Joseph were born free men 'cause I'm a free woman."

"*I'm* going to be a free woman someday too," I announced.

I loved the sound of my own words as they echoed in the forest. "No one is ever going to take my voice from me again."

"Well, then, don't let no one stop you, Mercy," she declared.

The furrows around her mouth became even deeper. "You think about that long and hard when we get back."

On the final stretch of path, the cow stayed just ahead of our birch switches, casting what I thought were suspicious looks in our direction. Knowing that we were almost home safe, Cate's high spirits returned.

"Next time I need a little rest, I'm going to put *you* out in that field, Mercy Girl," she threatened. "Then I'll pretend to go looking for you."

"That would be a good trick, Cate, but maybe we should have an uprising and tie up our mistress instead!"

We were carrying on so noisily that we didn't hear a hint of a whisper all around us: the leaves were murmuring as the wind began to stir. Then came a low rumble of thunder.

"What's that?" I asked, stopping in my tracks. I'd almost forgotten that sound during the long days of drought.

In the northern sky, clouds appeared near the horizon. They were dark as ink stains on Bryan's desktop blotter. Within seconds, lightning darted from those clouds, and for the first time in two months, a delicious rain began falling.

As we both began to run, Cate did her best to keep pace with me.

When we reached the homestead, we saw the twins racing in circles through ankle-deep puddles while Coffey tried in vain to grab them to bring them inside. Our gowns were soaked and clinging to our skin; water ran down our legs and into our shoes.

From the kitchen, the Hawk peered out at us in disbelief. With her swollen belly, she seemed to fill the entire doorway.

"Merciful God, have you two been swimming?" she demanded.

"At least you found the cow," she continued. "Maybe there's something in those old Indian ways after all."

Thank heavens I'd already learned a valuable lesson from Cate—how to prevent my true feelings from showing in my expression. Neither of us even smiled.

Later that night I put my arms around Cate and kissed her for giving me a sweet taste of freedom.

"I won't forget this until the day I die," I promised solemnly.

The next evening, I was surprised to see Coffey sitting alone behind the shed, eating clams and potatoes from a small iron skillet.

"No king ever had a better meal," he boasted, although he was barely able to talk with his mouth so full. "Cate walked all the way to the beach before sun-up to dig these up,"

"That's your Cate," I answered. "She always keeps her promises."

⁂

After that day the rains came again at natural intervals. The corn plants, which had emerged in thin, green threads through the fields, now grew thicker and expanded to an army of robust plants, standing at attention.

It was about that time that Bryan Palmes rode alone to Norwichtown to assist with writing someone's will. He stayed there for two days, lodged at a tavern where he spent all his money on cards, and then returned to the farm.

That evening, several hours before I took my meal with Cate and Coffey, I served a supper of salt pork and cabbage to Bryan, the Hawk, and her sons. To my surprise my master began giving Nat and Tim a detailed account of a scene he'd witnessed. The clack of the brothers' spoons against the wooden plates barely slowed as they listened to their stepfather, but I heard every word from the hearthside, having not yet eaten with my fellow servants.

As soon as he'd arrived in Norwichtown, Bryan had found himself on the edge of a jeering mob; it was so large that he couldn't see the object of their derision. A farmer standing by him said that two townspeople had just been tried and found guilty of adultery. Now the magistrates had decreed a public whipping.

"They gave the woman no less than twenty-five lashes, then made her stand for five hours on the pillory for all to see," said Bryan. "She was an innkeeper's wife, nearly fifty years old, they told me."

"What a disgrace for that old woman," the Hawk interrupted.

"The crowd kept shouting, 'Whore! Burnt-tail bitch!' and other curses too vile for me to repeat," Bryan continued, shaking his head.

When they'd finished with the woman, the mob had turned to her fellow sinner, treating him far more harshly. The magistrate gave the adulterer fifty lashes on his naked back. But his torture didn't end there.

For the final punishment, a blacksmith was called in to brand the man's forehead with a red-hot iron, fashioned into a crude letter "A." As the man screamed in agony, the crowd roared their approval just as loudly. At last, the offender was let go, presumably to tend his wounds in hiding.

I'd never heard my master use such a somber tone before. Perhaps he'd wished to gain favor with the Hawk by trying to sound like Reverend Jewett.

"Sinners will always be found out, sons. They'll be brought into the light like a fox smoked from its den. Never forget that it's *your* duty to bring them to their punishment."

He sounded as if he respected those townspeople for carrying out the punishments as an example to all. Yet he must have had some sympathy for the man, whose hideously scarred forehead would set him apart from others, just as Bryan was set apart by his crippled leg.

Tim and Nat had listened impassively at first, but soon Tim was leaning forward to catch every word.

"Well, I'm sorry I wasn't there to see for myself," Tim said sadly.

Nat, on the other hand, remained silent. He simply pushed the trencher aside and, with a gaping yawn, began whittling.

Later, as I cleared the greasy board on which they'd all eaten, I wondered what my master had been thinking as he watched such a grim scene in Norwichtown. Perhaps he already suspected that Nat had raped and killed Zeno. If so, was Bryan trying to set a trap for his stepson, to catch his guilty conscience? Or was he tormented by the sin of fornication that we'd committed together and so thoroughly concealed?

It was possible that Bryan felt each lash across his own back, believing that God knew of our sin in the canopy bed and would never forget us. If that were so, my master was probably waiting for his own punishment and would accept it when it came.

Yet there was another possibility I'd never considered. What Bryan had seen in Norwichtown would drive his restless spirit to do something that defied all reason: he would sin again.

And I would also.

The following night was as hot as an isle in the West Indies must be, languid and steaming. It wasn't possible to breathe, let alone fall sleep on my cramped wooden bench. I sought some air outdoors, where moonlight painted such a straight, shining path across the pond.

Barefoot, I climbed a short way up the grassy hill, hoping to catch a breeze. That's where my master found me, sitting on the large, flat stone that marked his first wife's grave. I'd never know if he was seeking me or her that night.

As Bryan drew near, he coughed slightly, perhaps so as not to frighten me. Heat had dulled my senses, so his sudden appearance didn't startle me as it might have in broad daylight. Not that I would have rested idle like that when there was work to be done.

I thought of the Hawk, seven months pregnant with his baby

and as swollen up as the mare I'd seen being led away on the day I'd arrived. My mistress was probably in their bed with a wet rag on her head and a feather pillow propped under her belly.

He seemed to read my thoughts.

"My wife is fast asleep, so I stepped out to smoke," he said, yet there was no sign of any pipe or tobacco.

I nodded. For months I'd longed for an opportunity to be alone with him, but now I'd lost my voice a second time.

"The moon is nearly full again," he observed, looking at the sky.

Then silence settled around us again for several minutes.

His gaze strayed to my body. I was clad only in my thin shift and was naked underneath. My hair tumbled down past my waist like a waterfall, catching the moonlight.

It was customary for a woman to keep her hair always hidden from sight under her cap. Perhaps he was more aroused to see my uncovered hair than the lines of my body.

He stood over me, so close that I thought I could hear his heart beating, but perhaps it was my own.

"You're more beautiful than ever, Mercy," he whispered. "I'm sorry I never told you that."

Not knowing why on earth I would do such a bold thing, or what I wanted, I gently pressed my lips to his hand, just as he'd once done to mine a year before.

Part of me wanted him to touch me again as he had that night in his bedchamber, but that was no longer enough. This time I needed to know that he had full knowledge of what he was doing, not like a man blinded by drink.

He sat down next to me on the stone, unmoving as the rock itself.

I waited.

It was a perverse notion, but the flimsy ribbon that gathered the neck of my shift seemed to beg to be undone. At last, Bryan slowly untied it. His hands found my breasts, and his mouth covered mine. My lips parted readily, as though I'd been dying of thirst and he'd poured cool water between them.

My master's embrace was even stronger than I remembered, strong as iron shackles.

I would remember every moment of that night—and the next five nights he came to me in the waning moonlight—but words we used in of our ordinary, daylight lives could not describe it. We were only two shadows, and shadows do not have such a language.

For those of you who would come to judge me so harshly, I could ask three questions. Were you ever sixteen years of age? Have you never acted foolishly or obeyed an impulse rather than your reason? And did you ever lie with someone on cool summer grass under the stars and feel as though you were, at last, fully alive?

If only I could answer my own questions, "Nay, not I. Never."

❧

Cate and I were scouring kettles in a wooden tub outside the kitchen door when she gave me a look that was as sly as a cat with a bird.

"Know what I heard while I was milking in the barn?"

"No, but I'm sure you're about to tell me Cate. And don't you dare spare a single word!"

Rolling her eyes, she divulged how she'd overheard Timothy speaking with his stepfather as Bryan was putting away his saddle after a day of riding.

She'd remembered almost every word and recounted the scene faithfully.

"Father, are we not all responsible for the sins of others, and are we not bound to bring them out into the light?" Timothy had asked.

Bryan had replied without hesitation.

"That is the contract we have with God and our fellow man, son. It's something you must have known since the age of reason."

Cate showed me how Timothy had clasped his hands together, as if seeking courage to continue.

Then all in a rush, Tim had said: "I saw your servant Mercy lying with a man on the grassy hill by the stone that marks your first wife's grave. It was in the dead of the night when I walked to the privy...."

"What?" Bryan had demanded in a flustered tone. "Well, who was it, son?"

"I couldn't quite see his face, sir, but I believe it was my brother Nat on top of her. He was *defiling* her. He hadn't come to bed that night and was out roaming the countryside."

"And how could you know for certain it was Nat if it were so dark?"

"Oh, I knew. The moon was out and I saw well enough. My brother had just boasted to me that Mercy recently let him have his way with her in a graveyard."

"What? Speak up, boy."

"He said they... they fornicated on the ground like animals, though his words were far cruder than mine."

Cate mimicked how Bryan's face had gone rigid, a death mask, then went on with her story.

"I thought our master might be having a fit," Cate observed, "but then he says, 'Tell your brother to meet me here in the barn.'"

Shortly after that, when Nat came back from hunting in the woods, Tim sent him to meet his stepfather straightaway. Nat never suspected what awaited him.

Cate paused at this point in her story and drew herself up as tall and narrow as she could. For a fleeting instant, I almost believed that she really *was* Bryan; the dark anger flashing in her eyes matched what I'd sometimes seen in his.

She lowered her voice to a growl.

"You must thank me, son, *thank* me that I will be the one to give you this whipping you deserve, not the Sheriff. And you're lucky it will be here in secret, not in front of the whole town!"

At first Nat had protested, "I never touched her! Mercy was the one who lured me with her lewd behavior!"

The instant that Nat had spoken my name, Bryan had grabbed an ox whip in his right hand. With his left hand gripping a ladder to the hayloft, he managed to knock the slow-moving Nat to the floor. Then he whipped the young man's back with such fury that even stalwart Cate couldn't bear to watch.

"They never saw me run away from my hiding place," Cate concluded, letting her voice trail away.

Of course, both Bryan and I knew that Tim hadn't seen his brother with me that night. No, the man I'd sinned with had been Tim's stepfather himself, a man he was asking for spiritual guidance. Yet Bryan had chosen to punish Nat anyway, perhaps out of self-hatred. Or had Bryan wanted Nat to suffer physical pain for what he'd done to Zeno?

Finally, I couldn't restrain myself any longer.

"Everything you heard Tim say today was a lie, Cate! He's a cowardly little liar who made up a tale to cause trouble for his brother. Nat's an even bigger liar."

She grabbed my arm and shoved her face close to mine.

"Oh, I want to believe you Mercy Girl. I'm already saying prayers for you every night and can't make them any longer! Coffey's waiting long enough for me to come to bed."

She added a final warning, "I've tried to help you, even take chances for you, yet you still been too friendly with the Devil."

We continued scrubbing the kettles in silence, our hands growing black with soot. Suddenly an idea came to me.

"Cate, you have to trust me! I'm going to need your help."

"I don't know," she grumbled. "Maybe you were better off when you had no voice."

"Listen, I'll tell you what really happened to me in the woods, what Nat did to me."

At last, I spilled the entire story of how Nat tried to rape me in the burial ground, not sparing any detail of what Zeno had witnessed.

"Then Nat went after Zeno when he couldn't have me. I'm certain he killed her that Sunday and left her in the corn crib. It wasn't any awful accident or sickness."

Cate cried with fresh grief, as if I'd opened an old wound, "Oh my poor little Zeno!"

"The master may have given Nat a good whipping, but that wasn't enough for murdering Zeno," I insisted. "He shouldn't be allowed to go free and hurt another girl or woman."

"But what can we do?"

"I couldn't speak out that night when Sheriff Christophers came for her body, but I can speak now. I've got to go to the sheriff's and tell him the truth."

Cate dried her eyes on her apron and turned to me.

"The Hawk's not watching me as close as you. That's because she hates you more than me. I can get into town easier than you can."

"But how will you do it?"

"The master's been sending Coffey all alone to cut trees on his woodlot. If I ride along in the wagon, I can slip away into town when Coffey's working. I'll talk to that sheriff man for you."

Early the next morning, when I came into the front chamber to open a window, the Hawk was rubbing a pungent salve on

Nat's back. The whip had raised long, red welts, and he moaned as she touched them. Perhaps Nat was just trying to gain his mother's sympathy, but he seemed dazed, if not chastened.

"I've never been whipped before, Mother," he whimpered in disbelief. "Father was never at home to do such a thing."

His mother was silent as stone, but when Nat pulled on his shirt and left, she spat out a few words in my direction.

"Don't think that I don't know, because I know *everything* that goes on in this house. I have my eye on you, Mercy Bramble. Cate too. That woman and her brood can't leave this household soon enough."

"Cate is a fine woman, Madam," I said. "As fine as any under this roof."

For the next few weeks, the Hawk kept Cate and me so busy that we were never able to leave her sight for even one hour. When Cate told the mistress that she was going to gather kindling while her husband cut trees in the woodlot, the Hawk refused to let her go with him. To our dismay, she even sent Nat and Tim along to chop wood with Coffey; reluctantly, the brothers accompanied him and worked all day until they were exhausted.

That evening, before retiring, I pleaded with Cate.

"So, what can we do now? We can't fly to the sheriff's house like two birds and sing our complaint through a window."

Cate was quiet for a moment, then told me her idea.

"Write a letter to him."

I reminded her that no one had ever shown me how to hold a pen.

"*I* write the letter," she announced. "We'll borrow a piece of parchment from the master's chamber. You tell me what you want it to say."

Since I wasn't allowed in Bryan's chamber, Cate had to wait for a chance to go in there. The next afternoon, the Hawk was sewing in the front room when her head dropped on her bosom and her hands fell in her lap; she'd fallen fast asleep.

Cate slipped into the bed chamber to complete her mission, securing a sheet of parchment, and an older quill pen that was not among Bryan's favorites. She also took a few drops of ink, pouring it into a thimble so he wouldn't notice his inkwell was missing.

Late that night, by candlelight, I told her what she must write and made her repeat it back to me several times:

Sheriff Christofers
It was Nat Way killed Zenobia Turner.

Cate was satisfied with her work.

"Keep it simple," she said. I agreed.

When the ink dried, she folded our letter, and slipped it into one of Bryan's precious envelopes. We didn't use sealing wax, since we'd be more likely to be discovered if any were spilled. On the front Cate wrote one word: "Sheriff."

For all of our planning, however, we soon realized that we'd reached another dead end. How would we deliver a letter?

"Give it to me. I'll find a way," I promised.

Only I knew that I'd be with Bryan again that night. We never set any times for our secret meetings; he simply came to me if he saw me waiting on the hillside.

After dark, I went to our meeting place as usual, carrying my letter; I placed it carefully on the flat stone, and waited. The moon was waning. It no longer had that full, radiant glory I'd seen a week before but only a dull glow that cast gloomy shadows.

Bryan finally labored up the hill after midnight, just as he'd done before. Without a word of greeting, he drew me roughly down to the ground, already slipping his hand under my shift and along my bare thighs. Even the weight of his body oppressed me, as though he meant to suffocate me.

It all came back to me, that awful day in the graveyard, and how Nat had tried to force himself on me. But then I became aware of the strangest sensations: the rolling of a ship at night, faceless shadows, men's laughter in the dark. Had this been my mother's fate?

With all my strength, I started pushing back. Bryan was caught unawares, and I rolled him off me with one quick shove; he might as well have been a sack of potatoes.

He groaned loudly as if I'd caused him great pain.

"For God's sake, woman, what is the matter with you?"

I pulled down my shift and sat up, reaching for my precious letter.

"We've been very close, close as a man and woman can be. Now I must ask you to complete a favor."

Trying to regain some dignity after being sprawled on the ground, Bryan drew himself up on one elbow and brushed off his sleeve.

"What are you implying?" he asked suspiciously. "I won't be blackmailed, not by any man, and certainly not by a woman."

"Just listen to me. Surely you must suspect that Nat is not blameless in the death of your servant, Zeno. I believe that he raped her, then took her life."

"And what makes you so certain? Did you see such a crime take place?"

"No, but he'd threatened to hurt her if I didn't give in to him first."

I told him how Nat had tried to force himself on me a few weeks before in the burial ground. If Zeno hadn't come along the path, my attacker would have succeeded. Perhaps Zeno had saved my life that day, I said.

Bryan rolled onto his back and heaved an enormous sigh.

"Please don't tell me he tried to take your *virtue*, Mercy. We both know you are hardly an innocent. And you've made your choices by free will."

Angered now, I stared at him, but could not see his expression in the shadows.

"You were the one who *took* that innocence, sir, then pushed me away and married another, even though you knew that I, that I…"

But I could not say, "I loved you."

Regaining my wits, I showed him my letter. He asked me to tell him its contents, since it was too dark to read.

"The letter says it was Nat Way who killed Zenobia Turner. It isn't signed. All you have to do is deliver it to Sheriff Christophers' house. He'll enforce the law and see that Nat is punished."

Bryan was sitting so still that I could hear his breathing.

"I despise Nat, if you must know," he confided.

"For what he tried to do to me? For lying to his brother Tim?"

To my surprise, Bryan laughed a little.

"Oh, perhaps. But he calls me the Cripple behind my back. I simply cannot abide that from anyone, least of all an oafish stepchild like Nat."

"Please, take this letter, Bryan. If not out of hate for him, then do it for love of me. All you have to do is leave it at the sheriff's door. He'll see how poor the handwriting is and will know it wasn't from you."

"I'm sorry, but I choose not to. What good will it do? The most Nat will get is a public whipping, and I already gave him one he won't forget.

Bryan took the letter and ripped it in two. I grabbed for what was left of it.

"I am not your servant, Mercy. It's quite the other way around, actually. I command *you*. And you will never be my equal."

Pulling myself to my feet, I started running downhill to the house, clutching the torn letter.

Bryan never came to me in the moonlight again. After that night, I'd believed that I was free of him. I soon found that he was still inside of me.

※

I'd saved my torn letter and could see that it was still readable. Although I pleaded with Cate one more time to have Coffey deliver it to the sheriff, she finally told me that they couldn't take the risk.

"Coffey's a black man, Mercy. He's in far more danger every day of his life than you will ever know. My children need their father here above ground, not below."

"So, we're just going to let Nat go free?" I challenged her.

She took both my hands and looked deep into my eyes.

"You wait. God will punish Nat someday. I know, because I've prayed to God to do it. I've asked Him to do it for you."

Although Cate urged me to burn the letter, I hid it in a secret place with my few personal belongings. Then I tried to return my attention to my daily work.

Despite the earlier drought, the corn crop was the best we'd ever seen. From sunrise to sunset, we servants labored to harvest it. No one could shuck corn faster and cleaner than Cate; her livelihood had always depended on it, especially during a famine year when she was a small girl. Many of her people had died.

"You never forget being hungry," she told me, patting her stomach. "Your belly remembers forever."

Neighboring farmers held husking parties almost every night, but none of us were permitted to go to hear music or to dance.

"Dancing leads to whoredom," the Hawk had warned us.

Our stern mistress didn't approve of what happened when the husking was finished, the fiddle music stilled, and all the rum kegs drained. On their way home, unwatched servants often paired off in the dark fields. Nightwalking, some called it.

"It's wise that a fine-looking girl like you stay away from any huskings," Cate advised. For such a pious woman, she had no end of stories about "the weak of flesh," and "lambs that stray."

We both knew that I'd already been guilty of nightwalking; I was thankful that she didn't remind me of that.

One night our neighbor Colonel Minor was holding a husking party just down the road. By prying open a kitchen window I could hear distant music and laughter. I pictured all the servants, arm-in-arm, spinning from too much drink.

That's when I saw something move between the shed and barn: two figures standing so close they looked like one. The taller one bent down and wrapped the smaller in a half-circle embrace, rocking gently back and forth. Cate and Coffey were dancing in the starlight, and he was stroking her long, unbraided hair.

How I envied them at that moment; no king and queen could be happier.

After the harvest, Tim departed for New Haven. He'd intended to rejoin the militia, but soon wrote home that he'd experienced "a revelation" and wished to study to become a minister. When she heard that news, the Hawk almost ruffled her feathers with pride, boasting to all of us about her son's divine calling. She even hired a seamstress—a young woman who now did the work my mother had abandoned—to make Tim a new frock coat. At great expense, she sent it with a post rider to New Haven.

Around that time, Nat told his mother that he wished to

sign on a vessel bound for the West Indies. Although many ships came and left port with fresh crews and cargo, he was never among them. The closest he came to a ship was an old fishing skiff that he kept hidden in the marshes. He sometimes drifted off to sleep in it while tied to the shore, too lazy even to cast a fishing line in the water.

I hated to see him enjoying any of life's pleasures.

"How is it possible that God allows Nat to walk around here so freely and enjoy the sunshine while Zeno is buried deep in the earth?" I complained to Cate. "Part of me wants him to go away forever; the other part wants him to stay and be punished."

It was only a matter of time, I thought, before Nat would start up his old behavior, stalking me as his prey. But days passed and he didn't start his old tricks again. To my surprise he even asked his stepfather if he could help me with final husking. Then he worked long hours at my side without causing me any trouble.

One day my curiosity finally got the better of me.

"Are you ailing, Nat? Do you have a fever?"

He shook his head, spit out a stream of tobacco, and assured me that he was quite well.

"If you're so hale and hearty, why haven't you gone out to sea?"

Nat wiped his dirty hands, gave me a long, sulky look, and sighed deeply as though I'd hurt him.

"You still don't understand, do you, Bramble? I thought if I stayed you might come to fancy me."

"Fancy you? Are you serious?"

"I was just playing the fool before to get your attention. A fellow like me doesn't know how to talk to a woman like you, only whores. Now I'm ready to act like a gentleman."

He took off his hat, placed it over his heart, and gave me a lovesick look.

"But if you truly want to make me happy, Nat, you should leave."

"Why should I go anywhere when I'm so happy here with you, Bramble?"

With his sweaty grip, he reached for my hand, pulling it to his heart.

"Come on, why can't we be sweethearts? Then we can marry and share a bed."

I snatched my hand away as fast as I could.

"Stop it, Nat! Do you think I could forget how you tried to rape me? How you murdered my darling Zeno?"

He swore that he'd only been having a little sport with me in the graveyard and that no one could ever prove he'd laid a hand on Zeno.

"It was all your fault anyway, Bramble. I gave you a choice, remember?"

"You're an evil man, Nat!"

"I'm really not so bad. You should live up to your name and have mercy on this sinner." Then, mild as a lamb, he folded his hands together in prayer and rolled his eyes heavenward.

"Doesn't Tim always say 'to forgive is divine?'" he asked mockingly. "But I really want to know, why don't you *like* me?"

"Even if you'd never done anything wrong, I would hate you, Nat. You're not a man I could ever care for. You're not..."

He cut me off before I could finish my thought.

"I'm not Bryan Palmes. Isn't that what you were going to say?"

His words horrified me. Behind his oafish manners, he was as sharp and cunning as his mother, the Hawk.

Now my head was spinning. I remembered an old nursery rhyme that Nat would recite to provoke me before trying to grab me.

There was a man in our town
And he was wondrous wise;
He jumped into a bramble bush
And scratched out both his eyes!

"Would you allow me to court you, Mercy?" He looked at me beseechingly through his matted hair.

Although I considered saying something charitable, I howled with laughter instead. Spreading my fingers like claws on both hands, I pretended to gouge my face.

"I'd rather scratch out *both* my eyes, Nat!"

The very next day, he re-enlisted in the militia.

Before he left the farm, he told me, "It's only for a while. Wait for me, Bramble. I know you'll come to change your mind."

Nat had walked no farther than the gate before he'd turned and shouted, "Time is running out, and you know it. You'll have no other choice."

He may have meant that there would be a shortage of husbands for me if I waited too long, but perhaps he knew something darker, something I'd yet to find out myself.

❦

In late September, Mrs. Palmes gave birth to her baby, a son she called Elijah. Cate served ably as midwife while I attended. It was an easy birth—far easier than two of Mrs. Holt's that I'd seen—but there was little rejoicing. Bryan took only scant interest in his new son; he grumbled about "the caterwauling" that disturbed his quiet study and woke him in the early morning hours.

I, on the other hand, could not have loved that baby more, even if he'd been my own. Each time I picked him up or swaddled him in his blanket like an Indian baby, his perfection overwhelmed me. His face, when not red from crying, was as pale and soft as petals of wild dogwood in the forest. The insides of his little ears reminded me of the seashell I'd found at the White Beach.

Even the Hawk seemed like a different person when she held Elijah or sang him songs; I was glad to see this change in her character, because no child should suffer from having an unkind or indifferent mother. She loved Elijah so fiercely that Cate took to calling her Mother Hawk, behind her back, of course.

It was during the final days of the harvest that I began to feel my natural vigor starting to fade. My motion became slower, and I found myself longing for day's end as never before. Then, one morning, I stumbled on my way to the barn. My legs felt no stronger than blades of grass, unable to bear my weight. My empty stomach churned as though I'd eaten rancid meat.

Somehow, with my head reeling, I made my way to Cate and Coffey's quarters, clutching my stomach. Cate was there with her boys.

Taking one look at my panic-stricken eyes she drew me away from the children.

"When was the last time you had Eve's Curse, the bleeding?" But she might as well have been talking nonsense.

"Whatever are you saying?" My mouth was so dry that I could scarcely speak.

"That you *may be with child*, God help us."

I burst into tears.

"I can give you a cure, Mercy. It's terrible, strong as poison, but it will make the problem in your belly go away—before the sun rises and sets."

Then she embraced me, tenderly stroking my hair as my mother had once done when I was a child, repeating over and over, "Oh poor Little Mercy."

I wept for only a few moments before I realized that my tears were as useless now as they'd been when I was seven.

"All right, Cate. I'll do whatever you bid me."

In the next two days the two of us hardly spoke a word to one another as Cate ventured into the fields and swamps looking for plants.

"Not easy to find anymore," I heard her mutter, shaking her head. "Very hard to find." Evading the eyes of the Hawk so that she could slip away to forage was even more difficult.

Then one night, after the master and mistress had retired and baby Elijah was asleep in his cradle, Cate and I met by the well.

"Here," she said, handing me something wrapped in a strange leaf. "Eat all of what's inside."

After a moment's hesitation, I forced a bitter mash of roots and leaves down my constricting throat. Then I waited.

Five days later, Cate took me aside and whispered, "So, is it gone? Has the bleeding come?"

"No, not yet, Cate."

She frowned so deeply that a great furrow seemed to split her smooth forehead between her eyes.

"That's no good then. You'll have to ask Hugo Moreaux."

I didn't have to wait very long for the homely old peddler. The next week, when I heard his wagon bells and saw him at the gate, I was the first to run and greet him.

No sooner did Hugo see me than he began singing a verse of "Charming Billy." Even though his heavy leather garments weighed him down, he managed to do a shuffling sort of jig while clapping his hands.

"Remember when I sang to you as a little one, Mercy?"

I nodded, but didn't join his singing as I'd used to do. Although I was ashamed to tell the old man about my problem,

I knew I had to do it quickly before the Hawk emerged from her roost to barter.

Hugo was still grinning at me, revealing many more gaps than teeth in his mouth, even more than he'd had when I was a child. It made him look like a ghoul or goblin.

"So, are you married yet, Mercy?"

"No," I stammered. "I'm not married, Hugo, but I made a big mistake, and now I need a cure." I rested my hand high on my belly as I spoke.

I was grateful that he didn't say a word to judge me; he was more interested in selling something from his medicine chest.

"You are in luck, today," the peddler said in a singsong voice. "I have something for your woman's problem."

He dug deep into a tin chest, extracted a small buckskin bag, and placed it in my palm.

"But I've already tried Indian medicine," I protested.

"This is pennyroyal and rue. Much, much stronger. But nothing comes for free, not even for a friend. So, what will you pay me?"

Reaching in the pocket of my apron, I found a small treasure I'd placed there the day before: one of old Mrs. Palmes' beautiful tortoiseshell combs. I'd borrowed it—no, stolen it—from the Hawk's dressing table the day before. She had so many combs in her collection I could only hope she might not notice one was missing.

"It's unlawful, you know, taking property from a servant without her master's consent," grumbled Hugo, but he pocketed the prized comb, just as my mistress poked her head out the farmhouse door.

That night I sprinkled the bag's contents into a bowl with some cider and spooned the mixture to my lips. It tasted far worse than Cate's remedy.

An hour later, I couldn't move my limbs or lift my head.

※

I lay in Cate and Coffey's quarters for three days, although my fevered mind made me believe it had been only three hours.

"A curse on that Hugo Moreaux and all his kin," muttered Cate, as she mopped my brow with a wet rag. "That baby be mighty strong if you come through this. Just pray to your Maker. Pray and pray, Mercy."

On the fourth day of my affliction, the Hawk appeared at the door of the shed but didn't come near me.

"I can send word for the doctor, but it's a long, long ride," she complained to Cate. She stood in silence with her arms folded.

"The doctor asks too much for leeches, which is surely what she'll be needing. No doubt she has an excess of blood in her," she declared.

But our mistress made no move to send Coffey for the doctor.

"It's after curfew anyway. Too late to send a slave out in the dark. We'll just have to see what God wills. Tell me if she worsens."

And she went back into the house.

For another three days, I lay on a patched, corncob mattress that was Cate and Coffey's usual bed. The two slept together on the floorboards without a single complaint, and I often saw them on their knees, praying for my return to health.

Day merged with night; I never knew the hour, nor was I always certain of my whereabouts.

Later I remembered hearing Coffey's low, soothing voice. He was always in at night of course—the curfew forbade Negroes from walking the roads after eight o'clock. To pass the hours, Coffey told stories to his little sons. A few were simple tales that he'd heard as a boy in Guinea, when his name wasn't Coffey but

Quafir, and when his face had been scarred deliberately, according to his people's custom. He never spoke of how he'd lost the use of one eye, and no one dared to ask.

Most of his tales were ones that he'd heard from other slaves and servants. As if in a dream, I learned how Captain Kidd had once buried a treasure on the banks of the Great River to the north. Before they hid the fortune in the earth, the crew had killed one of their own men on the lid of the treasure chest.

"And his ghost guards that treasure to this very day," said Coffey, making his eyes look huge and dropping his voice to a hoarse whisper. Then he'd grab the boys around the waist and hoist them, screaming, over his head.

No matter how many stories he told, his sons would always plead, "Tell us more!" Like the little men in tales of Mr. Gulliver, they'd climb on his trouser legs so he couldn't get away from them.

Cate told stories too, though hers were longer than Coffey's and often lacked a beginning, middle, or an end. She told of the last families of her tribe, whose hunting and fishing grounds once stretched from the Nehantic River west to the Connecticut River. Some were the last survivors of other tribes, including Pequots and Mohegans torn asunder by wars long ago.

Smallpox often destroyed whole families, and those who lived struggled to hold on to the few acres that they'd been granted. But Englishmen would send their cattle into the Indians' fields to graze, even after their corn and beans were up, ruining their crops. So many Indian men died from disease and warfare that women were often left to fend for themselves. That's how so many came to be servants, like Cate did and her mother before her, she explained.

"Then Reverend Adams brought the word of God to the Nehantic and changed our lives forever," Cate said. "He taught us how to read and write and told us the Lord had sent smallpox to punish us for our own sins."

By that time, I'd found the strength to speak. I wanted to know if their lives had been any better when our God replaced their Great Spirit.

"What happened to your people, Cate, your villages, and fields?"

"No more," was all she said.

Her sons begged her for stories about their great sachem, a man who'd once shot an arrow through the meetinghouse's steeple.

"That arrow stays up there today, through all the winter winds," she told her children proudly, pointing over her head. "If you ever feel afraid, just look up at that steeple and see that arrow. Know that the blood of brave warriors runs in your veins."

"And don't forget the blood of African kings," Coffey said proudly.

At last, many tales and stories later, I began to feel my strength return.

Soon I went back to the main house. Surely, I'd been mistaken about a child growing inside me. After all, my belly was only swollen from the poison I'd so foolishly taken.

Once again, I took on the heavy work of hearth and field and ate heartily every evening. All around me, autumn ignited the world with a heavenly fire, blazing royal gold and scarlet. The apple crop was free of blight—the best that the Palmeses had ever raised.

Baby Elijah granted me his first smile, or so I insisted to Cate. I was smitten with him but seldom had him all to myself to hug and kiss.

"Don't you let me catch you coddling him," my mistress would growl at me, sometimes snatching him out of my arms.

Once, as she did so, she'd narrowed her eyes and snarled, "You leave my sons alone."

I'd turned away quickly, sweeping a burning ember from the hearthstone back into the fire.

Seeing this, Mrs. Palmes couldn't restrain herself.

"God help us, you'll set us all afire!" she shrieked.

Picking up one of the corked glass vessels that were kept on hand in case of a kitchen fire, she shook it to make sure I'd filled it with water. Many a farmhouse had burned to the ground because of lazy servants like me, or so she reminded me again and again.

It was late one afternoon in October when I rode to the mill with Cate and Coffey, bringing a last load of corn for grinding. Coffey was in high spirits for once.

"Next year we'll ride wherever our fancy takes us. It won't matter if we come home early or late. We'll just do as we please." His words hung like a challenge in the air.

"And who do you have to thank for that?" Cate said with mock indignation.

She turned to face me. "The master says that come spring, I'll have worked all my seven years. For my freedom dues, he's going to give me this worthless old man, just like he always promised."

"Worthless? You're not likely to find a better man in this life, though maybe you'll meet a saint in the hereafter," Coffey shot back. "Besides, it's going to be a long, long winter where we're going. Who else you got to warm your old bones?"

Cate pretended to cuff him on his head, nearly falling off the wagon seat from laughing. Then she became very serious.

"Master Palmes says as soon as the snow's gone, we should go too. The Hawk's complaining that our boys are eating too much," said Cate. "He'll buy himself another slave, one who knows how to keep his mouth shut and keep his shoulder to the wheel."

"And what about me?" I asked.

"You'll be released from your bond at age twenty-one, Mercy. So, there's an end to this hard road for you too—for all of us—God be praised!"

Confident of being on good terms with the Almighty, she lifted her eyes and hands to heaven.

I rode on in wretched silence.

"I've no faith that I'll ever see that day," I said finally.

Cate and Coffey exchanged a glance, but I just kept staring back over the muddy path we'd just traveled.

At dusk, as we hauled home sacks of cornmeal from the gristmill, we heard shouts and barking from the town green. Half a dozen townsmen were drinking at the Fox and Grapes tavern after hunting wolves far up in the hills.

Outside the meetinghouse, hunters had nailed two wolf heads, dripping blood in long red streaks on the black planks. The magistrates would need to see these trophies as proof before paying any bounties the next day. Now the last of the huntsmen's wild quarry—a she-wolf trapped alive—was about to meet her fate.

In a frenzy, their dogs tore her apart in the dusty lane as their owners cheered them on.

CHAPTER V

ACCUSED

"The Lord spoke to me as He did to Eve;
Woman, what hath thou done?

—BOOK OF GENESIS, KING JAMES BIBLE

THE ICY DAYS of January came and went.

I ripped out the stitches in my shift and sewed up new seams to ease the midsection. Although my apron strings had to be tied at the far ends now, just barely meeting in the small of my back, my body's proportions felt unchanged to me. Had I viewed myself in a looking glass, I would have seen differently.

Mercy Bramble was destined to be a very solid woman, I believed, just like her mother. Perhaps all my months of working in the fields and carrying water had made me larger and stronger. The potatoes I'd dug from the earth last fall now satisfied my never-ending hunger; I kept some buried in the hearth ashes all the time.

My newly robust constitution spared me from winter's most punishing cold; for once I stayed warm in my bed on midwinter nights. February was strangely mild; snow started melting off the roof by mid-month.

"Thaw's coming early," Coffey told me one morning as he passed me in the kitchen with an armload of split wood. "Old Coffey and Cate will be just a memory 'round here soon. Her seven years are up next month."

Coffey was in such good spirits that I scarcely recognized him. He was practically singing.

"Just two free souls, rolling down the road with our own wagon, our own horse, and our two fine boys! Will you'll miss us, Mercy?"

Not waiting for my reply, he let out a booming laugh. The sound burst out of his lungs and spread in all directions, like a wave hitting rocks at the shore. No load seemed a burden to Coffey; he hoisted the heaviest logs as though they were pieces of kindling. If he'd moved an entire mountain that day, I wouldn't have been surprised.

"Master said he could have sold me for fifty or sixty pounds, as much as he'd get for five of his best horses. But he's true to his word and that piece of paper he signed. You see, Cate's going to buy my freedom."

"Yes, I know, Coffey," I groaned. "You told me at least a hundred times or more."

"And my boys will always be free men, thanks to their blessed mother being a free woman."

"But where will you all go?" I asked, trying to conceal my envy.

"Wherever Cate says we're going," he pronounced. "Could be west of here. Maybe far north in the New York colony to live with the Oneida Indians."

Coffey pointed in the general direction of the north pasture, as if their destination were that close at hand.

"But we got to go when the time's right: after snow melts off the roads but before spring mud gets too deep. The good Lord knows I'm ready right now!"

"And how will you feed your family without a master to provide for you?"

"Don't you worry. All we need is a little patch of corn and a scrap of roof over our heads. We'll do just fine."

Swallowing hard, I turned towards the hearth. The fire's scorching heat burned up my tears before I even realized they were forming.

Now Cate had her Coffey, the Hawk had my master, and everyone in the world was paired two by two since Adam and Eve. Since the law forbade me to marry while bonded as a servant, I'd be twenty-one when I was free to wed. All would think me a withered old maid.

And what sort of man would be left to be my bridegroom? An ugly, old bachelor like the gravedigger Benja Fargo? The peddler Hugo Moreaux, stinking of sweat and tobacco? Perhaps I'd sink so low that I'd have to marry the penniless swineherd who wandered the lanes with his pigs. I shuddered.

Often, I'd thought that marriage would save me from my servitude. Now I was starting to see that it might make my life even worse, especially if my husband were a cruel master.

"Do you think I'll be too old to be a bride at twenty-one?" I asked Coffey, but he'd already left for another load of wood and didn't hear me. He slammed the door so forcefully that he almost tore it from its hinges.

"It's like a jail in this wretched kitchen sometimes," I sighed.

Knowing the Hawk had forbidden me to do so, I gave the wooden cradle a push, hoping to prolong little Elijah's nap.

At that moment, something gave a peculiar lurch inside me.

I was rubbing my belly, lost in thought, when Cate came in from the hall.

She shook her head slowly and gave me such a dark look that I hardly recognized her.

"When you going to see the *truth* Mercy Girl, when it's so plain to me and to God above?"

Seeing fear in my eyes, she dropped her voice to a soft whisper, reached out, and spread both her hands across the bulge of my belly.

"I'll stay just a little longer here and help you when your time comes. Bring you to a secret hiding place and take good care of you and your little baby. Less pain for you, better for the baby."

I pushed her hands away.

"Don't worry about me, Cate. It's almost time for you and your family to go. If you wait any longer, your wagon will get stuck in all that spring mud Coffey keeps fretting about."

She wasn't saying anything, so I raised my voice. "Are you deaf, Cate? Aren't you listening to me?"

"No, *you* listen, Mercy. I'm going to stay to help you. That baby's as close to my heart as you are. She's even closer to me than you are."

"Did you say, *she*?" I asked in confusion.

"You're having a girl baby. I know."

"But *why*? Why does it matter so much to you, Cate?" Then I said something so bitter that it left a bad taste in my mouth: "After all, she'll be a bastard too, just like me."

My friend's dark eyes flared with anger.

"Don't you say that about her, Mercy!"

"You must be mad, Cate. Have you been taking one of your own potions or drunk too much of our master's beer?"

She narrowed her eyes. "If I didn't love you like a sister, I would slap you hard."

"Well, go ahead then. You're already hurting my head by talking in silly riddles."

At the very moment Cate was about to explain herself, the Hawk sailed into the room with a flurry of her black skirts and snatched Elijah from his cradle. Then she sat down on the bench to nurse him, making no move to leave us.

I had to wait until after the mid-day meal before the Hawk finally retired to her bedchamber for a nap; then we two servants had the kitchen to ourselves again.

"What's going on Cate? You've been acting as if you know something about this baby."

"I do know something."

"You always seemed to know so much about Bryan, even his private thoughts. It's as if the two of you were secretly brother and sister."

Cate's mouth dropped open. I'd stumbled upon a truth, but didn't yet know it.

"Tell me everything," I commanded. "Tell me now, or I'll no longer think of you as my friend."

"Be quiet and listen, then."

Gesturing for me to sit on the bench, she settled beside me and took my hand.

"Years ago, another Indian woman like me once lived here in this town. Her name was Katherine Garrett, but people called her Indian Kate."

"I remember hearing that name as a child, but it was before my time," I mused.

"This Kate was servant to one of the town magistrates and shared his bed sometimes in secret. Gave birth to a baby boy, half white, half Indian. Her master feared being whipped and fined for fathering a bastard, so he told her, 'Get rid of it.'"

I was starting to feel slightly sick.

"What did Indian Kate do?" I asked quietly.

"They say she killed that baby boy. Threw him into a flooded stream at night. She thought she was alone, but a watchman saw her do it. He charged her with murder, and locked her up in New London."

Everyone assumed that the tiny newborn had been swept away and drowned, Cate continued. But the next day a man and his wife were crossing a bridge when they heard his cries; they found the baby boy afloat, face up and still bound to his Indian cradleboard. Fearing that someone would take him away from them, they brought him home and hid him.

"So? What happened after that?" Even though I posed the question, something inside me had already figured out the answer.

"I tried to tell you once before, Mercy: that baby grew up here in this house. He grew up to be Mr. Bryan Palmes."

I pressed my hand to my mouth, not wanting to wake the Hawk in the next room with my outburst.

"Indian Kate was his real mother—but your master never knew this. Bryan wasn't her only child, see? About six years before he was born, Indian Kate had given birth to a girl baby. That girl's father was from Kate's own tribe, a man called John No Name."

"What became of that first child?"

Cate placed her hand on her heart.

"She's right here with you. It was me."

"So, you and Bryan had the same mother? Bryan's your *half-brother*?"

"Suppose some people they call it that, though Lord knows how a person can have a half a brother! To me, he's my full brother, my only living family."

Although I fought to control it, my voice trembled.

"Is there anything else you're hiding from me, Cate?"

"Well, I didn't tell you the story's ending yet. I got to go back to the beginning again when Indian Kate was in jail. They set up the gallows on Town Hill. Reverend Adams, he preached a long sermon. Then they strung up Indian Kate in a tree."

She stopped at that awful point in her story, but I urged her to finish.

"They made her daughter, Little Cate watch the hanging, just to teach her a lesson; then she was bound out as a servant. She was only seven."

"Oh Cate! Why did you never tell me how you'd suffered?"

She wrapped her arms around me; I wept for several minutes before she dried my tears with her apron.

"Now you know why I want to help your baby? My blood is in her veins. The blood of my mother, my brother too."

I asked her how she'd known to come to the Palmes' farm so many years ago.

"Before they took my mother to the gallows, they let us say our goodbyes. Her wrists were bound with rope; she couldn't embrace me."

Cate held her wrists together, her hands in two fists. Then, very slowly, she unclenched her hands, palms facing up.

"My mother showed me her hands just like this and whispered, 'Remember, these are your palms, Little Cate. One day you must go to the Palmes to find your brother.'"

Many years later, when she was a grown woman, Cate finally understood her mother's last words; the Palmes were owners of a neighboring farm. She went to Bryan and asked him to take her on as a servant, convincing him to buy her husband from her former master. Then she bore her two children there.

"Didn't you ever tell him he was your brother?"

"I wanted to, but didn't want to shame him or his parents.

The master has been fair to us. That's all I can ask of him," she said sadly.

"But wouldn't he want to know who he is? Or what he is?"

"Maybe deep inside he knows," she sighed. "The blood always speaks. It may talk in silence, but it speaks."

Having finished her story, Cate—who never appeared to grow weary after any chore—confessed that she was feeling tired and had to go lie down.

As she left the kitchen, I called out to her.

"You're right, Cate. You're the only one who can help me now, the only one who can help *her*."

※

How and when the Hawk had discovered my torn letter to the sheriff, I never found out. She must have found a little bundle of aprons and personal things that I'd hidden in a narrow space behind a kitchen cupboard.

As I was stirring a pot of corn pudding, waiting for it to thicken over the fire, my mistress appeared without warning at my side and waved the envelope under my nose.

"Who wrote this monstrous thing about my son, Nat?" she demanded. "Is this written in your hand?"

Flushing deep red, I told her that I didn't know how to write and couldn't even hold a pen.

"So, it was Cate then? Tell me the truth or I'll have you thrown into the street to fend for yourself."

She looked my body up and down in a way that convinced me she knew everything I'd been trying to conceal. All the changes going on inside of me were no longer the secret I'd believed them to be.

"I don't know what to say," I faltered.

"Well, go fetch Cate right now. I'll make her write something so I can compare how she makes her script."

"Please, Madam," I begged. "Cate is blameless. I forced her to write that note for me. But we could find no way to carry it to Sheriff Christophers."

"Go fetch her. *Now.*"

Even though I walked as slowly as possible, my heart was racing when I reached Cate and Coffey's quarters. It was wash day; dripping linen bed sheets hung from a dozen wooden racks. At first, I could barely see her through the wash bucket's rising steam.

"She found our letter about Nat," I gasped, "The one Bryan had torn in two. I'd hoped to piece it back together to give the sheriff one day."

Grim-faced, Cate dried her hands and trudged back to the house with me. As soon as we crossed the threshold, she folded her arms on her chest and looked squarely at our mistress.

"I wrote the letter, Madam. I did it for love of Zeno and to follow the Lord's commandments. The Bible tells us we should bring a sinner to judgment, and I…"

The Hawk cut her off in mid-sentence.

"Where did you get ink and paper?"

"I took it from the desk."

"It doesn't matter why or what or whatever," sputtered the Hawk, "You're a liar and a thief, Cate. I won't have you and your family eating our food anymore, not one crumb!"

She flung the envelope into the fire. It flared up for a moment and was gone.

"You'll all pack up tonight and leave this household tomorrow morning. Is that clear?"

"No, Madam. The master says my seven years will end next

month," Cate said stubbornly. "I promised him I'd work seven years, so I'm going to work all seven."

"Never mind what you *think* he'll say," the Hawk retorted. "What right have you to *think*? After I've spoken to your master tonight, he'll order you out of his house. I'll get your damned certificate of bondage from his desk and tear it up myself!"

Cate looked at her sorrowfully and shook her head.

"I've worked hard for him and now for you, Madam. Even helped you deliver Elijah when you needed a midwife. Now you treat me like this?"

Again, the Hawk told her to start packing. At last Cate obeyed.

Offering to help my friend, I followed her out of the house.

I didn't accompany Cate back to her quarters, however. Instead, I circled behind the barn and pushed open a back door that was seldom used. My mind was racing, trying to devise another way of helping Cate—and keeping her at the farm long enough to be my midwife.

My only hope was to speak to Bryan alone later that afternoon. Surely, he would listen to reason if I begged him to allow Cate to stay another month.

So, I waited for his return.

At first, I paced back and forth inside the barn but soon grew tired. My limbs felt stiff and awkward; my belly weighed me down like a load of stones. Trying not to think how close I was to the spot where we'd found Zeno, I spread my apron and lay down in the straw.

A strange peace came over me as I breathed in the sweet smell of hay and listened to the horses shifting in their stalls. Captain, the cat, rubbed his head against my shoulder, pleased that I'd descended to his level. In the rafters above us, mourning doves cooed. After nearly an hour, one of the mares began to whinny;

she'd caught a scent of Bryan's approaching horse even before I'd heard its hoofbeats.

I struggled to my feet just in time to meet my master inside the barn door and grab his mount's bridle.

Although Bryan didn't greet me, he continued to mutter as though we'd already been engaged in conversation. Falling forward in the saddle, he buried half his face in his horse's black mane—it was as wild as his own uncombed hair—and looked all around with a single, narrowed eye.

"Watch out now, Mercy," he warned, raising his forefinger. "These barn walls are tilting. I order you to make them stand straight!"

As he tried to dismount, his foot missed the stirrup; he tumbled, almost knocking me over. Then he steadied himself against the horse's flank and pulled himself to his feet.

"You're more than a little drunk, master. And in midday, no less."

"You'd be drunk too if your life was as miserable as mine," he groaned. "I married an old crone for her horses and her money, and now I have to look at her ugly face every night. Every... single...night!"

"You could have married me," I said boldly, "but instead you got me with child."

"What kind of man does something like that?" he asked in alarm, swaying slightly. "If I ever meet the blackguard, I'll look him right in the eye and say, 'You sir, are a bloody coward!'"

"Well, Bryan, I've already met that man. He's the same bloody coward who wouldn't tell anyone that his stepson murdered poor Zeno. He was too cowardly to send the sheriff a letter when I begged him to help."

Bryan began to look more sober but still confused. Though

I knew he might never remember our conversation, I was so emboldened that I simply couldn't stop.

"You told me you were my master, and therefore I'd never be your equal. But let me tell you this, Bryan Palmes. I *am* your equal. And do you know why? Because you were born a bastard, just as I was."

He half-fell against me, took me by the shoulders, and tried to shake me.

"What's that you're saying, Mercy? If you know something, for God's sake tell me now." The anguish in his voice made me think that he was returning to his right mind.

We sat down on a small workbench where Coffey often spent hours cleaning the carriage harness and other chores.

I took a deep breath and repeated the entire story I'd heard from Cate, sparing no detail about his origins and his true mother, Indian Kate. Several times he asked me to repeat myself, yet I could see from the shock on his face that he finally understood, he finally believed.

"Cate...my sister...or half-sister...what a strange, yet extraordinary revelation. And what you've told me about my birth would explain..."

His voice trailed away.

"Explain, what?" I asked, perhaps with more kindness than he deserved.

"Why I've always felt so *divided*, like two different men in one man's body."

He lifted his hands and stared at them strangely, as though seeing them for the first time.

The sun had set. It already was getting cold and dark inside the barn, and I knew that we must return to the house.

"When you go in, your wife will say that she has ordered Cate and Coffey to leave first thing in the morning," I said slowly.

"You claim to be the master of your house and everyone in it. If that is true, and you're not a coward after all, then tell your wife she made a grave mistake."

"She'll be very angry. Then what will I do, Mercy?"

"Demand that Cate and Coffey stay another full month. Say that Cate owes you the full seven years set forth in her contract, not a day less. You won't be cheated."

Bryan turned away and shook his head. My heart began to sink. As his reason returned, so had the dark, cowardly side of him, the side that could love no one but himself.

"And what if I refuse to do what you say?" he asked warily. "I won't take orders from women, not you, not my wife, and not this so-called sister of mine."

His face grew dark.

"If you must know, I've always been a little afraid of her," he confessed.

I told him that he had nothing to fear.

"Now Cate has too much power over me. If anyone learns that my mother was both a savage and a whore, it will be an abomination. I'll be shamed in the eyes of all in this town and congregation."

I swore that I'd never tell a soul; he only had to promise to let Cate's family stay another month until the end of her term.

"It has been vile enough to be called the Cripple Bryan Palmes all my life. I have no intention of becoming the Bastard Bryan Palmes as well."

That night I lay sleepless on my bench, not knowing what he would finally decide. At last, sleep overcame me. When dawn broke, Cate, Coffey, and their boys were gone. I feared that I'd never see them again.

"It's all for the best. They were both growing fat and lazy," the Hawk told Bryan later that morning. As they sat in the kitchen, neither one lifted a spoon to eat from bowls of bread and milk I'd set out for breakfast.

"We can do without extra hands till planting time. Then you'll get a new man, one who can drive a plow straighter than that one-eyed Negro ever did," the Hawk told her husband.

For once, I did not listen to the rest of their conversation. In my mind I pictured how Cate's family had departed long before sunrise, packing themselves and their scant belongings into a cart. In the harness was a skeletal nag called Bones, more dead than alive. He was, in fact, a dead man's horse, because Bryan had received him as payment for writing a dying man's last will and testament. Bones was the master's farewell gift to his servants.

Coffey had salvaged the two-wheeled cart from a heap of broken carriage parts behind the barn. Its wooden wheels were dry and worm-eaten—the spokes not much more than splinters—and I prayed that those wheels would last for their journey toward the New York frontier.

Joseph and Jonathan were their parents' most precious cargo, but I wondered what else Cate and Coffey had carried with them, perhaps things that no one else could see. Did they bring enough joy and hope to endure all the hardships that lay ahead? I was certain of one thing, however. Coffey would be guarding their certificates of freedom—signed by their former master Bryan Palmes himself—under his coat and over his heart.

I prayed that he never needed to surrender them.

❧

By mid-March I was no longer sleeping well at night. Pain would come and go in my lower back, but that alone didn't keep me awake; my nightmares did.

Whenever I began to fall to sleep, my mind invented many fantastic horrors. In one such dream I was trapped in a deep well, half submerged. In another, I'd sought shelter under a tree in a lightning storm, only to find that I was bound to it with ropes. One night, a wolf foamed at its mouth and chased me through the forest, and on the next, someone was burying me alive in a narrow grave.

To fall asleep meant that I would endure new tortures, so I'd lie awake instead, silently reciting the Lord's Prayer—the only one I knew by heart—over and over.

"Forgive us our trespasses, as we forgive those who trespass against us, and lead us not into temptation, but deliver us from evil…"

My appetite had been dwindling, but one day I heard the Hawk ask my master to dig up a load of potatoes that Cate and Coffey had buried in our root cellar months before. Bryan hesitated. He must have realized that this would have been Coffey's chore, not his, and bending down to enter a dank root cellar was likely to cause him pain.

"That's not possible. Send our servant to dig them out," he finally replied.

Fearing I might get stuck in there, I didn't want to go inside the cold, dirty cave of the root cellar either. But hunger got the best of me.

I told myself how good those potatoes would taste if I roasted them under the ashes, then ate them with a little fresh-churned butter. So, I'd picked up one of Cate's old gathering baskets and gone out to the root cellar.

The potatoes were all gone, I discovered. Perhaps Cate and Coffey had dug them up for their journey. Only a few heads of cabbage remained—black and wormy in parts—but I saved what I could for our supper kettle. After serving Bryan and the Hawk, I sat apart from them at the table's far end. Without the company of my fellow servants, there was no reason to eat at a later hour by myself.

After a brief prayer of thanks, we three ate in silence. In spite of my hunger, I found that I could barely swallow a few bites of pork and cabbage.

The household suddenly felt like a hostile place without Cate and Coffey; even having Elijah near was of little comfort. Unable to eat anymore, I lit a new candle for the table. Our shadows loomed against the wall, three flesh-and-blood strangers alongside them.

As I rose to tend the fire, a sharp pain twisted in my bowels. Before I could clench my teeth, a terrible groan escaped as if from someone else.

The two looked at one another, but not at me. Mrs. Palmes' mouth pursed into a knot, then stretched into a deep frown. Silent save for the scrape of fork prongs against their pewter plates, they returned to their meal.

Hours later, after midnight, I heard the master and mistress in their chamber and pictured them hiding behind those green drapes of their bed. I remembered how those curtains had once lured me, promising me such pleasure and mystery. Now that thought only sharpened the pain in my lower belly.

"You must go away for a few days, Husband. I will take care of this unhappy matter and bring it to its conclusion."

The Hawk continued speaking in a manner that I'd never heard her use before, using soft persuasion to command her husband.

"You can't change the ways of those in the lower order if they're not among the chosen. Just think of that Indian woman you sent away. She went to church with the rest of us, but she was a thief and a liar underneath."

"Perhaps we should inform the magistrates or the sheriff..." Bryan's voice trailed away.

She gave a short laugh. To me it sounded more like a snort.

"That won't be necessary. I know of only one remedy for a situation this dire."

"Then I think I'll go away for a few days. I'll go to Stonington and see about the Negro man left by Widow Livingston," said Bryan, choosing his words carefully. "The ice is gone from the rivers, and the rope ferry is crossing again. If all is well, I should return with Pompey—that is his name—in two days."

"That's a wise plan. This is woman's work now, so a woman must handle it."

I thought I heard him say, "God has given me a good wife," but I couldn't be certain.

As I lay down on my bench, pressing a wet rag to my feverish forehead, I heard Mrs. Palmes cite a line that must have been from her Bible, "Who can find a virtuous woman? For her price is far above rubies."

That was the last word I heard. Suddenly, it was as if thousands of those blood-red rubies exploded across my vision. I had lost consciousness, slipping from my bench to the floor.

The next sound I heard was the master's favorite mare whinnying as it left the barn at daylight. My mistress was nowhere to be seen; she must have taken Elijah into bed with her.

The skirt of my gown felt wet and sodden, but I didn't know why.

Now silence held sway; the small house might as well have been a vast, echoing cavern. The truth of my predicament struck me with all the savagery of the birthing pain. I'd seen Mrs. Holt give birth to two children and the Hawk bring Elijah into this world. I knew what was coming.

"Please help me, Mother," I whispered to the empty room, now blurred by my tears. "Please help me, Cate."

The first pain stopped as suddenly as it had begun, but as I tried to rise to my feet, more pain brought me to the floor like a blow behind the knees.

At last, I dared to appeal to the highest power I knew. "Please help me, God," I pleaded. But only silence answered.

The pain kept coming.

At first, it was like a wolf tearing at my entrails, but that didn't last long. Soon the pain became a giant fist closing around me, trying to squeeze out the contents of my belly. Crushed by such a monstrous force, I could no longer stifle my cries.

"My God, it's coming. It's coming right now!"

But I was wrong, so very wrong. It wasn't going to be that easy.

Soon I'd become a beast—a raging beast—no better than mares I'd seen struggling to push out a foal, their eyes rolling in fear. Pain blocked any thought from forming in my mind. All language failed. I wept uncontrollably.

At first my fingers bled from clutching the splintered planks of the floor. Later, when I looked at my hands, they were dripping red from a greater quantity of blood that pooled around me.

It was as if all air had been sucked from the room. As pressure in my belly grew stronger, my body tried to obey a solitary command: push out what was inside me, or die trying.

Neither past nor future mattered any longer; pain was my whole existence. Twice I blacked out and hoped that I had died, but each time I found myself awake and in no better circumstances than when I'd fainted.

Just when I thought that I'd pushed out my own insides and would be left like the empty shell of an egg, I saw a dark figure looming over me.

"Mrs. Palmes!" I gasped. "I mean, Madam..."

The unwilling midwife didn't conceal her disgust.

"There's no butter left, so I'll have to use hog grease," she grumbled, as if complaining to an invisible companion.

At last, the baby came.

The Hawk yanked out its body, cut its cord with a cleaver, and, with bloody hands, carried the baby outside the house. The last thing that I saw was the Hawk, framed by light in an open doorway. Her breath was a small cloud in the frigid morning air.

I saw the infant's breath too—it was as delicate as a white feather. Then my mistress placed her hand on its mouth, and the feather disappeared. She squeezed the child hard, as if to take its life.

Raising my arm, I tried to cry out, but a chasm of darkness had opened all around me. I couldn't tell if I'd fallen into that darkness or if something terrible had dragged me down, all the way to hell.

When I woke up, I called for a drink of water, but no one answered. My mistress must have gone to do the milking, I reasoned, since no one else remained to do it. The sun was high, and the cows were lowing in a pitiful way.

As I tried to raise myself from the floor, I could feel that the planks were damp, as though they'd just been mopped. My hands were clean, I noticed, but blood had dried beneath my fingernails.

When I heard a baby crying in the next room, it took me awhile to realize it was only Elijah.

At that same moment I discovered something right beside me, wrapped in my own apron. Inside that soft bundle, I saw the silky, raven-black hair and round face of my baby. Its curving eyelids were closed, as though in prayer or deep thought, and its tiny hands were drawn right up to its chin.

My heart almost stopped beating.

The lips were pursed tightly together, as if to keep a secret. I reached to feel for any breath; when I touched my fingertips below that small nose, I felt no breath moving there either.

Slowly unwrapping the rest of the bundle, I discovered a lovely baby girl. Cate had been right, as she always was. But this was not a rosy pink newborn; no, she was ashen gray from toes to fingers.

The child was cold and dead.

There was no time to think: I had to hide the baby from anyone else. I wrapped her tightly in my apron again, this time covering her head. Then I quickly slipped her into a place where the Hawk would never look during daylight hours: under the lid of her precious harpsichord. To secure it, I locked its brass clasp with a snap.

⁊

That evening, the stars came out like chips of ice in a sea of black.

To my surprise, Bryan Palmes returned at a late hour, travelling the last stretch of road by lantern light. Walking alongside the Bay mare was a gray-haired Negro man. I heard Bryan tell the Hawk that the old man was called Pompey, and she sent him to the slaves' quarters with the last serving of rotten cabbage for supper.

My master and mistress rose early the next morning. It was the Sabbath day, and the two left the farmhouse shortly after sunrise; they told me to milk the cows and to supervise the new man as he cleaned out stalls.

I moved through the day as in a dream.

"It's over," I told myself. "It's all over, and it will be forgotten. Perhaps, one day, it will even be forgiven."

I tried to forget the sight of Mrs. Palmes and what she did to the baby, and for a few short hours, I almost did forget.

Pompey wasn't inclined to speak to me any more than absolutely necessary. At first, I thought that he was deaf, or mute, or didn't speak our language; but when he finally began talking, he hardly stopped.

He told me a story of how his former master and mistress had betrayed him.

"My master, Mr. Livingston, had always told me that he'd grant me my freedom one day. *Manumission*, they call it," said Pompey. "I sure learned what that word meant. Said he'd sign a document to give me my freedom."

But old Mr. Livingston had died before making good on his promise, leaving no written record of it. When Pompey asked Widow Livingston to honor his master's wishes, and grant him manumission, she would only shake her head and pretend not to understand. She acted as though he were speaking the language of his forefathers in Africa.

It was a sad story, so I tried not to laugh when he imitated the old widow, cupping her hand to her ear and saying "Eh? Eh?"

When Widow Livingston had finally died, Pompey was listed as part of her estate along with a few gold rings, a silver drinking cup, and a damask tablecloth. Bryan Palmes had bought him from the family's oldest son, who said that he had no use for an old slave.

It was noontime before I remembered the sickening truth: I still had the child's body. She hadn't vanished like a bad dream or the pain of her birth.

There had been a hard freeze the night before, and I wouldn't be able to dig a grave by myself; it didn't seem right to ask Pompey for help. Although I remember trying to stay calm, I later realized that I'd been in what they call a state of hysteria.

Perhaps it was madness, but I decided to destroy the child's remains while the house was empty. A roaring hearth fire would consume everything, or so I thought.

Removing the bundle from inside the harpsichord, I hurried back to the kitchen. Then, hastily, I unwrapped the child and held her to the flame. Averting my eyes, I commanded myself to release her, to drop her behind the flaming logs.

But I began to retch. No sooner had I let her slip partway into the fire than I seized hold of her again. I acted so quickly that I barely felt any burns on my hands and wrists.

Now, half of the body was charred. Ashes dusted her doll-like face like a black veil.

"I can't!" I cried. Had I gone mad?

In my panic, I hadn't noticed Pompey looking through the window's diamond-shaped panes. He turned away so quickly that I didn't know what he'd seen, if anything at all.

I decided to hide the remains under my cot until I could bury her in a decent manner. I'd do so in a day or two, just as soon as the ground thawed, or so I hoped.

Several days passed, and I was carrying out all of my household duties again. I made sure that I came quickly whenever the Hawk called; I did as I was bidden. Aside from giving me her usual orders, the mistress never spoke a single word of reproach or sympathy to me.

My unfortunate ordeal was almost over, or so I believed. Life would go on.

Unbeknownst to me, the Hawk had gone to Reverend Jewett after service that Sunday and told him of some trouble she'd had with her servant. I learned of this many weeks later, from the fearful man of God himself. Without delay, the reverend had divulged that knowledge to one of the town magistrates.

The next afternoon I heard a slow, heavy knock at the front door.

When I opened it, I found two townsmen on the threshold. I recognized one as old Joshua Hempstead, who had often brought his Negro man to help Coffey mend fences or load a wagon with salt hay. His man was nowhere to be seen that afternoon. I knew Mr. Hempstead was an important man: shipbuilder, magistrate, justice of the peace, and a man of law as well. He even sold and carved tombstones.

From their conversation, I now learned that it was Mr. Hempstead who'd joined my master and mistress in their marriage bonds. The other man, a stranger to me, was younger than Mr. Hempstead; his expression lacked any hint of kindness.

Mrs. Palmes poured each man a draught of spiced rum from a decanter and then withdrew, leaving them with her husband by the fire. From the next room, I strained to hear their conversation, dismissing the notion that they would concern themselves with me in any way. Surely, they were here on important business, perhaps to offer my master an appointment of some kind, or to propose a location for a new gristmill on his property. Nevertheless, my hands started to tremble as I worked on some mending. Try as I might, I couldn't get any stitches in straight.

After half an hour had passed, my master suddenly appeared alone before me, leaning heavily on the doorframe. He looked at me without a word.

Last year, when those dark eyes had met mine, I'd believed that Bryan Palmes had found the soul deep inside of me and brought it to light. Now my body felt completely empty, hollow, soul-less.

Touching me for the first time since last summer, he stroked my arm. Then, with the lightest pressure, he quickly placed his mouth on mine. His lips were as cold as the glass I used to kiss on his painted portrait.

I pulled away.

"What is happening?" I asked, barely breathing and standing still as a statue.

"Mercy, you are wanted for an inquiry by these two gentlemen."

He took me by the wrist—we were so close that I could smell

the spiced rum he'd been drinking—and led me through the hall. If only he'd led me like this before Mr. Hempstead last year and made me his wife, I thought.

As soon as we stepped into the chamber, Mr. Hempstead spoke to me directly.

"Mercy Bramble, some say a bastard has been born in this house. Is there any truth in that?"

How could I answer that terrible question? I looked desperately at Bryan Palmes, but he no longer returned my gaze.

"Mercy, you're not the first servant to fall victim to temptation. You're not alone in this sin, but you must confess to God before us now. That is the law, plain as I can state it."

"Will I be whipped? I've no money to pay a fine."

Mr. Hempstead rubbed his forehead as though he were in pain. Then a fit of coughing seized him; we all waited for him to recover.

"Do you understand that it's a crime to bear a bastard? It's a lesser crime than some, but you're liable to pay a fine. If we find that you've *murdered* your bastard child, the crime is far more grave." He peered at me intently.

"If that is the case, you will pay not with a fine, but with your own life."

I could not answer, and suddenly his patience expired.

"Now where is the child? How do we know this accusation is true without seeing with our own eyes?" he demanded. "I don't hear an infant's cries, and Elijah sleeps here in his cradle."

"Speak the truth!" commanded Mrs. Palmes, who by now was listening at the doorway. Then she drew up behind me and whispered for my ears only, "How dare you bring shame on my household in this way, you wretched girl?"

I didn't answer her but addressed Mr. Hempstead in barely a whisper.

"Sir, the child was born without life, so I think."

"And what made you believe such a thing? How can you prove it wasn't murdered by your own hand?"

"I was in great pain, being ignorant of the ways of childbirth. For several hours I'd been ill with a terrible pain in my belly. The child may have died already in my womb."

"And what midwife did you call to your bed?"

I couldn't look at the Hawk, turning my eyes to the floor. Even though I was in such distress, I had no proof against her.

"None, sir. I was alone."

"If the child is dead, then where is the body?" the younger magistrate demanded, suddenly finding his voice. "There may be a greater crime here, one which we are bound to investigate. For if you took its life…"

My heart was racing faster than I ever thought possible without it killing a person.

"She's in a secret place, Sir. I had no wish to burden the Palmes with my private troubles."

"What in heaven's name did you plan to do with it?" pleaded Mr. Hempstead with outstretched palms. His eyes grew very round beneath his raised brows.

"In truth, Sir, I hadn't yet made a plan for that. Grief has taken over my reason these past few days."

Then, in five minutes it was all over.

I told them where I'd placed the body, and, having no other servant to take the order, Mrs. Palmes herself went upstairs to fetch it. I watched in misery as she handed the bundle to Mr. Hempstead, one hand pressing a handkerchief to her mouth. A ghastly smell now hung in the room, and my mistress, at last overcome, hurried back into the hallway.

"We shall inspect the body for signs of any violent action,

then give the little soul a decent resting place," said the old magistrate.

After a brief consultation about a coffin, my master gave them an old wooden box that Nat had used to hold musket balls and powder. It was the perfect size for my daughter's body.

"There's no need to worry about purchasing a stone for the burial ground," added Mr. Hempstead in a reassuring manner. "We make no markers for bastard children."

Thanking him for his trouble, Bryan bid the two men a warm goodbye as if they were old friends and they'd all just dined together.

Soon I heard the clank of an iron ring against the stone hitching post followed by a groan of wagon wheels. The men rode away into the darkness back toward town.

Late that night, I was awakened from a deep sleep by the piercing sound of a baby crying—I knew it was not Elijah—calling for me to take her back. Stifling my own cries with my quilt, I wept for my infant daughter for the first time. Then I buried her in the deepest part of my heart.

Someday I might be worthy of such a precious memory, but for now, I could hardly bear to live another day.

❧

Purgatory is a place here on earth, or so I discovered. It was where I must wait, not knowing what was to happen next.

A fortnight later, the magistrates finally came back to the farm. Without any explanation, they put me in a wagon and brought me to the meetinghouse. There, to my surprise, Reverend Jewett preached a lengthy sermon on my behalf while I sat among rows of churchgoers.

My sins were many, he said, thrusting a forefinger in the air as he counted each one. Temptation. Lust. Fornication. Bearing a bastard. Concealing its birth. Lying to my master and mistress. And finally, after a very long pause, *the murder of a bastard.*

"Seven sins!" he cried, in what sounded like a state of ecstasy. "Seven terrible sins!" He reminded his listeners that no boundary existed between sin and crime; both were offenses against the laws of man and Almighty God.

All of you, gathered from neighboring farms and the town, were staring at me now, but I couldn't turn my head to return your gaze. I feared that even the slightest motion might further condemn me.

Several hours later the magistrates returned me by wagon to the farmhouse.

"Keep her close," they warned Bryan sternly. "We'll be back for her soon."

The next morning when I rose at dawn to tend the fire, I heard a strange clamor outside: lengths of heavy chain dropping on the stone step. Hurrying to the window, I saw that Sheriff Christophers had arrived, bringing shackles for my wrists and ankles.

I ran back to where Bryan sat alone at the kitchen table, smoking his pipe.

"Please don't let them take me!" I begged.

He paused just long enough to give me hope. Then he replied quietly, "I can't. If I lost my reputation, I would lose *everything*. You understand that, don't you Mercy?"

I barely recognized my own voice, "No, how could I?"

The Hawk answered the door and brought the visitor inside.

The sheriff looked me up and down in a familiar manner, just as he had on that awful night when we'd found Zeno's body.

"We're taking you to jail today," he announced. "You're under arrest, and all your worldly goods and chattel are to be surrendered."

In a few minutes, Mrs. Palmes had gathered up my belongings in a blanket and handed them to the constable. I suddenly remembered my own mother leaving me with Mr. Holt many years ago, and then Mr. Holt leaving me with the Palmeses. The bundle that traveled with me hadn't grown any larger over the years.

"Thank God I can sleep now, knowing that my own child will be safe from her murdering hands," the Hawk confided to the sheriff. "I've heard a tale hereabouts of a servant who murdered her own babies, then her master's little son!"

They took me to the cart in shackles, half-stumbling like a hobbled cow. No one came outside to say goodbye to me. Only Captain, who was sunning himself on a stone wall, watched me curiously as I struggled into the cart.

The driver, a feeble old man in a three-cornered hat, touched a whip to the rump of his decrepit horse. The cart began a long, lurching pull to town, almost overturning on Town Hill's steep, rocky slope.

Looking all around me, I was puzzled to see how life could be continuing as if this were any ordinary day. The sky was as deep and pure a blue as a costly indigo. Soon, with spring's first warmth, apple orchards would start to bloom, but the promise of such beauty only mocked me and the ugly situation in which I was mired.

To lessen my fear, I turned my thoughts to Cate and Coffey and hoped that any road they travelled was less rocky than the one I journeyed on that morning.

In another hour or so we reached town. Even if I'd been blindfolded, I would have known that we'd arrived near the waterfront; seagulls screamed their curses overhead. On any other day I would have enjoyed hearing the gulls' raucous calls and watching their daring dives above rooftops and masts, but this was no time to observe such sights.

The cart stopped outside the jailhouse in Broad Alley. A short, plump woman with a red face stepped out into the alley to greet us. She grimaced, revealing yellowed, broken teeth.

"Now I have to care for a murderess too?" she asked shrilly.

My driver helped me off his wagon, holding the chains to one side so I wouldn't trip.

"I'm Faith Christophers, the sheriff's wife," the woman continued, as if she'd prepared a little welcome speech for me. "I take care of all you prisoners, not that you will ever thank me, and not that my husband has given me any say in the matter."

She looked me up and down. "You don't look as filthy as most of these scoundrels, but don't expect to be waited on hand and foot!"

Although at first, I had to bite my tongue, I managed to respond in a civil tone, "I'll do my best not to trouble you Madam."

"No one stays here long, of course," Faith continued. She'd raised my hopes for just a moment before dashing them. "In this town, punishment is swift."

Then she made a terrible gesture, as though an invisible noose had tightened about her neck. Her eyes grew wide, and her tongue extended from the corner of her mouth in a hideous fashion.

I turned away.

Surely there had been a mistake; Mercy Bramble was someone to be pitied, not punished. So why would none of you ever forgive me?

CHAPTER VI

THE JAIL

"Stone walls do not a prison make,
Nor iron bars a cage…"

—RICHARD LOVELACE

THEN ALL LIGHT disappeared.

The sheriff had slammed the cell door with far more vigor than was needed to secure it. I heard a heavy bolt slide into place, a key turn.

After a period of confusion, I began to look around the place in which he'd left me. Hardly any larger than the stalls in which Bryan Palmes kept his prize horses, the cell had a brick floor covered with straw, just like a stable might have.

A wooden pallet would be my bed, scarcely a hand's width off the cell's floor. It was so close to the fireplace—as yet unlit—that I wondered if I'd be safe in such a resting place. In order to keep out the cold, someone had stuffed dried seaweed into cracks in the walls. Its briny smell combined with the stench of an open privy, one that vagrants, miscreants, Sabbath-breakers, and horse thieves had been using for decades.

I would have been in total darkness had it not been for light that came through two narrow slits over my head, each on opposite walls.

By standing on my toes, I was able to peer through one opening and see the meetinghouse about a hundred paces away across Broad Alley. A greasy mix of lamp black and Spanish lead blackened its sides, hiding damage from The Awful Thunderclap; its doors and window trim were painted stark white. Such a severe-looking place was more suited to worshipping the Devil than the Almighty, I thought.

Squinting up at the steeple, I was excited see that a long arrow pierced an orb at its peak. Cate had been telling the truth about a sachem who'd sent it flying up there from his bow years before. Had he shot it simply to show his skill? Or was it truly an act of defiance, a warning to the white men who had built such an imposing edifice on his people's land?

Just beyond the meetinghouse was the burial ground where Mr. Palmes' mother lay. Memories of that morning when I'd found her on the floor came flooding back to me. My own body had still trembled from the act I'd just committed, yet I'd had to turn my attention to her body, already decaying. I'd never forget how her fingers had curled so tightly like the talons of a dead crow.

Looking at the graveyard, it was hard to fathom that my unnamed baby girl was buried there and that I was now a condemned criminal.

Through a gap in the opposite wall, I saw a dazzling blaze of blue: the harbor's shifting, shining surface, and open sea beyond. The limits of my vantage point framed this scene as though it were a miniature painting. A rope ferry and canoe tossed on the bright water. High above ships and wharves, gulls were making long, lovely turns in the wind, like flourishes that Bryan Palmes made with his pen.

When I tired of peering outside, there was nothing to do but sit on the hard pallet with my chin cupped in my hands. I listened to the privy flies' buzz and carts and carriages rattle through the alley. How often had I dreamed of having a few free hours to myself in which to do absolutely nothing? Now I could find no pleasure in it whatsoever, certainly not while lice were biting me relentlessly.

The sheriff had wrapped my ankles in a chain between two iron shackles, the kind used to restrain runaway slaves or bring them to an auction block. Even in the fading light I could see streaks of someone's dried blood inside the manacles and wondered who had suffered so terribly in these same chains.

Finally, darkness ruled; my first night in prison began.

As a rat raced back and forth through the straw, I crouched on the floor and wept. Perhaps crying was my only privilege at that point. It may have been forbidden to me as a child, but now I seized it as my right, one that no one could take away, not even here.

I'd thought myself completely alone, but later, from across the room, I heard someone snoring, probably a drunken vagabond who'd be released in the morning.

At last, I slipped from the cell's darkness and gratefully entered the greater darkness of sleep.

Shortly before dawn, I suffered a terrible nightmare that transported me back to the most dreadful scene from my life. Once again, I watched Mrs. Palmes and my baby against the doorway, tiny clouds of frozen breath forming from each. Mrs. Palmes' hand reached to cover the baby's mouth.

As I came to consciousness, however, I no longer saw the Hawk but only Faith's stout figure outlined at the door. She'd come to wake the sleeping vagrant and drag her onto the street.

"But I've nothing to eat!" the old woman protested.

"You can go beg for food, for all I care. And I'll thank God to be rid of you and your lice so soon, not like this other one. Now go!"

She shoved her into the alleyway.

"What about me, Faith? When can I be released?" I pleaded, leaping up to follow her as she went to bar the door again. "I can serve God better and longer than that old crone who's half dead already."

"Don't you know anything? You'll be kept here until your trial, and they won't hold your trial 'til Superior Court meets again."

"And how soon will that be?"

"Ask my husband, girl, don't bother me," she sighed. "The treasury will pay us well for food to keep you alive, and firewood too. Some prisoners can't be trusted with a fire, but we have no choice. Can't let you freeze, I suppose."

"No," I said, "that wouldn't be a godly way to behave."

Faith said she was going to fetch her husband from the tavern.

"Be careful. That man's a brute," I warned her. I pointed to a large bruise he'd left on my forearm the day before. Faith had already slammed the door, however.

The next day was the Sabbath, and through the gap I could see a slow parade of townspeople arriving for services across the alley. Among them were Bryan and his wife, the slave Pompey a few paces behind them. The Hawk carried Elijah under her cape to shield him from a light rain. I strained to see his sweet face, but his mother kept it well hidden. Just thinking about his fingers and toes, so fresh and delicate against the world's roughness, was enough to bring me a faint smile, the first since I'd been arrested.

My own baby would have had such rosy toes had she lived

past her first hour. Now such a thought was unbearable; the smile died on my lips.

On Monday morning Sheriff Christophers burst into my cell.

Fumbling and cursing, he went down on his hands and knees and raised the skirt of my gown. I wasn't sure what he was doing but tried to stand straight as a post. Finally, he produced a key to a rusty lock that fastened my chain. After what seemed to be an eternity, both chains and shackles came undone.

"The magistrates decided to let you go without these. You owe them your gratitude."

"Please tell them that I'm grateful."

"Of course, you may be shackled again when you're condemned, and you won't be condemned 'til your trial," he sputtered.

"My trial? When will that be held?"

He scratched his head and squinted up at the rafters.

"I recollect that Superior Court meets in September."

"September!" I cried in outrage. "But it isn't yet May!"

"Well, I can't make time go any faster, now, can I? You've placed a burden on Faith and me and all of us who've had the decency to obey God's laws."

He paused—perhaps waiting for me to offer an apology— but I gave him none.

"Let's hope there's enough in their damned treasury to pay me my due this time!"

The door slammed behind him, but it didn't stay closed for long.

Over the next few weeks, strangers kept showing up to see me, and I had no say in whether they gained entry. Even Faith began to grumble about fetching the key each time to admit them.

At first, I wondered what interest I held for all my visitors. If I had been still at liberty, few if any of them would have greeted me on the road. Soon I learned that they all shared a common purpose: to save my soul by any means possible.

In time I understood that I, Mercy Bramble, was of no real consequence to any one of them. Their real desire was to claim credit for saving me, and in doing so, to gain favor with the Lord and save themselves.

First came Reverend Eliphalet Adams, venerated for his missionary work among the Indians. I remembered many times when Cate had spoken his name with such respect, such gratitude for teaching her to read.

Stooped and white-haired at seventy-six, he gripped a stout cane in one hand, a Bible in the other. After Sheriff Christophers had dragged a rough-hewn bench into my cell to make him more comfortable, the old man began to read scripture until his own droning put him to sleep.

As he snored and wheezed, I peered at him curiously—he was, after all, the preacher who had stood at the pulpit during The Awful Thunderclap. Then I slipped the Bible from his palsied hands and began searching for passages that I remembered from my earliest lessons. To my astonishment, I now found hundreds of words and phrases that I recognized.

Two hours later the sheriff returned, shook the reverend by his shoulders, and helped him to his feet.

As he turned to leave, Reverend Adams pronounced in a quavering voice, "You have sinned mightily, woman. Pray to God for forgiveness before it is too late."

He didn't look at me again, not even towards the corner where I sat.

"I know not if I'm guilty of any sin or crime," I replied as respectfully as I could.

"Have you any husband, woman?"

"None."

He frowned, shook his head, and left with the sheriff.

Two days later, a more formidable visitor stormed into the quiet cell: Reverend Jewett himself. I hadn't forgotten his sharp reprimand on the day of Mrs. Palmes' funeral, calling for me to be silent. His frightful eyebrows, black and greasy as the side of the meetinghouse, were drawn together in permanent disapproval. As he came closer, I could smell his foul breath, like the vapors of hell that he so often described.

"*You* are not a member of the Church," he began, by way of greeting. "*You* have no right to expect God's salvation."

He shook his head with undisguised contempt.

"*You* are no better than godless heathen to whom Reverend Adams has preached the word of God. A base devil-worshipper cannot enter the Kingdom of Heaven. But none of those heathen women would have committed so vile and unnatural a sin as you have."

"But I don't know if I'm guilty of any crime, Reverend." My protest sounded much louder than I'd intended. I wanted to explain the circumstances of my child's birth, but he thundered right back at me.

"Only *God* gives life, and only *God* can take it away!"

He raised his fist as he often did during a sermon, but there was no pulpit to bring it down upon. His fist hung in mid-air as though he intended to strike me.

"Think on your sins, Mercy Bramble!"

His words echoed in my prison cell; then he was gone.

As I heard a bolt slide into place on the other side of the door, I sighed with relief. If only that door had a bolt on the *inside*, I thought.

As if in answer to my prayers, a few days passed with no visitors. Then someone I never expected came to call: the Hawk herself. At first, she looked so nervous and miserable that I almost pitied her. She stayed very close to the door as if hoping to take flight.

"Thank you for coming, Madam. It is a comfort." The lie came easily to my lips, since I thought that she might help me after all.

"My husband says it's our charitable duty to visit you, that you are still our servant and therefore under our protection," she said in a rush. "I say that we no longer owe you that privilege. And of course, murder will out. It always does."

"Madam, you know I did not commit murder," I whispered. "In truth, you are the only one who *does* know what happened that morning."

She shook her head sorrowfully, pretending not to have heard me.

"To think that my husband was all alone under the same roof with you before we married. And look what happened to his old mother!"

Then it was my turn to pretend not to have heard her.

I asked if she had any other news for me, but she'd brought me very little. As an afterthought, she told me that Pompey had been whipped for being out after curfew.

"My poor, long-suffering husband was summoned to bring him home after midnight. Half dead Pompey was from the whipping, but he learned his lesson."

"What a terrible way to treat old Pompey," I murmured, shaking my head.

"You must be speaking in jest," she said with a little snort.

Another tedious hour passed, the longest hour of my imprisonment so far. I asked about Elijah and everyone I could possibly think of, even inquiring about the cat, Captain and all the animals, one by one. Were the cows giving enough milk? Were the piglets growing bigger?

Finally, my guest rose from her seat and knocked sharply on the door, calling for the sheriff.

Before she left, she turned and said, "My son Nat wanted to come with me today, but I forbade it. Heaven knows why, but he thinks he fancies you. You're no better than that idiot girl Zeno."

"Madam, I surely don't deserve such harsh words."

"You have no brains and no backbone. You're just a selfish hussy. You've never done *a thing* to help anyone in this world but yourself. Fortunately, my husband can see that all too well now."

Her last words ran through me like a sword; she seemed to know exactly where to drive in the blade. This time I had no more breath to strike back.

She called for the jailer, but one of the guards appeared instead to slide open the bolt and release her. As the door swung open, I saw Bryan Palmes in their wagon, reins in hand, staring somberly straight ahead. Feelings of both love and hate filled my heart like two heavy stones; I could not move either one.

In spite of myself, I silently prayed, "Turn your head and look at me, Bryan Palmes! Look me in the eyes so I can see your rotting soul."

But his gaze never strayed in my direction.

"It's as if I've slipped into another world," I said aloud to myself. "It's far stranger than the travels of Mr. Gulliver."

Like someone in a dream, I believed I could no longer communicate with the rest of humankind. Invisible, I was a shadow next to others' flesh and blood.

Only when the wagon was out of sight did I shout my curse through the alley, "Damn you forever, Bryan Palmes!"

But I knew it was my master who had damned me.

❦

As my prison cell grew warmer with the season, a third minister adopted my cause and began coming to call. Matthew Graves had been sent from England to lead the town's Episcopal ministry, a small group of worshippers who were far outnumbered by Congregationalists.

Unlike all the other clergymen, Matthew Graves had first sent a message to me through the sheriff's wife.

"The young reverend asks if the prisoner would be so kind as to receive him, and at what hour, my lady," Faith asked me with a mock curtsy.

I tried to respond in a haughty tone.

"Please tell him that I'm very busy here in jail."

Faith guffawed loudly.

"But if he insists, please let him know I can receive a visitor at four o'clock tomorrow."

From the first sight of him I knew that I wasn't going to hear another stern reproach or angry tirade. Much younger than Reverend Adams, the Reverend Graves was meek and mild compared to Reverend Jewett.

At twenty-three years of age, Matthew Graves was a recent graduate of divinity school; Faith told me that he barely had enough confidence to raise his voice to his small group of followers. He seemed woefully unprepared for being in a jail cell with a prisoner, let alone an accused murderess.

Upon arriving, he stood for several minutes before discerning the whereabouts of the bench. Since my own eyes were well accustomed to such dim light, I was able to study him awhile before he'd even noticed me.

Here, truly, is a lost soul, I thought, far more lost than myself.

Although Reverend Graves was tall, he carried his head quite low in an angle of exaggerated humility. He had a long neck with an Adam's apple, a narrow face, and pale locks that drooped just past his shoulders. Something about his unblinking gaze reminded me of the turtles that poked their heads from the pasture pond in late spring. But unlike those silent water dwellers, this creature finally stammered a few words to me.

"I never thought that you would look so, so…"

"So unlike a criminal, Reverend?" I ventured.

"No, I meant, I didn't expect you to be quite so *beautiful*."

I'd never heard so much kindness expressed in a single word.

To my astonishment, my visitor handed me a handsome Bible that he'd carried tucked under his arm.

"You can read, I suppose?" he asked anxiously.

"I only know my letters and a few words," I replied sadly. "My first master started to teach me, but my second master did not wish to continue my lessons. One of my fellow servants helped me, and I was starting to make progress on my own. Then all this happened, and, well, they brought me here."

"How terribly unfortunate for you," he murmured.

"There was never any paper or pen given me, and a servant has precious little time for lessons." I felt compelled to add, "I did try to read a primer once, starting with the letter A. I even remember its first passage:

In Adam's fall
We sinned all…"

He asked permission to sit and carefully brushed off the bench so as not to dirty his breeches and coat. Then, taking a deep breath, he mustered the courage to look right at me. Although not quite knee-to-knee on the bench, we both felt a sudden start at our proximity. He smelled like freshly milled soap.

"I hope that I don't appear too bold by coming here to counsel you. After all, I'm a stranger to you and most of your townsmen." He placed his hand on his heart and tried to smile a little. "And having finished my divinity studies only six months ago, I'm sure that there are men far wiser than me."

When locked into my gaze, his grey eyes had a curious way of growing wider and wider as he spoke.

He cleared his throat. "So, I have come to beg a favor of you, strange as that may sound."

When I asked what favor that could possibly be, he explained that he was writing a series of sermons on the nature of sin and needed me to grant him several interviews. He wanted to gain a better understanding of my transgression and *why* I had chosen to sin.

I stared at him blankly, but he forged ahead.

"I've read Cotton Mather's great work on sinners, *Pillars of Salt*. Now I'm looking for notable sinners among people of our own colony so that I might write of them."

"And how can I help you if I don't understand my own sin? No one ever baptized me, Reverend, and I'm very poorly schooled."

He dismissed my objection with a wave of his hand.

"I need your friendship, Mercy, if I may call you by your Christian name. I don't have many friends on these shores yet; they seem very hard to find in this town."

He took a deep breath and eagerly continued.

"In return for your friendship, I'll give you instruction in the Scriptures. Then, every week, before the Sabbath, I'll also practice my sermon for your ears only. You can tell me your opinions without prejudice."

Having no reason to refuse, I told him I accepted his offer.

Then Reverend Graves bid me farewell and called for a guard to release him. I hadn't even thanked him for his gift of the Holy Bible.

Sometimes I thought that the walls of the cell must have had ears, and that my enemies could hear everything I said, because the very next day, the Reverend Jewett reappeared. He wasn't pleased that I had my own Bible and immediately tried to take it away from me.

"There are others in my Congregation far more deserving of the Lord's book," he insisted. "It will only lead to confusion, since you lack instruction and will misinterpret the sacred texts."

Recoiling from his grasping hands, I drew the Bible back to my chest.

"Stay in the place that God has set you, woman!" he warned. "Don't meddle in affairs that are reserved for men, and bow to their superior judgment."

"It was a gift from Reverend Graves," I said firmly, surprised by my own boldness.

"A gift from a fool, you mean. The young reverend is so green that it makes him blind. And his band of ignorant followers are not among the chosen."

Having no other defense, I turned and pressed myself against a wall, with the Bible at my breast.

"You shan't have it, Reverend! It's mine now."

He stopped short of wrestling the book from me but launched a final attack with words instead.

"Read it, then! Read all you want. Read how the ungodly shall perish, Mercy!"

But I forgot his cruel words the minute he called for the guard, and the door slammed shut.

Hunched on my pallet, I began sifting greedily through lines of scripture, searching for words—and then groups of words—that I might remember seeing in Bryan Palmes' Bible. The words were like hidden gems; I began stringing several together into a beautiful necklace, one that only I could see sparkling about my neck.

For the first time in weeks, the hours flew by on their own without my trying to count them. If I could read this entire book and find a way to help myself, wasn't it possible that God might decide to help me as well?

Deep inside of me, a flutter of hope dared to stir, gentle as a butterfly wing or a baby's breath.

漎

I was halfway between sleep and wakefulness one night when I heard someone whispering nearby. The cell was so pitch black that I couldn't even see my hand as I reached to steady myself against the wall; I stumbled blindly before finding my balance.

"Mercy," hissed the voice.

I didn't recognize the speaker, nor could I guess whether it was man or woman, adult or child. Then a gentle tapping started outside the wall.

"Who's there?" I asked, my heart wildly beating.

After a profound silence, the whisperer spoke again; it seemed as if he or she were struggling with words that had been committed to memory.

"Friends are close by. Going to set you free."

"Who are you? Who sent you here?" I squinted in vain into the dark through the narrow crack in the wall.

"I'm nobody," said the whisperer. I heard retreating footsteps, then silence.

Five nights later, the strange voice came again.

"Come over here, Mercy."

The moon was full, illuminating the alley. A pair of enormous brown eyes had appeared very close to mine.

"What's your name?" I asked.

"I'm Zeke, from Colonel Minor's farm, just beyond the Palmes' place."

From the pitch of his voice, I guessed that he was no more than fourteen or fifteen years old.

"Don't you know it's unlawful for slaves to be out after nine o'clock?"

"Oh, I stay in the shadows. And I know when the watchman's coming 'cause I see his big lantern light shining."

"So, what do you want from me, Zeke?"

"Cate and Coffey sent me with a message. They're only about ten miles away in Saybrook now. They want to help you out of here."

"But they already left for the New York colony. What keeps them here so long?"

"Farm work for a man with a broken arm. They'll be there for a month, they say, just 'til they're paid," Zeke reported. "They have plenty of friends to carry messages from farm to farm."

Zeke coughed a few times.

"Cate said they're real sad."

"Whatever for, Zeke?"

"They're both free now, but you're not anymore."

"But I've *never* been free since I was a small girl, Zeke. I've always been a servant, bonded to Mr. Palmes, and to Mr. Holt before that."

"But you wasn't a slave to no one."

The messenger fell silent, allowing me a moment to consider his words.

"Coffey can hide you in the same barns and root cellars used by runaways. He'll put you under the boards of their wagon, then take you away with them on a night with no moon."

With a heavy sigh, I put my face in my hands for a few moments and weighed my choices. Surely the town fathers and clergymen would somehow protect me—just as my masters had supposedly looked after me all my life. Perhaps I'd be harshly reprimanded, but I didn't think I needed to hide in barns and cellars like a runaway, risking further punishment or some injury.

"There's no way out of this jail. Zeke. Go back and tell them that Mercy isn't going to run away or get them in trouble Do you have that?"

Zeke sounded disappointed.

"All right, but Cate said you'll need something powerful to protect you. To give you courage. She says you must be like the she-wolf, not like the sheep."

His slender hand and wrist slipped easily through the opening, handing me a small object. Then his hand disappeared and Zeke also.

It was too dark to see what he'd given me—the item seemed both soft and hard in places—so I slept with it clasped in my hand.

As a single ray of morning light slanted into my cell, I found that I held a wolf's claw, a tuft of gray fur still attached. I slipped it inside my bodice so that no one else would ever see it.

❦

Soon, from inside the cell, I could see the trees beginning to turn green and smell the warm earth of late spring. I pictured myself back on the farm, preparing to plant pole beans when the horns of the moon were up.

As I came to fully understand that I'd be imprisoned until September, my hope of an earlier release had vanished. At least for the present, I had to accept that I was going to be penned in like a farm animal for five more months.

When Reverend Graves sent word that he'd be coming to visit again, I was glad to hear it. For the first time since my arrest, I wondered if I smelled badly. I was accustomed to bathing at least once a month—even though I'd heard that water exposed our flesh to diseases—but Faith hadn't brought a washbasin in weeks. I'd all but forgotten to ask for it. In any case, the smell of the streets was so strong that it overpowered all other odors.

Reverend Graves looked weary. He said that he'd been tending to his maiden sister who lived with him. She'd taken ill a week before, and he'd stayed at her side every night, through fits of her terrible coughing.

"The doctor came to bleed her, but she still didn't improve," he lamented.

The reverend's face was pale and drawn from lack of sleep; even his hair needed combing. Nevertheless, he wanted to talk.

"You know, Mercy, you and I have one great thing in common."

Heaving a sigh, he drew his hands up under his chin in the shape of a church steeple.

"We both have names that others like to ridicule," he said. "How many times have I been told what a *grave* man I am or heard that my sermon might send someone to an early grave? And you, I suppose, a Bramble, are forever teased that you might stick to someone or that you were in need of weeding out."

His tone was so mournful and serious that for the first time since I was imprisoned, I fought the urge to laugh.

"Yes," I agreed. "I'm afraid that's all true."

With a slight smile, the reverend placed his hand on his heart and recited a line from memory: "But what's in a name? That which we call a rose by any other name would smell as sweet."

"What an odd saying."

"It's a line from a play by the late Mr. William Shakespeare. Are you familiar with him?"

"No, but I suppose he was an Englishman," I observed, trying to sound knowledgeable. "My first master, Mr. Holt, warned us all many times that plays and play acting are as sinful as dancing or playing the fiddle. He used to say those pastimes could pave the road to hell."

"Ah, but Mr. Shakespeare's words are quite heavenly," the reverend persisted, rolling his eyes upward. "When I returned to England two years ago, I saw his Romeo and Juliet on a stage in London. Though I confess it was rather removed from my studies at the time."

"So why *did* you risk your virtue by going to the theater, Reverend?"

My visitor suddenly looked uncomfortable.

"I'm only a man, I suppose. A man of God, but a man, nevertheless. And young men are known to do foolish things."

"Young women too," I murmured.

Then, as if waking from his dream of London, he said, "Let us pray."

He bent his head and began to recite the Lord's Prayer.

"Now open to the Psalms, Mercy."

I took the Bible and opened it at random, not knowing where to turn. But the book fell open instantly to the first Psalm.

"That must be a good sign!" he cried. His face had lit up from within, reflecting a hidden joy.

"A sign of what, Reverend?"

"That we two are going to save your soul by teaching you the Lord's word!"

He pointed eagerly to a line of text and asked me to read it. I recognized the word "tree" right away, and also "river."

"Read it!" he urged. "Read about the man who follows God's laws."

For the very first time in my life, I read aloud without faltering, the words flowing together without any pauses.

"And he shall be like a tree planted by the rivers of water."

I would never forget the miracle we'd just witnessed; it came from deep inside me after so many years of failure.

I, Mercy Bramble, could read at last, and no one could ever stop me.

※

This was the tale I heard from Reverend Graves, who heard it from one of his followers, who heard it from any man or woman with breath to speak.

One night while I slept in late midsummer, a storm blew in from the Atlantic and bore down on New London. As the storm raged, a crew of Spanish seamen and their captain had fought in vain to keep control of their vessel. In one terrible moment, the ship had struck a reef just west of New London's harbor. The site wasn't far from the White Beach where I'd spent an afternoon with Cate.

Playing the Good Samaritan, a local captain used his own vessel to offload the Spaniards' heavy cargo, allowing their ship to be towed safely into port.

Soon all along the coast and far out into the countryside, every soul was talking about the shipwreck; even Reverend Graves couldn't wait to tell me what he'd heard. From the narrow gap that served as my window, he pointed out its mast to me, still flying the flag of Spain.

"The ship's cargo is worth a king's ransom," he said. "The chests are filled with gold Spanish doubloons and cases of the finest indigo."

The townsmen had offered to store the Spanish treasure in a warehouse near the wharves.

"No less than six armed guards—all men of different trades— were ordered to stand guard. But two days later, when officials came to unlock the doors, all the chests had been stolen. Every one!" the reverend had reported to me.

The guards who'd failed in their duties were rounded up at gunpoint and thrown in a jail cell opposite mine. Now six more men and a constable now stood watch outside to make sure that the guards-turned-thieves did not escape.

Although I could only see their shadows through gaps in my wall, I could hear the prisoners' conversation quite plainly. Hour after hour, they shouted, cursed, and scuffled with one another.

For the first time in months, my thoughts strayed from my own troubles, wondering if these men were guilty or innocent of any crime. I barely remembered to ask Faith my daily question: "When is my trial? Shouldn't it be any day now?"

She'd answered me with feigned indifference, "Why should I care how long you're locked up? My husband's being paid as long as you're here, so you're putting some very fine meat on our table every night."

At noontime, Reverend Graves arrived bearing good news: against all odds, his sister Joanna had fully recovered from her long illness. He thanked me for my prayers on her behalf.

"It's clear that your prayers are powerful. God must be listening to you."

He'd brought me a meat pie Joanna had baked; I made him promise to tell her that it was the best meal I'd ever had.

For more than three hours we studied the scriptures together, and I delighted him by reciting an entire psalm that I'd committed to memory. Ever since he'd given me the Bible as a gift, the act of reading had become more natural for me. I felt as though I'd finally found the missing treasure that I'd been seeking all my life.

"You have a natural *gift* for studying scripture, Mercy, more so than any of the ladies of my church."

His eyes glowed with excitement behind a new pair of spectacles.

If I did have a gift, however, it must have been the power of seeing right through him. I was beginning to see that his feelings for me went beyond that of teacher and student.

We concluded our visit in our customary way, with the reverend standing before me, rehearsing his next sermon as though he were standing before his congregation.

"It's a fine sermon, if not your best," I told him. "I only wish that I could see and hear you deliver it to your congregation on Sunday."

"Someday you will hear me preach to the multitude," he promised. To my surprise, he took my hands in both of his.

"I'm certain of that, Reverend. Of all who have tried to counsel me, I believe that only *you* can help me."

"*God* will help you, not one of His poor subjects like me."

Perhaps he felt what little warmth there was to my hands and was reluctant to take his away. I couldn't help but remember how my master used to stroke my hands with his slow, absentminded caress. The memory made my heart begin racing—or was it from the reverend's touch?

I slipped from his grasp. Something great was troubling my conscience. Something I'd never spoken with him about before.

"Reverend," I asked, "What is the greater sin—to commit a wrong oneself or to go along with someone who commits a wrong and stay silent?"

My hand pressed my heart, trying to slow its rapid beating.

"What crime do you mean?" he asked calmly. "The one of which you are accused?"

Suddenly it felt as though a door had closed between us; I wasn't ready to speak of my child's death to him after all. In recent days I'd begun to wonder if I bore more guilt than I'd first realized. After all, I did nothing to protect my newborn child from the cold-blooded actions of the Hawk. Was that not a sin in itself? And why hadn't I done more to protect Zeno?

To change the course of our conversation, I stammered out a half-hearted confession.

"I once went somewhere that I shouldn't have gone, to the White Beach. A fellow servant lied for me, saying that we were going to look for a lost cow."

The words were scarcely out of my mouth when the reverend cut off my confession with a wave of his hand.

"Dismiss the thought and save your strength for greater battles with man or Satan," he advised.

Then he said goodbye rather hastily, already walking toward the door. To my surprise he took a large key from his coat pocket and gave it a little shake.

"I must remember to give this back to Madam Christophers," he muttered to himself.

"What's that you said?" I called out. I couldn't take my eyes off the key.

"Oh, the sheriff's wife was kind enough to let me in but she asked me to hold the key this time until she returns."

"But why on earth did she do that if she is my jailer?"

"The good woman said she was heading to the tavern to fetch her husband and that she was too weary to walk all the way back to their house with the key. Nor did she wish to risk losing it by carrying it through the streets. Surely, I could be trusted to hold the key for just an hour, or so she said."

He lowered his voice to a whisper.

"Don't tell anyone but I carried it halfway home with me the last time, I was so distracted by our visit. Of course, I returned it to her."

"But if you'd kept it, you could have opened my cell at any time?"

"Yes, in theory, but there are always guards, Mercy. Please don't think that I'd be so weak as to make such a mistake! That would be a criminal act!"

"I'm very sorry, Reverend. It was only my curiosity."

"And of course, Madam Christophers always slides the bolt. I'm actually locked in here with you right now like a fellow criminal! Until I call a guard to come and release me that is."

To make his point, he shouted for a guard, and footsteps approached. Then, with a slight bow, the reverend slipped out the door.

No sooner had it closed than I heard a lock turn and a bolt slide into place.

Darkness was already falling, and I saw that a watchman was making his rounds by lantern light. The shadowy figure of the reverend stood for a while in the alley as if he wanted to come back and spend another hour with me. Soon he was hurrying towards the sheriff's home to return the key.

That night I had a strange dream in which I saw the reverend kneeling for his evening prayers at a bedside. Instead of reciting the Lord's Prayer, though, he was repeating something that he'd once told me from a play by Master Shakespeare: "My only love springs from my only hate."

❧

CHAPTER VII

SEEKING REDEMPTION

Forbear to judge, for we are sinners all.

WILLIAM SHAKESPEARE

It came as no surprise when the thieves of the Spanish treasure, under armed guard, all escaped three days later. The six men—tradesmen, merchants, and farmers—simply returned to everyday business as if nothing had happened. I heard talk of arresting and jailing the second group of prison guards for letting the first group escape, but that rumor quickly faded.

In truth, it was hard to find a clean conscience anywhere in town; many God-fearing, law-abiding men and women had carried off some of the treasure and hidden it in their homes. Even the magistrates were entangled in the web of lies, yet no one could single out the wrongdoers.

Observing these events as a prisoner gave me a kind of false hope. If New Londoners didn't honor their own laws—and their memories were so short—perhaps they'd have only passing interest in my situation as well. My trial might be overlooked in the chaos, and I would be set free.

Or so I believed.

I even dared to dream of what I might do on my first day of freedom, roaming the town and country to see what I might find. Faith had told me about a strange and wonderful animal that everyone was clamoring to see. When the Spanish ship was sinking, several crates of precious indigo had burst open, washing the contents through lower decks. That was how a white Spanish stallion had been dyed entirely blue.

At the height of the storm, a sailor had opened the main hatch to let the panicked creature swim away through the waves. A farmer claimed that he'd found the blue stallion galloping up and down the White Beach; now the man was taking it from town to town and charging curious souls a penny to view this marvel up close. I pictured myself stroking its sky-colored mane or petting its nose, just like I used to do with Rosie. Although it gave me comfort to think of the Holts' mare, part of me now blamed that old horse for all my troubles.

"If the Holts' old mare hadn't stepped in a hole and broke her leg, none of this would have ever happened to me," I once complained to Faith while she swept out my cell.

"You made this mess yourself, dearie. Don't blame the poor horse!" she scolded.

For all the news that reached me about goings-on in town, I still heard nothing about my future trial. Neither the sheriff nor his wife could tell me when the court would be held, although I asked them every day.

Finally, Sheriff Christophers informed me that the presiding judge had fallen gravely ill. A few weeks later he told me that a recent storm had felled many great trees on the road from Hartford, so a judge who'd been appointed to replace the sickly one couldn't travel to New London. Then the governor had decided to change the month for Superior Court to meet. The sheriff wrote the governor a letter to inquire about a new date, but it could be weeks before an answer arrived.

Meanwhile, September was slipping away, and not a soul listened to my entreaties.

Autumn was never a season to be trusted along the coast, or so I'd come to believe. The other three seasons were usually true to their character, but fall could be madly unpredictable. It was like a false friend who comes offering a beautiful gift, only to destroy it, right before the recipient's eyes. No sooner had October given the trees such brilliant, red and gold adornments, than it sent gale winds to tear them away.

Nights were colder; soon ice would still the river's surface. Like fine lacework, thin patches of ice covered the ruts in the alley each morning until wagon wheels broke through each delicate creation.

It reminded me of how frost would line all the furrows in the Palmes' cornfields. After harvest time, nothing stirred but a few crows, walking imperiously through each rut in search of an old kernel. In stillness, the world awaited the first snow; after it fell, broken cornstalks made a pattern like crooked stitching on a white linen sampler.

I'd always thought those sights were the harbingers of hardships to come, but now those barren fields would have seemed a kind of Eden compared to the confines of my cell. For a chance to run free through that wasteland with gray skies above me, I gladly would have sold my soul to the devil—if he hadn't already claimed it.

The jail had grown quieter, and my visitors less frequent, but one day strangers' voices roused me from a daydream. It sounded like a small crowd had gathered just outside my cell door. Rising from the tangle of their conversations, I heard a beloved voice that I'd so often longed for.

It was my mother's.

Desperately, I removed a rag from the crack in the outer wall—I'd put it there to block the cold—and tried to get a look at her. At first, my heart soared when I saw the woman who had given me life seventeen years ago. For a moment I even let myself believe that she'd come to bring me home, as though collecting a wayward child from distant relations.

But learning the real reason for her visit would soon extinguish that hope.

When Faith swung open my door, the former Mary Bramble was waiting outside.

My first impression was that the early frost had somehow coated her as well. My mother's hair had gone as white as cinders under her cap, like ashes from a fire that had burned very hot. Her black cape was severe but sturdy.

Part of me wished to run to her and cling to her skirts as I did when a child. With tears rising, I moved to embrace her, but seeing her with so many strangers, decided against it.

"*That* is my daughter," she said, nodding in my direction. She had six companions: a man and five women.

"Who are all these people, Mother?"

"This is my husband's cousin, Mr. Bartholomew Paine, who has come by sea from Long Island. He's a very learned teacher and a leader of the Children of God," she explained quickly. "And these good ladies are all his followers who are here to pray with you."

Clad in black capes and caps, and all with prayer books in hand, these women were so plain of feature that it was hard to distinguish one from another. The younger ones may have been quite old, and the older ones quite young.

I'd started to ask how she came to be in the company of these strange people, and why she placed more trust in them than in church members of our own town, but Mr. Paine interrupted before any words were out of my mouth.

"We come as friends, but before we can pray with you, you must first confess your sins."

He spoke very quickly; he hadn't come to listen.

"God will turn a deaf ear unless you come to him with a clean heart."

"Amen!" chorused the women.

They were so insistent that I almost complied with their request for a confession—after all, I'd been trained to obey orders above all else—but something made me pause. A voice inside me was urging, "Speak up, Mercy."

"Mother, I will pray with them if you wish it, but only if you grant me a favor in return: you and I must speak in private first. It has been many years; surely you can spare me a few minutes."

Although Mr. Paine became quite agitated, my mother agreed. She fluttered her hand at the flock of women until they backed out into the alley.

I walked behind her and shut the prison door. At first, she wouldn't look me in the eye.

"Must I be alone with you, daughter? You've fallen so far into Satan's pit that I'm a little afraid to be in here with you."

I had no reply, so she sniffed the air and covered her nose.

"How do you bear the stench of it?"

"I scarcely notice anymore, Mother, but let's not waste precious time; I have so much to say. For seven years you cared for me and kept me from all harm. Then you sent me to live with strangers, and they gave me away to other strangers. Why did you do such a thing to your only child?"

She pressed her lips together, making a line as straight and thin as one drawn with the tip of a sharp knife.

"That's the way of the world, Mercy. Your father was gone,

and I had nothing but my two hands and a sewing needle. No man would marry a widow without property. I wasn't even a member of the Church and couldn't attend services because I hadn't been saved."

"Then why didn't you have me baptized? Didn't you see that you were condemning me to such a lowly station in the eyes of others?"

She still avoided my gaze, looking towards the floor.

"A man must hold his child for the baptism ceremony. I had no one to do so."

Her voice began to rise. She insisted that she'd tried to give me a good life by bonding me to people who had property, since I would have had none of my own.

"What was so wrong with that?" she asked defiantly. "I did it for you. And now you've thanked me by bringing a bastard child into the world and taking its life!"

"Mother, I swear to you I didn't murder that precious baby. She was either born dead or harmed by another woman's hand after I'd fainted."

She turned her head so I couldn't see her face.

"Perhaps it would have been better if I'd done the same when you were born," she murmured, "or found someone to do it for me."

"Are you telling me that I had no father?" I demanded. "That I was misbegotten?"

My mother whirled around and at last looked me straight in the eyes. She spoke as though spitting out a poison she'd been carrying in her throat for many years.

"I wanted you out of my sight because you were a constant reminder of my shame."

Stunned, I fell to the floor and sat there in silence as she continued.

"You had no lawful father. Two sailors forced themselves on me one night during the voyage. I was only a girl of fifteen and never saw their faces in the dark. Now do you understand why I tell people my first husband died on shipboard? Why I'd rather *die* myself than to have my husband Elisha know the truth?"

I looked up and wiped away tears.

"It doesn't matter anymore. I always loved you Mother; I love you still. Promise you'll speak up for me! Tell them you'll take me home with you!"

For a moment the hard line of her mouth began to soften.

"No one can bring a grown child home. But I'll speak to my husband and see what we can do if you are called to trial."

I thanked her, grabbing her hand to kiss it before she drew it away.

"Now, if you have any love left me for me, Mercy, please let my husband's cousin enter with his followers. Elisha is a decent man, and I must follow his wishes today."

She moved to open the door where the group was still waiting outside and told them that they could now enter.

Mr. Paine cleared his throat loudly as they assembled.

"Open to Joshua, Chapter Seven, verse nineteen," Mr. Paine commanded. The women eagerly opened their prayer books.

He began to read in a loud voice that was more suited to a large meetinghouse than a small cell.

"And Joshua said unto Achan, my son, give, I pray thee, glory to the Lord God of Israel, and make confession unto him; and tell me now, what thou hast done; *hide it not from me.*"

The chorus of women recited, "And Achan answered Joshua, and said, indeed I have sinned against the Lord God of Israel."

Mr. Paine struck his palm against the open page of his Bible.

"Do you see how simple it is? Achan confessed and so must you, Mercy Bramble," His look was piercing.

"Must I confess to man or God?" I asked boldly.

"To *both*," came his answer with absolute authority.

My cell was so crowded that I could scarcely breathe. Only the teacher and one woman could fit on the narrow bench with me; the rest had to stand along the wall. Looking like a row of ravens, they shifted from one foot to another and eyed me warily.

I looked to my mother for reassurance, but she'd already slipped out the door without saying goodbye. A memory came flooding back: being left on that doorstep at the Holts' so many years ago. Now I was both abandoned and betrayed.

Mr. Paine did not waste time or spare his words.

"If you do not confess, the Lord God will be angry. And those who are innocent will suffer His terrible wrath as though they were among the damned," he warned.

"Little children of this town will be taken with the pox, cows will not give milk, and other grievous misfortunes will befall us all until this sin is confessed!"

By degrees, his face grew redder and redder behind the black stubble of his beard. It looked as though he were being heated in a blacksmith's forge.

What if Mr. Paine were telling the truth? I thought of baby Elijah and pictured him inside a tiny coffin, being dragged deep in the woods to the smallpox burial ground.

"And if I were to confess, will your prayers travel to God faster than mine?" I asked.

Grabbing her bosom with bony, spotted fingers, the oldest woman blurted out ecstatically, "Oh yes! We're your friends, and we have nothing but love for you. If you confess, you'll find sweet, sweet forgiveness!"

"Let us pray, Children of God," intoned the teacher, "that Mercy will be the Devil's counsel-keeper no more. That she will break these chains the Devil used to snare her, and that she might speak the truth and free her soul."

"Amen!" came the enraptured chorus.

Still, I was reluctant to believe them.

"You're not the first to come to this cell to minister to my soul. How do I know that you deserve my trust? I've never even heard of the Children of God before, so your teachings are unknown to me."

"The Children of God," Mr. Paine said firmly, "are Apostles of Christ. Ours is a sacred mission, and we would not divulge your confession to anyone outside these four walls. If you confess to us now, in private, it will go *straight* to God and never be heard by mortal men."

Mr. Paine laid his hand on his heart. Speaking in the most intimate way, he leaned in so close to me that I felt his breath on my face.

"I will tell you a secret, Miss Bramble. We are far, far above your magistrates, you see, and they know it well."

A strange gleam appeared in his eyes, and he pointed heavenward.

"We're closer to the angels, at God's right hand! But you can't begin to fathom that holy bond until you've confessed any prior sins to us and prayed."

For five or six hours they took turns reading from the scripture, not stopping for any rest. I began to grow weak; perhaps it was from hunger and thirst, but it seemed that these people were taking my strength by the hour.

"Don't be afraid, Child! Don't be afraid!" one of the nameless women kept whispering near my ear.

"We're your friends, your only friends, Mercy," another said sweetly as she held my hand in hers. Her hand felt soft, but bloodless, like that of old Mrs. Palmes.

"We're your *family*, poor girl, your sisters in Christ."

"We all made a long voyage from Long Island to be here with you. We are your family, those who come to your side in time of need."

The weight of several hands pushed gently on my shoulders, just like the tide had pushed me on that day at the White Beach. How good that deep caress had felt. How soothing it had been to surrender to a greater force—to let go of everything that weighed me down and float free of my cares—just that once.

As my cell began to dissolve in shadows, I let my head drop and closed my eyes. Soon the voices were pleading passionately.

"Give us the power to pray for you, and we can do anything!"

"Confess that you have done this thing, and it will be absolved by God's grace! Even if you're not certain, simply make confession unto Him and He will clear all confusion!"

"Your prayers will be answered and you'll be released. You'll be free! Absolutely free like we are!"

"Did you do it Mercy? Did you put your hands on its mouth?"

These plain-faced women were lulling me to sleep. Their pleas became gentle crooning, like that of mourning doves in the rafters of the Palmes' barn. I'd always loved that sound and the feeling of peace that it had brought me.

Only half conscious now, I wondered why they kept talking about a mouth. Was this one of their religious riddles or symbols? A reference to something in the Scriptures? I remembered how I'd touched that tiny mouth to feel for her breath. Is that all my inquisitors wanted to know?

"Did you do it Mercy?"

"Did you do it?"

"Did you put your hands on its small mouth?"

Without any warning, Mr. Paine started shouting and waving his arms as if a demon had possessed him. His spittle wet my face.

"Confess! Confess, woman! Tell us now! Did you put your hand on its mouth?"

The walls seemed to collapse around me and then blow apart again; I fell to the floor in a trance. All was quiet and dark.

Then someone who sounded very faraway spoke a single word: "Yes."

It was only a whisper, but that word reverberated as though an arrow had sliced through the room and still quivered where it struck. When silence closed around me, I realized that I'd been the one to speak that word.

Mr. Paine rose so abruptly that the bench clattered backward against the wall. The sound roused me from my trance, reminding me that I was still a prisoner.

"That is all!" he declared. His prayer book snapped shut like a hunter's trap.

The women looked at one another silently. Then, with heads bowed, they fled from my company just as one would from a madwoman or a leper.

Still crouched on the floor, I thought that I heard Mr. Paine speaking with Faith in an agitated way. The noise of the street, as people returned from Saturday market, prevented me from hearing him clearly.

Before the light faded altogether, I opened my Bible; I'd kept the Holy Book better protected lately, having once seen a rat gnawing at its pages. It seemed a miracle that I could read entire passages on my own now, even without Matthew to guide me.

Thumbing quickly through the text, I looked for the passage from the Old Testament that they'd first read me, Joshua, Chapter Seven. I wondered what had happened to Achan after he'd confessed his crime of thievery to his father and the Lord. Did his neighbors pardon his sin and embrace him once again?

My eye found the passage, but it took me a while to read, word by word.

"And Joshua said, why hast thou troubled us? The Lord shall trouble thee this day. And all Israel stoned him with stones and burned them with fire, after they had stoned them with stones. And they raised over him a great heap of stones that remains to this day."

⁂

The next morning, somewhat earlier than usual, Faith brought me bread and beer mixed together in a bowl. She smiled at me in a way that I found very odd.

"So, you finally decided to make a clean breast of it, did you?" she asked in a kindly manner. Was it your mother who told you to confess?"

"I don't know what you mean, Faith."

Not fully awake, I ached all over, as though I'd been beaten.

"That gentleman from Long Island said he heard your confession yesterday. He promised the magistrate that he or his followers would appear as witnesses at your trial and swear to what you'd said."

"*What* did you say? That Mr. Paine is a liar!"

"Mind your tongue, dear."

"But he claimed that my words were for God's ears only!" I cried. "He said that confession was just something they did, like an old custom, so that their prayers would be heard!"

Faith patted my knee and spoke to me like I was a child.

"Come now, Mercy, you know that our Lord would never listen to any prayers of yours."

"And why not?"

She rolled her eyes.

"You aren't even *baptized*. God has no time for you, because you haven't been saved. You must have known all along."

"But how can that be, if God is so good and merciful?"

Faith's smile grew wider.

"Why should He waste His precious time when He's already so busy saving souls and punishing the wicked?"

"But surely He'd have pity on a servant girl like me…"

"A man's head may be turned by a pretty face, but not Almighty God's. No silly wench could ever tempt Him to change His own commandments!"

Faith snorted with laughter.

"Now I must get on with it. As my dear mother used to say, 'A man works from sun to sun, but woman's work is never done.' Not that you ever have to lift a finger around here!"

She slammed the door and bolted it.

Even in my torment, one thing was becoming clear. Baptism would make me the equal of everyone else in the Congregation. If it were truly the key to gaining my freedom—and salvation itself—then I must be baptized, no matter what the cost.

Later that same afternoon, when old Reverend Adams paid his weekly call, I spoke my mind to him right away.

"Please, Reverend, you must baptize me with all due speed."

After the elderly man listened to my appeal, he waved his hand weakly. Then, between fits of coughing, he described the difficult training that I'd have to undergo beforehand.

"I'm just too old and sick to take on such a task anymore," he wheezed. "You must find a younger, stronger man."

Though I knew in my heart that Reverend Matthew Graves would readily consent to baptize me, I feared that he'd been shunning my company these past few weeks. Then again, as a newcomer from England, perhaps he didn't wield as much power as the older clergymen did, those they called "pillars" of the Church. I needed the highest authority to intercede with the Almighty, and Reverend Graves was just a novice, after all.

Still, I felt a pang of disloyalty to the young reverend when I begged Faith to summon one of "the pillars," to my cell: the formidable Reverend Jewett.

To my surprise, he appeared the day after he'd received my message. Not wanting to anger him by wasting his time, I spoke up as soon as he entered my cell.

"I wish to be baptized straight away, Reverend."

"That's not possible!" came his reply, quick as the crack of a whip.

"Of course, I'm prepared to study and work hard for it."

"No! I cannot take anyone into my Church unless he first makes an open confession of any crimes he has committed."

Perhaps he didn't know about the Children of God's visit, I thought. Even if he did, he was unlikely to recognize the authority of those outsiders.

I folded my hands and clasped them to my heart.

"Don't you believe, sir, it is your sacred duty to baptize me if I am willing?"

"Woman, you are a sinner, and I would sooner cut your throat than administer that sacrament to you."

Then Reverend Jewett narrowed his eyes under his immense brows and lowered his voice to a hoarse whisper. Even Faith, who certainly was eavesdropping at the door, couldn't possibly have heard him.

"I have no reason to think that you are a true believer, you wretched woman."

"But I'm a *changed* woman, Reverend, one who has put her sin far behind her!"

I seized my Bible and shook it vigorously, right under his nose. "I pray *five* times a day now that I've seen the path of Christ."

"Your prayers will only be an aggravation to you when you're burning in hell."

He brushed off his sleeves as if to be rid of me.

Then, the reverend was gone. I imagined that he was annoyed with himself for having wasted more of his valuable time.

※

Reverend Matthew Graves began calling on me once again.

Soon we resumed our reading of scripture as zealously as we'd done last spring and summer. Amazed that my ability to read was blossoming more each day, he proclaimed that it was a blessed miracle, a gift from God.

The Psalms were my favorites. I believed that only a person like myself—someone who'd been imprisoned by circumstance—could have written many of them. Now the verses spoke to me directly.

> *"Have mercy upon me, O Lord, for I am in trouble: mine eye is consumed with grief, yea my soul and my belly...*
> *For I have heard the slander of many; fear was on every side. While they took counsel against me, they devised to take away my life.*
> *But I trusted in Thee, my Lord: I said, Thou art my God.*
> *My times are in thy hand: deliver me from the hand of mine enemies, and from them that persecute me."*

Late one afternoon in the cold heart of winter, Reverend Graves and I had just opened my Bible when I offered to select our daily reading. Instead of choosing a favorite psalm, however, I opened to the Song of Solomon in the Old Testament, having already marked that page.

Leaning forward so the hearth's meager glow could illuminate the pages, I began reciting in a hushed voice.

"Let him kiss me with the kisses of his mouth: for thy love is better than wine."

He immediately broke off my reading.

"Not the Song of Solomon!"

I told him I believed the song must have been written by a woman who was kept a prisoner. She was sealed behind a wall in a garden and could not see her beloved.

"But the Song is an allegory for man's love of Christ, Mercy. It's not meant to be understood *literally*." He shook his head in disbelief. "No Bible text would be so profane."

But I resumed reading, savoring the verses.

"I rose to open to my beloved; and my hands dripped with myrrh, and my fingers with sweet-smelling myrrh, upon the handles of the lock.

I opened to my beloved; but my beloved had withdrawn himself, and was gone... I sought him, but I could not find him; called him, but he gave me no answer."

The reverend caught his breath sharply. I felt breathless too, but kept reading.

"The watchmen that went about the city found me, they smote me, they wounded me.

My beloved is white and ruddy, the chiefest among ten thousand.

His head is as the most fine gold, his locks are bushy and black as a raven..."

I faltered when I came to that verse. It called to my mind the image of young Bryan Palmes. How many hours had I held his miniature portrait in my hands, worshipping each raven black lock of hair upon his forehead?

Why hadn't he loved me as I'd first loved him, and why had he withdrawn himself, like the mysterious beloved in the Song?

"His mouth is most sweet; yea he is altogether lovely. This is my beloved, this is my friend…"

But Matthew Graves finally stopped me.

"Don't do it, Mercy! Don't be fooled again by the temptations of the flesh."

Gently, he closed my Bible, took it from my hands, and set it down beside me.

"It's best that I go home now," he said.

After a hasty prayer he bid me goodbye, promising to return the next day.

Although I'd never been in a theater or seen a play, I imagined that Matthew looked like an actor preparing to make a dramatic exit from the stage. He stood by the door and called for a guard to let him out. Although he waited patiently several minutes, no one responded. Then he began to call over and over for Madam Christophers, banging the door with his open hand.

After about an hour he said mournfully, "It's no use, is it?"

"Is it possible they've forgotten you? Maybe they've fallen asleep."

"What kind of jailers are so forgetful that they lock up innocent visitors?" he asked, still banging the door in frustration. "Now I'm imprisoned here until morning!"

When the cell grew completely dark, Matthew had to stop his pacing or risk walking into a wall.

"Please, Mercy, lie down if this is the hour that you're accustomed to retire," he bid me politely. "I had no intention of intruding like this, so you must pay me no mind whatsoever."

I stretched out on my pallet. Even though I kept on my garments, I felt very awkward.

Matthew took something from his pocket: a piece of wax candle. He crept over to the fireplace and leaned in to catch a smoldering ember. Soon a small circle of light embraced the two of us.

Clearing away any straw, he set down his precious candle on the bricks. Then he studied me intently.

With a tender skill he'd no doubt learned while nursing his sister, the reverend took a cloth from the washbowl and began bathing my face. At first, I thought his gesture was a kind of strange custom, perhaps a practice of his Church, but then I saw the soiled rag. Heavy chimney smoke—constantly backing up into my cell—had streaked my face, but I hadn't known to wash it.

He looked at me as though seeing me for the first time.

"I'll watch over you until you fall asleep. The candle's wick is short, and the tallow no bigger than a shilling," he apologized. "It won't last us more than a few minutes."

He nodded toward the other side of the cell. "That bench is wide enough for me to lie on while you rest."

I thanked him and needed no further urging to close my eyes.

Although I longed to sleep, my mind unleashed a flood of questions, as it always did when I lingered on the edge of slumber. I recalled each minute of my mother's recent visit and wondered if she would defend me when called to do so. And what would the Hawk say in Court?

Questions about Bryan Palmes tormented me the most, however.

By the terms of my indenture as a servant, my master had denied me the right to marry for another seven years. And since I was legally sworn to obey him, was it a crime that I'd obeyed him so well on that first night we lay together and those summer nights that followed? Hadn't he betrayed *me*, by failing to protect me as he'd sworn to do as my master and by abusing his authority?

Bryan Palmes was the real criminal, I decided, not Mercy Bramble. Nat and the Hawk were criminals too. Now it was time to take charge of my actions. In order to free myself from ties that still bound me to my master, I needed to accept responsibility for my own desires. A voice told me that I would never again be the helpless victim Bryan Palmes had found in his bed.

Sitting up on my pallet, I looked straight at the reverend kneeling beside me in the candlelight. My blood stirred strangely, as though a separate being were awakening inside me.

"There's none in this world knows where you are," I said very softly.

The candle was about to expire, but in its golden light, Matthew Graves looked like an ordinary young man to me, not a pious minister. A reflection from the dancing flame ignited his dark blue eyes like stars above a calm sea.

"Even God might be looking elsewhere at this lonely hour," I whispered.

He took my hand; his was trembling.

"Don't deceive yourself, Mercy. God is always watching. He sees us now here in your prison cell."

"But even the Lord expects we will stray sometimes."

"How can you possibly know that?" he begged, staring away into the darkness.

"Forgive us our trespasses, as we forgive those who trespass against us. Is that not meant to be our *daily* prayer?" I asked. "Doesn't God *expect* us to fail, seek forgiveness, and fail again?"

For a long time, my companion sat motionless, saying absolutely nothing.

When he finally gave me an answer, he didn't do so with words, yet his meaning was perfectly clear. He took my face in his hands and pressed his lips on mine.

"I love you, Mercy Bramble, and I will...never...ever...leave...you," he said, placing separate kisses between each word.

Then, just as twilight covers the earth below, his body covered mine. With surprising strength, he lifted me as though I weighed nothing at all.

He didn't behave as Bryan Palmes had done on our first night together. My master had taken me to the point of madness; when he had no more to give, he extinguished that flame with his indifference.

Now, with every kiss and every touch, Matthew Graves gave me reason to hope, to love, and to be loved even more. I wanted to learn everything about this man—body and soul, chapter and verse. I wanted to know everything.

Three hours later, the candle still burned, its flame blazing even higher and brighter than when it was lit. Matthew rose from our bed and lifted the bit of candle from its pool of wax.

"How extraordinary! It's as if the devil himself were in that candle," he exclaimed. "I've heard such strange tales."

"But they're just ghost stories."

"Maybe it's a sign that we're meant to be with one another. Perhaps we should run away tonight!"

I reminded him that we were both locked in together.

"Please don't consider such a foolish act or risk your life for me," I pleaded.

"My God, it's inhumane to keep you almost a year without setting your trial. Look at me, Mercy. Tell me that you wish us to be together forever!"

I shook my head. "I cannot answer since I do not know my own future."

He said nothing but I saw pain in his eyes.

"How I wish I had set you free that night I had the key in my hand," he groaned. "My mind was shackled to a belief that I must always do the right thing, but it's not shackled now!"

At sunrise the door swung open, and Faith entered with my meager breakfast. Her mouth dropped when she saw Matthew standing in the middle of my cell. He grabbed his hat and hurried past her into a freshly fallen snow that covered the alley.

"Good day to you, Madam Christophers. I trust this abominable negligence will never happen again."

❦

The days that followed were endless and empty. For lack of company, I'd formed a habit of speaking to myself. Although I believed that I might be going a little mad, it lifted my spirits to express myself so freely without fear of punishment.

After a week, the reverend finally returned. His face was flushed as red as a few apples that he carried in a small, tightly woven Indian basket.

"A gift from my sister. The last of the harvest she'd saved in our cellar."

As soon as Faith had secured the door and apparently retreated, Matthew collapsed on his knees at my feet and buried his face in his hands.

"I've betrayed your trust in every way! The Lord knows how much I wanted to be the one to save your soul, but instead I've risked damnation for both of us."

Tears streaked his face. As he doubled over his knees, his spine made a bony ridge under his thin wool frockcoat. I touched his shoulder to comfort him, but he wept in a manner that would have moved the most hardened of criminals.

"To think that I wanted to learn about the soul of a sinner so that I might write my foolish essays! Am I some kind of *idiot*?"

He laughed bitterly, then began choking and couldn't continue.

"Reverend, it was only the night vapors that made our will as weak as our flesh," I consoled him. "We must put this behind us and save our strength for greater battles, just as you once advised me to do."

He finally nodded in agreement, his face growing somber.

"Ask whatever you want from me. I'll do anything to earn your forgiveness while I also pray for the Lord's. I'm *your* servant now, Mercy."

"I could never see you in that way, Reverend, but there is one great favor I must ask of you."

His face brightened at last, and he rose off the floor to share my bench.

"Ask anything you want of me, but please call me by my Christian name: Matthew." When I promised I would do so, he insisted that I tell him my favor.

"You *must* baptize me as soon as possible! Only then do I have a chance to be saved."

No longer red from shame, his face had returned to its customary pallor, but his eyes were shining. A handsome young man looked back at me with newfound resolve.

"Oh yes, of course I will administer the sacrament to you!"

"You should know that two others have already refused me— Reverend Adams and Reverend Jewett. How cruel it seemed to be denied by men who live to save souls. It's a matter of such great importance to me."

"Baptism is of great importance to all Christians, Mercy. It's more than just washing of flesh with water; it's our covenant with

God and our union with Christ. It will deliver us from death itself!" Matthew explained, as if he were in his pulpit.

At that moment, I saw how much he loved to teach and how he'd been born to that calling.

"But I've never baptized a grown man or woman, only innocent babes in arms who have never sinned," he reflected, looking doubtful.

"You've already baptized me, in a way," I said smiling. "Remember how you took water and bathed my forehead?"

"But I didn't speak the words, Mercy! That would have been blasphemous indeed. No matter how kind your words are today, I shudder to think of our sin."

We both fell quiet for a while.

"Do you think anyone even said a prayer for her, Matthew?"

"A prayer for whom?"

"My little child. The one who lies in the burial ground."

He looked so startled that I wondered if he'd forgotten her part in my story; my daughter was like a page that had been torn from a book or a line crossed out from a ledger.

"In honesty, I do not know. Though she was given a Christian burial of course."

"But what has happened to her *soul*?"

"Did the little girl have a name?"

I stared ahead, not blinking. He may have feared that I'd been struck deaf or taken by a fit.

"Please tell me your dear sister's name, again Matthew."

"She is Joanna."

"Then that is my daughter's name too. She would have grown to be a beautiful woman, one who is pure of heart and could never be corrupted."

As though we'd made this gesture a thousand times before, our hands reached out and met. Then it was my turn to weep, while he appeared quite unmoved. My tears stopped as suddenly as they'd begun, and I dried my eyes with his handkerchief.

"How soon can you baptize me?" I demanded.

"Be patient. Our studies will give me more reason to visit you, provided the sheriff will allow me. I'll bring you more books and passages to memorize every day."

He stared at me searchingly.

"Now you must help me, a fellow sinner," he said, his voice filled with anguish. "The terrible truth is that I once sinned before, with an innocent girl in London, a deacon's daughter. I didn't come to the colonies of my own free will—no, I was sent here, no better than a convict. You should know this, that you were not the first."

"It doesn't matter, Matthew," I comforted him. "Nor were you the first for me. Now we're equals in God's eyes."

"And the devil's as well," he whispered. "May God help us both."

He got back on his knees and gestured for me to join him.

"We must pray together, Mercy. But first, close your eyes…"

CHAPTER VIII

MY TRIAL

Wherein thou judgest another, thou condemnest thyself.

—*Romans 2:1*

FEBRUARY BROUGHT SOMETHING that was far more devastating than fierce winter winds: news that I would have no trial until the Court met in September, seven months away.

The Sheriff told me this himself.

My piercing scream would have deafened him, had it not been contained inside my own skull. No one, not even Matthew, would ever hear those cries.

The news unleashed a terrible war inside me: now anger attacked my older, lingering fears. My rage was like a strong, young warrior who rises up against an old warlord, one who has grown weak but still keeps inflicting pain. Soon I saw that these two opponents were evenly matched. Neither anger nor fear would surrender claim to my battle-scarred heart; I had to live with both.

As winter lingered on, I was twice as confined as in other seasons, both by the jail itself and by unrelenting cold and snow that pressed around it. The fireplace should have burned day and night, but wood was scarce. Matthew himself often arrived with sticks of precious firewood under his arm, his Bible under the other.

At long last, the harsh season finally slipped away. It left behind scattered patches of snow that looked like petticoats blown from a clothesline.

Except for a fortnight when he lay ill, Matthew visited me faithfully several times each week that spring. To his delight, I'd memorized more lengthy passages of scripture and recited them flawlessly. Afterward, he would praise me lavishly.

"You have a natural *genius* when it comes to memory, Mercy." Then he added in a hushed tone, "If only you had no memory of my sin against you."

Pretending not to hear his whispered comments, I'd keep reciting in a strong voice so that mine would be the only one Faith could hear if she were eavesdropping—and she usually was.

One afternoon in May, when April rains had finally stopped, and new leaves were tracing the distant hilltops with emerald green, the reverend told me that I'd completed my course of study.

"Are you ready to be baptized, Mercy?"

"Oh yes!" I responded, overjoyed that I'd be saved at last.

After praying awhile in silence, he told me to kneel and clasp my hands. Then he'd recited a lengthy prayer and asked if I were ready to receive Christ into my heart. At last, he took a few drops of water from a vessel and let it fall onto my forehead.

"Mercy, I baptize thee in the name of the Father, and of the Son, and of the Holy Spirit."

"Amen."

I kept my eyes closed until I no longer felt water trickling over my eyelids. But as soon as I opened them, a wave of doubt swept over me.

Rising from my knees, I looked out through the crack in my

wall. Before I could restrain myself, I cried, "But the world looks exactly the same!"

"The world is no different now, but *you* are, Mercy," Matthew said. He spoke as if to a child, offering a sweet reward for good behavior.

"In God's eyes you're among the chosen now. If they ever allow you to leave this place, you can worship every Sabbath with all the others, and God will always hear your prayers. Now you truly belong to the Church."

Even as I thanked him, my doubts would not subside.

"Oh, I am one of the chosen, surely," I told myself. "Chosen to rot forever in this jail."

After Matthew left for home, I watched the alley, hoping that he might return within an hour as he often did. He wasn't a man of grand gestures, yet his small kindnesses were growing on me. In the same way that daisies turn their faces, slowly following the sun's path, I felt myself turning more in his direction.

Spring changed rapidly to summer; the days were even hotter than that year our well had run dry. The air, usually lively with a sea breeze, was dead calm.

About that time, a ship's passenger who had just sailed from New York was so ill with yellow fever that the captain put him ashore in New London. The passenger was dead by the next day, and soon seven in town had died, four of them small children. All servants were warned to stay at home, but of course, I had no choice but to stay where I was.

Faith often spoke with the Hawk when my former mistress came into town; afterward she would tell me what was going on back at the farm.

"Your mistress says Elijah's sick and can't keep anything down. His fever's so high she lets him run about the yard naked, like an Indian baby."

But soon he could neither run nor walk, Faith had reported. Three days later, she told me he was dead.

"No! You're lying, Faith! You're telling me a tale just to make me suffer!"

I pushed her towards the door and told her to leave me alone. Late that night, I prayed for Elijah's soul and for that of his father. Even Christian charity couldn't bring me to pray for the Hawk, so I asked for forgiveness for my shortcomings at the same time. Worst of all, I couldn't forget what that dreadful Mr. Paine from Long Island had told me months before: that little children would suffer and die if I didn't confess to my sins. My forced confession that day—or whatever it had been—hadn't stopped the ravages of yellow fever after all.

The next day I watched in the distance as Old Benja Fargo dug three small graves, each barely one scoop of his shovel; one was for Elijah. Children's graves were not as deep or wide as those for adults. Knowing that he'd be paid only two shillings a piece for them, he'd probably dug three to help make up the shortfall. They would be used soon enough.

A hundred years before, the town's founding fathers had realized that this hilly, rocky place would be no good for planting; it commanded an impressive view of the river, however. Those early settlers knew that only their dead had the leisure time to contemplate nature from this vantage point. The departed souls could watch the tidal river flow and graceful ospreys dive for their prey.

I later learned that Mrs. Palmes was already expecting another child—that may have eased her sorrow over Elijah—but I wondered if her husband grieved at all. By my count, he'd conceived three children by three different women and lost them all: Abigail's baby, mine, and now the Hawk's. Maybe that was Bryan's true affliction, not his crippled leg. All his other gifts—

for writing, for riding, and for giving pleasure to women—could never make up for that curse.

If I ever mastered the art of writing with pen and paper—just as I'd now learned to read—I vowed that I'd write a book about my master someday.

"Perhaps I shall call it "The Wretched Curse of Bryan Palmes," I announced to my empty cell. Writing my book would be like the sachem shooting his arrow through the meetinghouse steeple. I'd leave a lasting message for all to see.

"It will be my final Mercy's Rebellion," I promised myself.

To fill the nighttime hours, I struggled to decide what to write about Bryan's character. Should I condemn him for his shameful acts, or portray him as a broken man, deserving of the reader's pity and forgiveness?

Just like Bryan had once dragged a huge stone over his first wife's grave—a stone no man could possibly move with his own powers—I began to move the heaviest of stones in my own heart.

⁊

Sometimes I prayed that they'd forgotten my trial and moved on to more important matters like settling the complicated business of last year's Spanish ship affair. But as late summer days unraveled one by one, Faith reminded me that my case would be heard in Superior Court, come fall. Her husband finally confirmed the date: the twenty-fifth day of September.

My cell had only grown darker and drearier as the months passed, but at least it was always warm after dark, the summer heat being trapped inside. Night after night, I lay sleepless. My confused thoughts were as aggravating as the lice that bit me relentlessly; both ruined my attempts to pray.

"Our father who art in heaven. Our father who art. Our father who…"

On most days I awoke to the sound of sea gulls quarreling with one another above the jail, but one morning I heard men's voices outside. Matthew was having an agitated conversation with Sheriff Christophers—I couldn't call it an argument because the reverend was too even-tempered to argue.

In recent months, the sheriff's wife had readily agreed to unlock my cell and let Matthew visit me whenever he asked, no matter the hour. Now, as my trial neared, her husband was denying him that privilege.

"*I'm* charged with keeping this jail in order, not my wife," snarled the sheriff. Although I couldn't see him, I pictured him jabbing his thumb into his own puffed-up chest. He had plenty more to say.

"It was her fault you got locked in here that night, but I'd be the one to be punished, see? You can't go waltzing in and out of a prisoner's cell at all hours. Not in *my* jail."

"You are interfering with my Christian ministry, sir!" shouted Matthew.

"And how do I know you're a true man of God?" the sheriff countered. "The bloody Separatists have been hounding me every day. They say you've no authority to visit her and that you baptized her when you had no right to."

"Why in God's name would you listen to those false prophets?"

"They say you wouldn't know God's word from a horse's ass, Reverend."

"That's utter blasphemy! Don't you understand? The greater sinner she is, the greater need to pray to God for her pardon. So help me, I shall write to Governor Wolcott if you deny me!"

When he heard the Governor's name, Sheriff Christophers finally unlocked the door. Giving the reverend no more respect than a tinker or fishmonger, he bawled, "Half an hour. That's all you get."

Matthew rushed inside and dropped to his knees next to me. Too weak to rise and greet him, I offered him my hand, but he drew back.

"Our time is short, Mercy, so I dare not touch you. You cannot know how I long to do so."

"Just take my hand, and I'll be happy, Matthew. Nothing else ever came to pass between us, only the tender care you've given me in recent months."

"How I wish I could believe you."

"Two people might believe that they both dreamed the same thing, but those are dreams nevertheless, just visions," I comforted him.

His face brightened like that of a child listening to a story at bedtime.

"Maybe you're right. It's like those old tales of witchcraft when several minds were possessed by the same delusions."

Excited, I leapt to my feet.

"If I'm truly reborn in Christ, as you said, then the old Mercy Bramble doesn't exist anymore, isn't that true? Those were *her* deeds, not mine; the Lord washed them away by my baptism. We should forgive one another and pray together as two who are reborn."

He stretched out his hand and pulled me gently back down to my knees. I felt his warm breath and his heart heaving.

"But first, close your eyes," he whispered. I silently obeyed.

His lips grazed mine as gently as a salt breeze from the river, but then he pulled back. He looked at me so intensely I had to cast down my eyes.

"Now that your trial is only a few days away, there's something I must know. We've spoken of your baby girl, but you've never told me if you raised a hand against her."

My heart sank.

"Are you asking if I'm guilty of a crime, Matthew? Does it matter now that I'm reborn and we forgive each other?"

Without warning, his face darkened with anger.

"Yes, by God, it matters to me! I deserve to hear the truth! From the first day we met, you have sorely tested my faith, Mercy Bramble."

"And you've done quite the opposite for me; you've helped me *find* my true faith," I declared. "You gave me knowledge and showed me I'm free to ask questions."

"What difference has it made?" he asked, his voice now calmer.

"From here on I needn't accept everything that is expected, or taught, or even forced upon me."

"But you still haven't answered my question about the baby, Mercy."

I turned my face to the wall, took a deep breath and began my story.

"After I gave birth on that terrible night, I'd fainted from pain. When I awoke my child was dead and wrapped in a cloth beside me on the floor. I have reason to believe she was born alive, but my mistress had already taken her from me."

"But what happened next?" he pleaded. "Surely you remember."

"The night was cold and dark. I never saw what happened outside the door. I have to live with the knowledge that even if I couldn't rise from the floor, I could have tried to stop my mistress. *I should have raised my voice to stop her.*"

Matthew became highly agitated again. I'd spoken the truth— as he had demanded of me—but he didn't want to hear it after all. Immediately he began calling for the guard to let him out.

"Some things cannot be fully known, Matthew. It's like seeing through a glass darkly, like it says in the Bible. You can't imagine the long hours I've wrestled with my conscience about this."

"Now that you've cursed me with these ambiguities, I must wrestle with *my* conscience."

"Will you speak up for me at my trial, Matthew?"

He gave me no answer but his departing back.

The day before my trial began, I could hear crowds gathered in the street. It surprised to me to learn that many people had walked and ridden many miles from the surrounding countryside to attend the court session.

My hands and feet felt numb when a key turned and the door swung open. I'd hoped to see Matthew, arriving for a few hours of prayer, but was sickened to find Nat Way instead. Although he was clean and freshly shaven, his narrow eyes reminded me of the beast he was inside, the animal that had killed Zeno.

"Just hold your tongue and listen to me, Bramble," he said, raising his hands as though to block me from striking him. "I have something important to say."

"Nothing you could say would be important, Nat. But I can't run away from you this time, so let's hear it and be quick about it.

"My mother wrote you a letter for me, but I told her I had to speak for myself. Perhaps you think she's a crazy old shrew, but she is my mother."

He tried to take my hand, but I slapped him away.

"I've nothing to offer you, Mercy—the Cripple has taken all my mother's money and I have no property now. I'd bring you fresh game; you'd never be hungry a day in your life."

I asked him what on earth he was talking about.

"Come on, we understand each other, don't we? We're two of a kind."

"How can you say such a thing to me? You're a *murderer*, Nat.

"And what are you, then? They think you have blood on your hands, and they'll soon make you to pay for it."

He took a deep breath and loudly blew it out; it sounded like air rushing from a bellows to revive a dying fire.

"I want you to be my wife, Bramble."

"That's ridiculous, Nat," I retorted. "I've nothing but loathing for you."

"Look, I have no secrets from you, so you already know the worst," he admitted with a shrug. "It can only get better between us."

He pulled a crumpled sheet of paper from his pocket.

"Is that your mother's letter? Read it to me."

He squinted and began reading very slowly.

"To My Servant Mercy Brambel,

My son Nat has found you to his liking for some reason and requests your hand in marriage. No doubt this comes as a great surprise to one like you. I would not oppose such a marriage, being as it would give our household your services for the remainder of years that you owe us. I am willing to testify in court that a certain infant was born without life, but will do so only if you accept Nat's offer today.

Your Mistress,
Madam Eliz. Palmes

Before he could stop me, I tore up her letter into tiny pieces and threw it on the floor.

"Give her just one word from me, Nat. Tell her Mercy Bramble says, '*Never!*'"

His mouth twisted into a grin.

"I don't give up so easy. Just wait and see, Bramble."

❧

The day of my trial dawned. The morning was bright and clear after a fog had lifted from the river. At Matthew's urging, I'd been fasting for several days so that both my head and heart would be strong for whatever lay ahead. But instead of waking clearheaded, I felt a fever starting to burn; a strange dizziness came over me as well, just as it had when I took Hugo Moreaux's terrible poison.

When the sheriff led me outside, I almost regretted having to leave the protection of the jail's four walls. The vastness of earth and sky overwhelmed me, the light, blinding. My eyes must have looked like mere slits, or the tiny cross-stitches on the face of Zeno's cornhusk doll.

The thought of Zeno hurt so much that it almost brought me to tears. I thanked God that my hands were unbound, and I could shield my eyes with them.

A bystander immediately asked in a loud voice, "Is she blind? Did the Lord strike her blind?"

Outside the meetinghouse, I could see well enough to realize that at least a hundred people had assembled. Those who couldn't find a seat in the pews had gathered outside, shoulder-to-shoulder.

"Make way, make way for the prisoner!" the sheriff barked.

I smelled a pungent mix of sweat and tobacco as he dragged me through the mob. Stubbornly, the men and women refused to yield more than a few inches for my passage, as though they wished to crush me to death then and there, as Achan was crushed under stones.

I'm quite certain that some of you were in the crowd that day.

As soon as I entered, I looked out a small window and saw the jail in which I'd been confined. From this vantage point, it looked like a harmless place, almost quaint in its small dimensions.

This was only the second time that I'd set foot in the meeting-house, which served as both a courthouse and the Congregational

Church. I'd first been taken there to hear Reverend Jewett rail against me in April of last year. It seemed a lifetime ago.

The sheriff ordered me to sit on a bench in front of the judge.

"You must call him Your Honor, do you understand?"

I shook my head, yes.

The elderly Judge Thomas Finch was wearing a bright red robe and curled white wig. The heavy weight of his headpiece appeared to have wrinkled his brow like a bulldog's.

At his side were four assistants. To their left, twelve men of the jury had already assembled; the harvest was over, so all men were now free to serve as jurors. I recognized a few faces. Some men had bought horses from Bryan Palmes. Others had traded goods with Mr. Holt long ago, but at least half were strangers to me.

An assistant called their names from the bench: Colt, Leeds, Lord, Packer, Branch, Starr, Whipple, and so on. Among the hundred or more people I saw a few familiar faces in the pews and in the gallery above. Mr. Holt was there, as well as Nat Way, and, to my great surprise, Bryan Palmes.

The judge brought his gavel down so hard that even a few men in the pews jumped a little.

"In New London, in the colony of Connecticut in the year of our Lord 1753 in the reign of His Majesty King George the Second, this court is hereby called to order!"

His words set off a panic in my breast. Fearing that my heart might stop, I pressed one hand against it, lowered my head, and closed my eyes to pray.

When I opened my eyes, the scene had become very unclear. The pounding of blood in my ears drowned out the judge's voice. Under a window on my right stood three ministers—Adams, Jewett, and Graves—all with prayer books in hand. Only Matthew Graves nodded and raised the fingers of his right hand from his prayer book, as if to bless me silently from across the room.

"By the new act of Parliament, Superior Court for the County of New London shall be held on the third Tuesday of the month of September. Superior Courts to be held on the day fixed for their sessions are hereby fully empowered to hear, try, and determine, all matters, causes, civil and criminal, according to the law, that shall come before them as aforesaid," droned the judge's assistant.

Conversations had ceased. Someone shouted to the crowd outside to be silent as well. A stray dog kept barking, and through the door I saw someone strike it with a walking stick to drive it away.

"Mercy Bramble, an inhabitant in His Majesty's name, has been charged with the murder of her bastard child by placing it in a fire, a year ago last March twenty-first. We will examine the charge of this violation of the laws of God and this Colony."

Cries erupted from the back of the hall. "Whore!" "Murderess!" but no one individual seemed to have produced them. Faces in the crowd emerged from the shadows like pale white masks.

"To the Sheriff of New London, in His Majesty's name you are commanded to summon the accused, Mercy Bramble, an inhabitant in His Majesty's name, accused of murdering her bastard child on the day of its birth, at the home of her master Mr. Bryan Palmes...."

The judge heaved an enormous sigh and continued.

"An unknown knave had carnal knowledge of the accused, and thereby begat her with the child with which she was pregnant. Neither her master nor mistress had any suspicion of this matter, the accused being not a large woman who was able to conceal her fallen condition and thereby deceive them for many months. A year ago this March she delivered a bastard child alone, without a midwife or any other woman present. And, when the Palmes were not at home, on the Sabbath day, she put the infant in the fire, which was the cause of its death. She brought disgrace to her master's home, even after her master and mistress had provided for her welfare so generously."

Rolling through the pews like thunder, exclamations of outrage echoed against the wooden walls.

Judge Finch called for silence.

The sheriff guided me in front of the pulpit, and the judge leaned down to scrutinize me. There was no place to hide from that stare.

"Mercy Bramble, do you swear to testify and to tell the whole truth and nothing but the truth?"

I nodded and kept my face lowered so that that the edge of my cap blocked the stares of the hundred pairs of eyes. In the pocket of my apron, my right hand closed around the wolf claw that Cate had given me, testing one of its savage points with my finger and coming very near to drawing blood.

"You will answer yea or nay, Mercy Bramble. Are you married?"

"Nay, I am not, Your Honor."

"Do you have a father or mother?"

"A living mother only. She told me my father died aboard ship in the Atlantic when we sailed from England, and we were indentured to pay off our passage and his."

"Did you tell anyone that you were with child?"

"Nay, Your Honor."

"Did you give birth to a bastard child last March?"

"Yea, I did, to my great sorrow." My voice was shaking.

"Did you cry out for help in your travail?"

"Nay."

"Will you name the father of your child here for the court?"

"Nay, I cannot."

"And why is that?" he shouted. "Did you lie with more than one man?"

"I cannot say."

"Why not?"

"For common decency," I whispered.

The judge drew himself up straight. Then he exhaled with great force, just like a bull had once done before it sent me running from a neighbor's pasture.

"Did you put the infant's body in the fire and thereby take its life?"

"She was already dead at that time, sir."

"Are you claiming she was born without life, then?"

"I swear, I know not the answer. She looked like she was without life when I awoke from a faint and could see her clearly."

"Where did you hide the bastard child's body?"

"I closed it up in a harpsichord, Your Honor. Then later under my cot."

All the voices in the room were rumbling so loudly that it was now hard for me to hear the judge.

"Why did you not tell your master or mistress?

"I was too afraid, sir."

"And what, in God's name, did you intend to do with the body?"

"I planned to bury it in a few days when the ground thawed."

The judge did not disguise his anger any longer.

"Do you wish to make a mockery of this court with your foolish sounding answers?"

"Nay, I would not do that."

The jurors exchanged long looks. One whispered to a man alongside him. A woman's voice cried from the back of the meetinghouse.

"She's a liar! Satan has her in his power!"

Swaying slightly, I grasped the rail before me so I wouldn't collapse.

"May I sit down now?"

The judge did not answer my question but posed another.

"Mercy Bramble, the law of this colony states that concealing the death of a bastard child is punishable by death. Do you know this?"

"No, I do not know that particular law, Your Honor, but I'm an unschooled servant."

"That is no excuse," Reverend Jewett roared from the side of the room. "We are *all* servants, servants of the Lord, our God!"

Judge Finch turned to his assistant and spoke in a distressed whisper that was loud enough to hear from where I sat.

"I've seen such a case as this with slave women or Indians or even the Irish. Never have I seen *an Englishwoman* brought before me for this crime."

Then the judge raised his voice again, as though I were deaf.

"Can you tell me the seventh commandment, woman?"

"Yes, of course. I've been baptized and have studied the scripture. 'Thou shalt not commit adultery.'"

I silently thanked Matthew for teaching me all the Commandments and hoped that my reply would gain me some favor.

"And what about the sixth commandment? Can you tell me that as well?"

"Thou shalt not kill."

"So, you are not unschooled, as you first claimed, Mercy Bramble, nor are you mad or insane. Do not try to deceive this court. Several good men of this town have seen the infant's body and were charitable enough to give it burial. Let us not trouble them any further. Will you confess now to its murder?"

I raised my voice at last, shouting over the heads of all assembled.

"No! I cannot confess, because I did not murder her!"

The murmuring started again and quickly mounted to a roar.

The sheriff called for order as though he were breaking up a brawl in the streets.

Then the proceedings began again; minutes rolled into hours.

Repeating much of the same sermon he'd preached before my arrest, the Reverend Jewett was asked to describe the corruption of my character and give a summary of my offenses.

"Each of her sins led on to greater sins, until she committed the most heinous crime of all: the taking of human life, *murder*. Like this young woman's name reminds us, a sinner is a weed, *a bramble*, that must be plucked out by the roots from God's garden in order to save the rest of us!"

The crowd murmured in agreement. A woman shouted, "Pluck her out!"

At last, the judge called for recess. Under guard, I was allowed to leave the courtroom and use the privy. Before I was returned to the building, Faith handed me a piece of cornbread to fill my empty stomach. It was dry, and tasted of ashes, as though it had been dropped in the hearth. I couldn't swallow it.

Returning to my pew, I heard one of the men on the jury say to another, "God forgive me, but she is a pretty creature for one so wicked."

The judge began reading.

"I have before me a list of those witnesses who will testify in this trial. Elizabeth Palmes, wife of Mr. Bryan Palmes, master of the accused. Mary Bunce, mother of the accused. Mr. Timothy Way, a student of divinity. The Negro man known as Pompey. And Mr. Paine of Long Island, a teacher, and several of his followers."

I wondered why Bryan Palmes was not on the list. Did they think him unfit to testify? Or had he bribed someone so he wouldn't have to speak?

The judge turned to Sheriff Christophers, "In His Majesty's name you are commanded to summon Elizabeth Palmes."

The Hawk rose on signal and met the sheriff halfway before approaching the bench. Although she was now five months gone with another child, there was little change in the rest of her angular frame. She kept her shawl pulled tightly around her as if she feared that her soul might somehow fly out of her body if not restrained.

The judge warned Mrs. Palmes that she must speak the whole truth and nothing but the truth. Returning his fierce glare, she swore that she would do so.

"To determine whether Miss Bramble was the cause of her infant's death, witnesses will first address the character of the accused," the judge began. "Was she a good subject of our Majesty the King? Was she God-fearing? Was she sober? Was she chaste? Did she deliberately bring disgrace on her master's household and all her fellow townspeople? Did she…"

But my former mistress could no longer control herself. She interrupted the judge's recitation.

"Your Honor, this servant's conduct has caused a great disturbance in our family. She's not only immoral—as you can clearly see by her giving birth to a bastard—she is lazy and a thief as well."

The Judge Finch nodded. "Go on."

To my horror, Mrs. Palmes described the theft of her tortoiseshell comb, the one that I'd traded to Hugo Moreaux for a remedy that had almost killed me. My mistress had never mentioned the missing comb before; it was as if she'd saved her accusation for just this moment. Then she told them how I'd defiled several books by cutting out their pages.

I hung my head, but not from shame; no one must see my growing anger.

"Is there anything else that would be instructive to the jury regarding her character?" Judge Finch asked respectfully.

Mrs. Palmes grimaced.

"Your Honor, I'm a God-fearing woman, and I know very little of those who worship Satan, but I'm told that this servant keeps objects in her possession that look like tools of the Devil."

"And what would those be?"

"A piece of burned wood with Satan's image and a wolf's claw like those that heathen Indians might wear around their necks."

She had barely finished when a woman screamed: "Succubus!"

A murmur rippled through the meetinghouse. The judge called hoarsely for order, and Mrs. Palmes raised her voice again. She gestured toward her husband, who was seated, stone-faced, in their pew.

"And my husband's dear, departed mother was in this servant's care when she dropped dead for no reason at all one night!" The Hawk paused to let the full effect of her words take hold.

"She left an old woman to die alone. Some say it looked as if she'd been poisoned. I'd heard stories of servants who poisoned their masters or mistresses and was never able to put this thought from my mind. I wondered if we were harboring a serpent under our roof."

The assembly stirred as one; a few had heard such stories too every now and then.

I closed my eyes so tightly that I almost believed I was back in the darkness of the jail. My cell would have been the lesser evil between these two dreadful places. When I had the courage to open my eyes, I found the courtroom in shadow. All the faces were gray and drawn.

Suddenly, I called out just as someone would from a nightmare. Though my rising fever may have dulled my reason, I found my voice at last.

"Mrs. Palmes is the serpent! Ask *her* if she is a murderer, Your Honor! Ask if she took my child's life on the morning she was born! She pretended to take my baby out and clean her at the well, but she stopped my child's breath before her first cry!"

The crowd was struck dumb for a few seconds but not the judge.

"Silence! I won't tolerate the defamation of a decent, God-fearing woman in my court. The servant is on trial here today, not her mistress."

Ignoring Judge Finch, several in the assembly asked if I were not insane and perhaps should be sent straightaway to the madhouse.

As I tried to shrink back into myself, I thought of those little periwinkle crabs that I'd seen at the White Beach on that day not long ago. How quickly they'd pulled back into their shells to hide. I, however, was fully exposed for all to see.

Judge Finch ordered the sheriff to help Mrs. Palmes to her seat, but she yanked her arm away from him and stood her ground a little longer.

"If this woman is hung, Your Honor, who will compensate my husband and me for the loss of our servant?" she demanded. "She owes us two more years of service, so it's only fair that the town should pay us a fair price."

"Sit down, Mrs. Palmes!" the judge bellowed. She quickly returned to her seat.

Next, he called Mrs. Mary Bunce to the stand.

It wasn't until the woman stood up that I recalled my mother's married name. As she took the oath, all I could think of was our recent conversation. A wave of love rose inside me, rising above our present circumstances.

"Mary Bunce, how do you know the accused?"

"I'm her mother."

"What is your husband's name?"

"Elisha Bunce."

"Is Mr. Bunce the father of Mercy Bramble?"

"Nay, not he."

"Can you vouch for the character of your daughter?"

She shook her head and drew down the corners of her mouth.

"Nay, I cannot. Not anymore."

"And why can you not?"

"You see, I bound her out as a servant when she was a girl of seven. I was a poor widow who couldn't feed or clothe her in a proper manner on my own. I wanted her to have a better life."

A murmur of sympathy went through the pews.

"Did you see to it that she was baptized and properly schooled in the scriptures?"

"No, I trusted that was the sworn duty of her first master, Mr. Holt."

"Were you aware that a rogue had carnal knowledge of your daughter's body and begat her with child?"

"Nay. How could I? I lived far outside of town by then."

"Did you know that she took her child's life when it was born?"

"Yes, I suppose that I knew."

"And how did you come to know that if you did not live with her nor see her?"

"They told me she confessed as much to that man and his followers."

She pointed straight at Mr. Paine, leader of the Children of God.

The meetinghouse resounded with the cries: "Her own mother! Her own mother swears that she has committed murder!"

To my surprise, the judge sent her back to her seat, and the cries died down.

While the judge conferred at length with his assistants, the jurors became restless and began talking amongst themselves again. Rain started to fall; I swore that I heard each drop hit the roof, until almost drowning out the proceedings below. Finally, Judge Finch's voice rose above the din.

"Sheriff, in His Majesty's name you are commanded to summon Mr. Timothy Way to stand before this court."

Staring at me mournfully, Timothy rose shakily from his seat next to his mother and approached the bench. He placed a hand on the Bible and took the same oath as all the others.

"State your name and occupation, Sir."

"My name is Timothy Way. I am a student of divinity at Yale College."

"How did you come to know the convict Mercy Bramble?"

"My mother is the mistress of the accused criminal. She is the wife of my stepfather Bryan Palmes, who is master of this servant. I lived in their household for a while when my mother, formerly a widow, was newly married."

"Did you witness the accused murder her child?"

"No, I did not, Your Honor. I was in New Haven for my studies."

"Did you know Mercy Bramble was with child?"

"No, I did not. But I knew that she was guilty of the sin that brought the bastard child into this world: the sin of uncleanness." His answer set off low rumbles through the assembly, but once again, the judge called for silence.

"How did you come to know about such a lewd and shameful act, Mr. Way?

"I had the misfortune to witness her being defiled by a man."

"And who was that man?"

A wave of dizziness almost sent me tumbling out of my seat. Would Tim speak his brother's name in court? His stepfather's?

"I do not know," answered Tim, dropping his voice. "Perhaps another servant, a slave, or even a common vagrant. She sometimes spoke to one of the peddlers in a very familiar way."

None present, including myself, would have ever suspected that a divinity student could tell a falsehood so easily.

"And where did you witness this ungodly act?"

"On a grassy hill behind the farmhouse where my mother and her husband live. I suppose they thought no one would see them at that late hour, but there was bright moonlight. Miss Bramble and the man were lying together on the ground."

"And in what manner did they behave?"

Tim hesitated.

"Dear Lord," I prayed silently. "Please let me die now! Take me now!"

"The man lay directly upon Miss Bramble's body, the skirts of her gown being pulled up above her waist." He gestured awkwardly to demonstrate the skirt's position. "Of course, she was half naked at that time."

Every person in the meetinghouse gasped for breath. Men leaned forward as if they were all one body, while women shrank back into their seats, covering their faces.

I saw Matthew spring up and leave his pew, almost falling as he tripped over another man's leg. At the door, he had to push through a wall of listeners to get out.

I wanted to cry out, "Don't listen to his lies, Matthew!" but he'd disappeared.

The judge called for silence.

"Did Miss Bramble offer any resistance or show any displeasure at this lewd conduct?" asked the judge.

"Nay, I saw none."

Timothy sighed and shook his head sadly as though he and the judge were old acquaintances having a private conversation over a pot of tea.

"There was no question in my mind that her virtue was sullied. Satan had her firmly in his grasp."

"Tell us, Mr. Way, did you actually see Satan himself?"

"No."

"Then how do you know such a thing to be a fact?"

"I felt his awful presence. Satan was right there with her, as though he were having carnal knowledge of her himself!"

"That is all that we require from you, Mr. Way. You can be seated. Call the Negro man Pompey to the bench, and then we'll be done with this for today."

After taking the oath, Pompey told the court who he was: a slave who would have been a free man had it not been for the false promise of his former master in Rhode Island.

"Your former master is quite dead, I understand, and he is certainly not on trial here today," said the judge impatiently. "We are here solely to learn the truth about Miss Bramble's crime. Tell us, Mr. Pompey, when did you come to live with Mr. Palmes and his wife?"

"I came when Master Palmes bought me from Widow Livingston. Can't say exactly when, but I remember it was still mighty cold. And it was one day after Miss Bramble had her trouble."

"And what made you remember that particular fact so clearly?"

Pompey drew his hand slowly across the back of his neck and took a deep breath while he gathered his words.

"Well, Judge, I saw her the next day, when she thought herself was alone. I seen her plainly through the little window pane by the kitchen door."

Pompey held his hands out in front of him to show the measure of an object.

"She had a little *person* in her hands, no bigger than a loaf of bread."

Cries of horror rang out in unison.

"And then what happened?" Judge Finch inquired.

"Oh, that was a terrible, terrible thing, Judge. I saw her put that baby right in the kitchen fire. Right into the flames."

Several women were already sobbing; how I wished that they'd stop.

"Are you certain? And did she leave it there?" asked the judge.

"No, sir, she snatched it back out as if she didn't even feel any burning. Didn't see no burns on her after that neither."

"Did you know what she was doing when you witnessed this gruesome sight?"

"No, sir. I thought it was some kind of witchcraft, so I kept far away."

As Pompey's voice trailed off, the judge fixed his eye on the jury and spoke to them sternly. He pointed straight at Pompey.

"Listen to me well, gentlemen. Though he is a black man, the jurors will respect this man's word as a *Christian*. You may go now, Mr. Pompey."

The slave darted a look at me before returning to his seat up in the gallery above. His dazed expression gave no clue as to his true feelings.

After Pompey's testimony, I felt that all hope was unraveling; there was not a single thread left for me to seize. Worst of all, Reverend Graves—my Matthew—was nowhere to be seen in the meetinghouse.

The rain had stopped as suddenly as it had begun, but the sun shone for only a few brief moments before it set. Once again, a gusty wind came up and began to slam the unlatched shutters. A storm of words swirled all around me.

Then both the jurors and the spectators started returning to their horses and wagons in the street.

"What's happening Sheriff Christophers?" I wailed. "What will my fate be now?"

"Who knows?" he snapped, probably impatient for a pint of ale at the Fox and Grapes. He spat out a plug of tobacco, just missing my shoes.

"A dozen fools can't reach a simple verdict anymore. Men have lost their reason these days."

Then he walked me back to jail.

❦

I spent a sleepless night in my cell, and though I wished him to come to me, Matthew had stayed away. By morning I was so weak that Faith had to lift me from my pallet and force me to drink some cider.

On the trial's second day, rain started falling as soon as I entered the meetinghouse, blurring my view of the outside world. I watched the proceedings unfold in a haze, caused by my rising fever.

Judge Finch called the Children of God to the stand, one by one. None of the five women had changed in the slightest manner since the day when they'd questioned me so deviously.

"I'm Hannah Smith of Long Island," said the first in a sweet, high-pitched voice. "My sisters and I are followers of Mr. Paine, and we sailed to New London by ship. It wasn't a long passage, but the water was rough, and some of us became quite ill." She pressed a lace handkerchief to her lips.

"I did not inquire about your health," snapped the Judge. "Did you have any knowledge of the accused before her imprisonment?"

"We did not, Your Honor. We'd heard news of her crime and wanted to bring her counsel and solace through our prayers."

Her eyes became wider, her voice even sweeter. "She confessed her crime very openly and willingly to us."

"And how was that confession made?"

"We put forth a simple question to her: 'Mercy, did you put your hand on its mouth?'" Hannah Smith pressed her fingers across her mouth. "And then the prisoner answered us plainly, 'Yes.' There was no mistaking it. She confessed freely before God and man. God and woman, I suppose."

Next the judge called each sister—for they were indeed, all sisters—to the stand, and asked if each had heard Mercy Bramble's confession.

Each, in turn, answered, "Yes, Your Honor, I did."

How I wished that those high collars on their ink-black dresses would choke each of their skinny necks!

At last Judge Finch summoned the final witness: an old woman whom I didn't recognize. Only when I heard her voice—deep as a man's—did I remember the drunkard who'd shared my cell for a few hours. Remarkably, on the first night of my imprisonment, she too had heard me confess to the crime of murder.

"That one over there was talking in her sleep, she was," the old crone declared.

After she was dismissed, the jury grew silent. A potent mixture of weariness and excitement stirred in the air. Rain kept battering the rooftop. Wind slammed a loose shutter over and over; no one went to secure it.

"That's the Devil himself out there! He's come to claim her!" cried the old woman who'd just testified against me.

Had I been having an ordinary nightmare, I could have ended it simply by forcing open my eyes, but they were already wide open. By the time the jury had withdrawn, a fever had taken full possession of my body.

I waited with my head bowed low. My hands were clasped

tightly to pray, but my parched lips did not utter a single prayer. When the judge and jury returned, I struggled to comprehend what the assistant was reading.

"This twenty-sixth day of September 1753 in the county of New London, in the Colony of Connecticut, said Jurors upon their oaths testify that the accused Mercy Bramble on the twenty-first of March 1751 at New London, feloniously, willfully, and with malicious forethought did kill and murder her infant. Her actions were a violation of the peace of our Lord the King, his Crown, and his dignity, and contrary to the laws of this Colony."

When I looked up, my gaze locked instantly with that of Matthew Graves. Having entered without my noticing, he stood braced against the far wall as though he alone must hold it upright.

Now the assistant fell silent, and Judge Finch took charge.

"The jury has brought the following verdict. The jury finds that the defendant, Mercy Bramble, is guilty in the manner and form of murdering her bastard child at the time of its birth. She is hereby sentenced to death. She must be brought to an open and convenient place, and she will be hanged by the neck between Heaven and Earth until she is dead."

The silence was more profound than any I thought possible among the living. I could hear my own heart beating. Then, all at once, bedlam erupted: shouts, whispers, cheers, laughter, prayers, and weeping.

"Order!" the judge howled.

He turned to face me.

"Mercy Bramble do you have anything to say about this sentence? If so, speak now."

Remembering how the single word "yes" had brought me such great trouble, I was tempted to say, "no." I also thought of everything I'd learned about Christ, and all that He'd endured for the sins of the world.

Standing up, I looked at every man and woman present. Then a loud, clear voice rose out of me. My words were slow but deliberate.

"God, who is the searcher of hearts, knows I am not guilty of this crime. Though none of us is all-knowing, as He is, shouldn't we follow His words and forgive my trespass, 'as we forgive those who trespass against us?'"

Not one of you answered. Not a single soul.

"Gentlemen of the jury, you are dismissed!" shouted Judge Finch.

Like a blacksmith striking an anvil, he raised his gavel over his head and smashed it down.

Succumbing at last to my fever, I collapsed. The last thing that I saw was Matthew's hand, reaching out to me as I slid to the floor.

CHAPTER IX

BETWEEN HEAVEN
AND EARTH

"If I cannot move heaven, I will raise hell."

—Virgil

After the trial, I had nothing to be glad of except for one thing: most of you now went about your own business again and no longer concerned yourselves with mine. Men and women would wait until my execution day before they thought of me again, and on that day, I would be only a diversion, a kind of entertainment.

On the day after my sentencing, old Reverend Eliphalet Adams passed away at the age of seventy-six. The man who had survived the Awful Thunderclap so many years before had caught a fever, and despite taking large doses of quinine, had died of ague and bloody flux. When the jailer told me that the reverend had died, I said a prayer for his soul and thanked him for teaching my friend Cate to read when she was just a girl.

Weeks passed, and each day seemed as long as a year as I waited for an announcement of my execution day. After my sentencing, I'd received no more visitors except for Matthew; he was still waging his private battle with Sheriff Christopher over his right to access my cell.

Late one afternoon, I heard Matthew pleading with my stubborn keeper.

"You *must* admit me at once, Sheriff. I've been charged with making a written record of the criminal's final statement, which I must read in church next Sunday."

The printer Timothy Greene also had requested my account so that he could set it in type and print it in a booklet. He planned to sell copies at my execution, making an honest profit for himself while ensuring that others would learn from my example.

"What do I care about you or Mr. Greene?" sneered the jailer. "The judge has ordered me to carry out the prisoner's *death sentence*, not give her a bloody tea party with her minister."

"This is an outrage, sir!" sputtered Matthew. "An affront to common decency!"

"Who knows, Reverend, maybe she'll let you in between those pretty legs now, since they'll be up in the air soon enough!" The sheriff laughed. "Would've had her myself anytime, but my wife would string me up faster than she could truss a capon."

Peeking through the crack, I saw that Matthew had worked himself into a rage. His hands were fists inside his coat pockets; it looked as though he would rip apart the seams.

"God will punish you for your lack of charity!" cried Matthew. "He will *smite* you down harder than I ever could!"

The threat of divine punishment made Sheriff Christophers relent at last; he took a key from his coat and walked the Reverend to the door. It was a very solemn Matthew Graves who entered my cell. He told me that I was to dictate my final statement that afternoon; a scribe apprenticed to Mr. Greene would record every word.

When the frail-looking scrivener arrived several hours later, I was already feeling weary, and I hadn't yet spoken a single word.

The scribe shivered as he sat down on my bench.

"It's so cold in here, I fear that the ink will freeze in my inkwell. That has happened to me more than once," he fretted.

"This account will go to Mr. Timothy Greene's shop to be set and printed, of course. Perhaps he'll be so kind as to give you a copy when it comes off the press."

He looked at me expectantly, pen in hand.

"Where shall I start?" I asked.

"Tell us your name, something of your early days, and what circumstances led to the crime for which you were sentenced."

As I began to tell my story, the scribe wrote it all down in fluid strokes.

Although I'd read of many wonders in the Scriptures—water turned to wine, the parting of the Red Sea, and even the raising of the dead—it was no less miraculous to see my spoken words made visible to others. I'd wished so passionately that someone had given me such power by teaching me to write; now I would have to take that desire to my grave.

At first my statement had only a crude structure. Then my words began to take on form and purpose, however, like rushing water from a stream that is captured in a gristmill's orderly wheel. So, in my mind, a great wheel was slowly turning; I felt its power going to work.

One memory kept forming and disappearing like mist on a river: The Hawk was standing in the doorway, holding my baby in her claw-like hands without even a swaddling cloth. Pausing there, she turned to look down on me where I lay on the floor. I saw a small cloud of breath suspended in the morning air, no bigger than the puff of a dandelion.

Suddenly the vision was no longer clouded: it was as crystal clear and finely etched as frost on a glass window.

Mrs. Palmes was a murderess; she'd taken my newborn's life with her own hand. Of this I was certain, but I still couldn't remove all blame from myself. Had I *allowed* my mistress to kill my child, conspiring in her death by my silence, my lack of action? Perhaps that was the true reason I'd lost consciousness after giving birth.

The child was already dead when I first examined her; I'd only held my hand near her mouth and nose to see if she'd been breathing. But now these agonizing doubts wouldn't leave me alone. I should have raised my voice to save her life; now no one could save mine.

Choosing my words carefully, I leaned in close to be sure that the scribe had them correctly.

"I, Mercy Bramble, have been accused of murder, for which I am to die: and though I am not conscious that I committed this crime, I ought to suffer for it, because I may have had it in my heart."

When Matthew broke his silence, I jumped slightly. I'd almost forgotten that he was next to me. Now he leaned in closer, but not so close as to arouse the scribe's suspicions about us.

"What about the doubts you've shared with me in private, Mercy, that another had a hand in your child's death? Are you willing to die for the smallest chance, the mere possibility that you harbored any sinful intent in your heart? Surely you were exhausted by the act of birth, and frightened too."

"Yes, I was in pain and truly terrified that night."

"Our God tells us, 'Thou shalt not kill.' But He's given us no commandment, 'Thou shalt not ever contemplate if thou *might* kill.'"

Even as he tried to reason with me, his eyes were half wild.

"Please don't question your faith any further on my behalf, Matthew," I pleaded. "Who knows where the true boundary lies between our thoughts and actions? I was wrong not to speak up. That was my crime."

I asked the scribe to pick up his pen one more time.

"Please write this as my ending: *I pray for the Reverend Graves, who has been the Good Samaritan to me. He brought me to a sense of my duty and the error of my ways. May he shine like the sun in the firmament for his charity to my soul.*"

Then I paused; the scribe needed a fresh sheet of paper, because Matthew's tears had blurred the last few lines.

"Now you must record my response to her!" Matthew insisted to the scribe. There was desperation in his voice.

"Write this down exactly as I say: *The Reverend Graves is grateful to the prisoner for shining light upon his own beliefs and restoring his faith in the greatness of the human spirit itself...*"

But the scribe cut him off.

"I'm sorry, Reverend, but Mr. Greene gave strict directions for me to record only the prisoner's account today and none other. I mean no offense, but he warned me that you clergy-men tend to be long-winded. Mr. Greene can only print a very short booklet."

On the following Sunday, Matthew read parts of my statement after his sermon. A few of his followers rose from their pews and walked out of the assembly, he said, but most of them had stayed.

Later that evening, as he recreated the scene for my benefit, like an actor might do on a stage, I thought how his listeners were no doubt pleased by his performance. Perhaps they were thinking that their young minister had backbone after all, even if he'd been deceived by a murderess who mocked every virtue that they professed to hold dear.

Matthew had added just a few embellishments to my statement, including a warning to any impetuous youth who might follow my example and "fall into the snares of Satan." And, in a phrase that particularly pleased him, he'd spoken of the "cruel love" of parents and masters who overlook their children's or servants' sins.

I was curious about one thing he hadn't mentioned, however.

"From your high pulpit, could you clearly see all the faces in the assembly? Did you recognize my master, Bryan Palmes?"

Matthew confirmed that he'd seen Bryan sitting alongside his wife who was great with child.

"In all our time together, Matthew, you've never asked me to name the father of my child. Why is that?"

"You did not need to name him. I recognize a man's cruel love when I see it."

"And how is that possible?"

"It's like a reflection in a looking glass. Because I have so much weaknesses in myself, I can see weakness in another man, just by looking in his eyes."

"So, weakness is truly one of your strengths," I said with a slight smile. He managed a smile too before he responded.

"See? You've taken everything I'd known for certain in this world and turned it upside down. You're not a bramble but a rose. Like the thorn of that beautiful flower, you prick at my conscience until I can see the whole truth."

He took my hands and brought them to his lips.

"How I love you, Mercy Bramble.

❧

November arrived with gusty northeast winds from the Atlantic. The jail's roof was leaking now; on some nights the cold rain soaked my bed of rags. I was glad that Joanna Graves had sent me a woolen shawl that she'd woven and also a full sheepskin to keep me warm.

Little if any outside news reached me now, but I knew that my last day was drawing near. Every morning Faith would fix her gaze upon me and pose a question that I would hear again and again in my final weeks.

"Are you ready, Mercy?"

Every evening, townspeople would gather outside my cell door and bang their fists on it. I couldn't see their faces, nor did I know their voices. They would shout, "I'm praying for your damnation, Mercy!" or "Are you ready?" or "Don't you have anything to say to us?"

"I will say it to God now," became my repeated reply. "I'm done speaking to men," but it seldom satisfied those invisible strangers beyond my door.

On the seventh of November, a well-worn envelope appeared on my cell floor, just a few inches inside the door. In all likelihood, a messenger had picked it up at the Fox and Grapes; such missives were left on a tavern table until someone who knew the recipient offered to deliver it. Perhaps a night watchman had pushed the letter beneath my door.

The envelope was addressed "To Mercy Bramble, New London," in a childish, rounded, handwriting.

I lifted the sealing wax, unfolded the letter, and read silently:

Dear Mercy Girl,

Both boys are doing lessons and saying their prayers. We always pray for you. Coffey works hard all day and says we can buy a few acres soon. You were a good friend and not a bad woman as some said. My mother's blood was in your child and in your child's father.

Love bears all things, believes all things, hopes all things, endures all things. I tell you that was true even if I had not read it in the Bible.

I will never forget you,

Your sister, Cate

I read her letter three times, giving thanks that I'd had such a fine friend in this world.

Later that same day, Sheriff Christophers lurched into my cell. Without even a greeting, he told me bluntly, "The twenty-first of the month is the day they chose for your hanging. There's nothing you can do now but pass the time and pray it passes quickly."

"What choice do I have, Sheriff?"

"None that I know, but mind your tongue. It's an abomination you've brought to us, calling for a punishment the likes of which no one has ever seen before in this town."

"What do you mean, Sheriff? Others have been hung for their crimes here. I saw such an awful hanging when I was a child."

"Oh, but there's never been a *white* woman taken to the gallows! Now we'll see if a fair-skinned one dies quicker or slower than the dark-skinned do."

He scratched his head as though puzzled.

"Of course, no one can tell how many women may follow you in these sinful times. I'll be a busy man in my old age."

❧

It snowed on the fifteenth of November, just enough to dust the roads and rooftops. Matthew arrived with snow on his great coat, a garment that I recognized as my own mother's workmanship. How strange it was that he wore a coat of her making. Yes, he recalled, he'd hired a woman three years ago to make it for him, and yes, her name might have been Mary or Molly. The coat was the same color as storm clouds that had brought snow that day.

Gently, I tried to brush away the fine snow that clung to the dark wool like a constellation of little stars on his shoulder, but it melted at my touch.

As always, Matthew had brought his Bible. We'd planned to select a passage for him to read on my execution day, but I told him that I'd already chosen one: the sixteenth Psalm.

"But the Psalms are joyful," he protested, "and how could you be joyful on the day of your death?"

"I'll be seeing the Lord, Matthew, just as you promised. Besides, I want everyone to see what a great teacher you've been to me." Eagerly, I began to recite.

"I have set the Lord always before me;
because He is at my right hand, I shall not be moved.
Therefore my heart is glad, and my glory rejoices;
my flesh also shall rest in hope…"

Suddenly Matthew set down his Bible, and with a look of reverence, unwrapped my shawl. Kissing the tops of my breasts where they met my gown, then my neck, and finally my lips, he stopped the psalm in mid-verse.

For a moment, I feared that the Lord might strike us down, just as He'd killed the man with the Awful Thunderclap. When

I broke away from Matthew's embrace, he slipped to his knees on the floor.

Tears rose in his eyes, yet they didn't seem unnatural or unmanly to me anymore; they were pure as rain. Placing his right hand on his heart, he appeared to try to slow its racing—or to gather his courage.

"With God as my witness, I'm asking you to be my wife, Mercy."

Maybe, after all these months, Matthew Graves had finally lost his reason, yet his words were the most beautiful that I'd ever heard spoken.

"But that isn't possible!" I cried. "And even if it were, we have only six days left on this earth together, not even enough time to publish our intent."

He seized my hands.

"Am I not a man of God? Surely the Lord is the only one who needs to hear our secret vows. Take me as your husband, in your heart, and I'll never seek another as long as I live."

"But there's no church, no witness…"

"Our two souls will build that church around us."

He waited for my answer.

Through my tears, I looked into Matthew's eyes and no longer saw the lost soul who'd entered my cell nearly eighteen long months before. Instead, I saw my Charming Billy, the joy of my life. He was my protector, but also my captive, bound to me forever as Coffey was to Cate and she to him.

"Of course, I'll take you as my husband, Matthew, for now and for all eternity!"

That night, through the gap in the wall, we stood arm in arm and watched a full moon rise over the river. It cast a shining net of silver across the water.

❧

Matthew had advised that fasting would bring me spiritual solace, so I'd stopped eating any food and only drank tea twice a day. At first, sharp hunger pains lanced my belly and kept me from sleeping, but after two more days, I had no desire for food at all.

The Lord's Prayer repeated in my head a hundred times a day. Late one night, instead of reciting, "In the name of the Father, and of the Son, and of the Holy Spirit," I invented words of my own: "In the name of my master Bryan Palmes, and of his stepson Nat Way, and of the holy Reverend Graves, I will burn in hell for their sins forever. Amen."

Then I had to pray for forgiveness for speaking such blasphemy.

I had no way to mark the hours but knew when Matthew was seated beside me. One night, while I lay sleepless, I heard a baby crying. Frantically, I searched the darkness with my hands before realizing that there was no child in my cell.

And always, in the late evening, I'd hear a violent thumping at my door, as men stopped to mock me on their way home from the tavern, calling me a whore and other names. I feared that the mob would batter down the door and murder me for sport, just as I'd once seen dogs tear apart a she-wolf. On one occasion, hunger deceived me into thinking that I was on the outside of the door, shouting abuses at myself inside.

But soon I felt no more hunger; I'd begun to starve to death.

Faith told a physician that I might die before my execution, only two days away, but he didn't come inside to see me. Though Matthew had first advised me to fast for my spiritual benefit, he now implored me to take some sustenance. He even brought me foods from his sister's kitchen.

"You're my wife now, at least in my heart, and I love you like Abraham loved his wife. I beg you to eat."

But I just pushed any food aside, sickened by the sight of it. That night I saw an angel, all clothed in white.

Neither man nor woman, it stood at the end of a long, winding tunnel, one that stretched beyond the jail itself. I wondered why I hadn't noticed this passageway before. The figure radiated such dazzling light that it annihilated my prison cell walls. When I shut my eyes to stop the pain from its blinding glare, the vision still remained, clear and bright as the burning tree of my childhood.

Without a sound, the angel reached out its hand to me. Although nothing solid touched me, I felt it seize my body from an unseen place, as though my heart had an invisible harness. Perhaps it was my soul that the angel pulled on so mightily.

As we entered the tunnel of blazing light, a familiar figure turned to look at me: I caught a glimpse of Zeno's pale, heart-shaped face and saw a faint smile on her lips.

Then the tunnel of light collapsed into itself, like water rushing down a hole. The apparition vanished as suddenly as it had formed.

What was the meaning of this vision?

For all the glory it had shown me, I knew that I didn't want to die as another victim, like Zeno, my baby girl, or even Indian Kate had done. That's when I realized the many things I *did* want: to see bright waves again as they met the shore; to feel Matthew Graves' arms around me; and to hear a child's laughter, my own precious child's.

I wanted to live on *this* side of the tunnel, not beyond it.

For the first time since I was imprisoned, I began seeking a way out. I frantically ran my hands under the door. I pried at any loose boards until my fingernails bled. I swore fouler oaths than the thieves of the Spanish treasure had done. And I cursed myself for not escaping when Coffey had offered to carry me away in his wagon one night. I could have stolen away to a new life on a quiet farm near Cate and Coffey's settlement.

But after a few hours of this panic, I finally fell into a state of half-sleep.

When I awoke, I felt someone slowly stroking my hair the way my mother had years ago when I was very ill. At first, I feared that it might be the angel, returned to claim me this time, but it was only a mortal man lying next to me. Faith had taken pity on Matthew and let him into my cell just before daybreak.

In my mind I heard a phrase from the Song of Solomon: "This is my beloved, this is my friend..."

When the morning of November twenty-first dawned, I woke up alone. I prayed in silence, knowing that it was my last chance to make peace with God. There was no escape, no turning back.

On the farm, November had always been "the killing time," the month when we slaughtered animals for winter. I remembered how I'd boil water in a huge cast-iron kettle, then roll my sleeves and get down to work. Cate would kill the first pig with a knife through its heart, then boil and scrub to remove its bristles before we'd start butchering.

It was work, that's all that it ever was, another chore. I had no time to pity any creature or think about its pain as the knife found its heart. Now here I was, penned up and waiting for someone to slaughter me.

Faith was the first to arrive.

"I've come to convince you to eat. You'll have to walk and ride a way, and you don't want to faint in the crowd."

Then to my surprise, she took my chin in her hand and spoke

to me as gently as an older sister might. "That body the Lord gave you needs food, and it's not right to starve yourself, even on your last day."

She offered a bowl of bread crusts soaked in beer, and I took it. Somehow, I lifted a spoon to my lips and swallowed without choking, then raised the bowl and sipped the bitter beer.

When I'd finished, she took something from her apron pocket, but held it back a moment.

"Are your hands clean?" she asked, just like a fretful mother.

After I'd extending my palms for her inspection, she handed me a small pamphlet, printed on crisp, clean paper.

"That printer Mr. Greene left it for my husband this morning."

Immediately I saw my name in bold type and the long title that the scribe had invented a few weeks before: An Extraordinary Account of Several Occurrences and Remarks Concerning a Certain Mercy Bramble.

The book smelled of fresh ink—I brought it to my nose and inhaled deeply. The odor was sharp, even acrid; it seemed to come from another world, one with different ideas and, perhaps, the freedom to express them.

"They'll be selling copies today at the gallows, and I thought you might like to read it first. After all, it's all about you," Faith said quietly. I heard a touch of respect in her voice.

"I suppose it gives an account of the hanging," I mused, "even though it hasn't happened yet."

"Oh yes. That's what people will want to read."

When she left me, I read every word from first page to last, even all the sermons. Then I closed the cover, closed my eyes, and tossed the pamphlet onto my pallet.

A few hours later, they all came to get me: the sheriff, the magistrates, and two other men appointed to assist the proceedings. Reverend Graves—my beloved Matthew—stood without speaking, and for once he was straight-backed like a soldier, ready to march into battle.

Hastily, the sheriff showed me my death warrant before putting it back inside his vest. He'd tied a noose already and slipped the rope loosely over my hair, displacing my linen cap. Clumsily, he tried to replace it, but I set it aside. I would go to the gallows bareheaded, I'd decided, my fair locks tumbling down my back in waves.

No one tried to bind my hands.

For a few moments I held the rope—as if to admire the workmanship—then let it hang at my side. The crowd would expect to see it; as part of the spectacle, it served as a warning to all would-be sinners. I could tell that the rope was a new one, just bought at a chandlery. Like newly mown fields or fresh cut timber, the smell of woven hemp was pleasing to me, but I'd have no use for my senses anymore.

I was dressed in the same gray, woolen gown that I'd worn since my trial weeks before; beneath it was my only linen shift, worn so thin in the past year that it had become transparent. I donned my heavy cape and pulled it all around me to hide my body from view.

Tucked inside the bodice of my shift, beneath tightly drawn ribbons at my breasts, I carried Cate's letter of forgiveness. The night before, I'd taken all my other treasures—my black splinter from the lightning tree, my shell from the White Beach, and my wolf claw—and hidden them below a loose brick in the floor.

My Bible I'd returned to Matthew.

"Do you not wish me to place it in your hands when you lie in your coffin?" he'd asked me gently. I told him to give it to another needy soul, then made a more important request.

"It would please me if you buried me with one of your quill pens in my right hand and a sheet of your best parchment paper in my left. It was my greatest earthly desire to learn to write, Matthew, but perhaps I will learn in the hereafter."

With a somber nod, he promised to comply with my wishes.

A wagon was waiting on the town green, they told me; I must walk there through Broad Alley with Sheriff Christophers at my side. The streets were strangely empty in mid-day. As if to answer my unvoiced question, the sheriff informed me, "Most people have headed up to the gallows already, to the crossroads above Joseph Bolles's farm. They want to find a good place to watch."

"How many are there?" I heard myself ask weakly.

"Dozens, no, maybe hundreds by now."

Several farmers and their families had traveled more than twenty miles to see justice served, he told me. They'd made a camp in a grove of hemlocks last night.

"You could see their campfires from here," he said excitedly. "And someone played a few ripping tunes on a fiddle. Heard there was a juggler too. Or was it a magician?"

At noon, a steady, cold rain started falling; it would make the road muddy and slow our progress. I didn't lower my head as I stepped outside the jail, nor did anyone try to shelter me. Two seagulls cried overhead, dipped their wings as if in farewell, and headed towards the Sound.

When a wagon came into view, I was astonished to recognize one that belonged to Bryan Palmes. Seeing his two finest black mares in the harness caused me more of a shock than the plain, pinewood coffin—my eternity box—across the cart's floor.

"Mr. Palmes paid for the coffin, you should know," said the sheriff as he helped me into the wagon. I accepted his hand and took a seat, relieved that I wouldn't have to stand shackled to a rail as some prisoners were forced to do. No one could stand upright when riding on such a stony road.

Matthew climbed up right beside me. I looked around for my master but didn't see him anywhere in the gathering crowds.

A magistrate picked up the reins, and the horses leaned into their harness. The sheriff mounted a horse to ride alongside.

"Don't be afraid," whispered Matthew, perhaps ashamed that he was only trying to comfort himself.

At that moment I made a decision. I couldn't shoot an arrow through the meetinghouse steeple, like the Indian sachem had done, but I could hold my head high. Mercy Bramble would show no fear that day.

Matthew told me that the rain clinging to my hair and body gave an illusion of unearthly light.

"I shall write of this day," he promised. "Those who come after us will know what barbarism you suffered here."

I shook my head. "No, my story has already been written and printed by Mr. Greene. Not a single word can be changed."

Then I stared straight ahead past the driver.

Our wagon began to ascend a steep hill on the town's northern boundary. At its summit, I turned around to look to the distant horizon. From my cell, I'd only been able to see one small section of the river. Now, at last, I could see where it was flowing, out far past the White Beach to the sea.

In the last half a mile, we hadn't seen a soul except for old Benja Fargo. Nodding to me as if this were an ordinary day, he hurried on toward the burial ground with a shovel on his shoulder. Perhaps I would lie close to my infant daughter or to my fellow servants, Hannah and Zeno.

I remembered coming to Gallows Road when I was small and seeing the unfortunate slave's execution. In all these years I'd never traveled any farther from town than this. It still would have seemed a desolate wilderness had it not been for the crowds.

A mob was gathering up ahead, waiting to get a look at me.

They were of all ages, all races—white, Indian, and slave. The surrounding hills were heavy with mankind, but a festive spirit had set the air humming. Merry greetings rang out between travelers in the chill air. Many who'd camped under the hemlocks had tethered their mounts from lower branches, and it looked like a fair for trading horses.

From the corner of my eye, I caught a glimpse of something that I would have marveled at on any other day: the magnificent stallion, dyed blue with Spanish indigo. Even a blue horse did not distract anyone from what they'd come to see: the figure of Mercy Bramble.

The crowd was already restless. It was almost three o'clock, and they'd been waiting many long hours when the rain grew heavier. When the shouting and pushing started, there was no way to control it. Six times our driver was forced to bring the horses to a stop. Riding alongside, Sheriff Christophers swung a short whip to clear the road, but no one paid any attention to him.

A group of men began pounding the wagon sides, howling insults at me. Soon their target shifted to Reverend Graves, however. Matthew made the mistake of standing up and shouting, "Let he who is without sin cast the first stone!"

When several men grabbed the sideboards and shoved them even harder, he tumbled clumsily to the wagon's floor. The horses reared in panic, their massive bodies colliding in their harness.

In the midst of this chaos, I began looking for the gallows. Faith had told me that a wooden structure would be erected at the road's highest point so all could look up and see my execution clearly. But our wagon suddenly stopped in the middle of the road where several hundred people had gathered. Still, I saw nothing resembling any gallows that I'd pictured.

Here slaves stood shoulder-to-shoulder with well-to-do merchants. A few wealthy townsmen had brought their wives by carriage to give them a closer look. I found myself wondering if the women regretted having to wear their capes in the chill, preventing them from showing off their extravagant gowns. Tucked into their wraps or clutched in their white kid gloves, they all had copies of Timothy Greene's book.

I recognized the printer's apprentice who was selling a stack of pamphlets.

A few Indians in buckskin trousers stood near groups of drunken soldiers, sailors, and their whores. Children ran everywhere, elated by a holiday from their lessons and farm chores.

Try as I might, I couldn't find Bryan Palmes anywhere.

"Here's the spot!" cried the sheriff to our driver. A gigantic oak spread its long branches before us as if to block our passage. I finally realized that there were no gallows, only a hanging tree.

The sheriff was pointing to a large branch that grew perfectly horizontal to the road in one portion, then turned straight upwards. The smooth limb bulged like a blacksmith's upper arm.

Once again, Matthew leapt to his feet and, shouting over the riot, tried to read from my last statement.

"As a servant of God, I'm commanded to read you this woman's last mortal testimony! It is her final prayer and admonition to fellow sinners."

This time, three men grabbed his legs and pulled him roughly to the ground.

"I shall not be moved!" Matthew shouted. He shielded himself from several kicks aimed at his head. I tried to call out to him but found that I had no voice.

"You can carry your speech to hell, Reverend! That's where this murdering bitch is going today."

"Shut your lying bone-box or we'll string you up too, Reverend!"

Roars of laughter erupted.

The miller waved a copy of Timothy Greene's book in Matthew's face.

"We already bought the bloody book, Reverend, so we don't need no more of your jabbering today!"

Then, as if they'd heard a signal, two men dragged my coffin across the wagon boards with a loud scraping noise. It made a platform a foot higher than the sides of the cart.

"Tie her up! Hang her up!" a woman screamed.

A group of children joined hands and chanted, "Kill her! Hang her up!"

To my astonishment, Matthew stood up yet again. Blood now streaked his shirt.

"The condemned woman has chosen a Psalm for today…"

But this time a burly man seized him from behind, dragging him farther away from the wagon. I feared that I heard bone breaking as the huge man crushed his ribs.

Right behind the struggling men, a woman shouted at Matthew's attacker, "Leave him be, Elisha!"

In that churning sea of bodies under me, I recognized the person I'd loved and longed for my entire life: my mother. Why had she bothered to come after so callously betraying me, first with the Children or God and then again at my trial?

"Oh Mercy, please forgive me," she gasped. I never should have forsaken you, my only child."

I found my voice only seconds before the cart lurched forward and left her behind.

"Mother, I forgive you. You gave me life, and I can ask for nothing greater."

The last thing I heard from her was an anguished question she directed to the entire crowd: "Who would believe that men could be so cruel to a woman?"

Now I heard someone else shouting above the din.

"Bramble! Bramble! Look over here!"

Amid so many taunts, it was almost a blessing to hear my real name, but it gave me no comfort when I realized that it came from Nat Way. Hadn't he tormented me enough? Astride a skittish horse that stepped sideways through the crowd, Nat had brought along his hunting gun, which swung carelessly from his shoulder.

But something else seized my attention.

One of the magistrates was throwing the rope up over a branch. He shouted, "Step up on your coffin, prisoner!"

I did as he told me, removing my shoes and stockings before planting my feet on the coffin's wet lid. The magistrate tied a knot to secure the rope; another man tested to see that it was fast. When he signaled that it was ready, a loud cheer went up.

Then, at once strangely obedient, the multitude cleared the way, and two men who'd been holding fast to the horses' halters stepped away in silent compliance. The restless mares shook their heads as if to say, "Let's get on with it."

The wagon, which had been rocking so violently that I could barely keep my footing, suddenly grew still.

Looking over the crowd I remembered Indian Kate, the grandmother of my baby, and what she'd told her little daughter Cate at the gallows. I raised both hands before me.

"Remember this: these two palms have never sinned, but two others have. *Bryan Palmes* was the father of my baby, and it was his wife, *Elizabeth Palmes*, who murdered her."

The crowd's roar almost drowned my voice, but some of you had understood. Then I pressed my hands together and spoke the words I'd chosen to be my last:

"Lord Jesus, receive my spirit."

There was a murmur of approval—the first that I'd ever received from any of you—but no one dared to say "Amen."

I quickly unfastened my heavy cape and let it fall into the wagon bed. It landed there, brown and sodden, like a crumpled milkweed pod. Would I just blow away in pieces now, like the silky insides of that lovely weed?

Then, as the crowd still rumbled in mass confusion, I peeled away my wet grey gown and let that drop as well.

The thin white shift underneath was one I'd worn night and day for almost two years; it covered me no better than strands of a spider's web. The rain soaked its remaining threads, rendering them completely transparent.

Now every one of you could see my swollen breasts and every curve of my flesh as rain streamed down my hair and body. Naked in all of your eyes, I stood there boldly, in the form that God had given me, awaiting the end.

Shocked silence ruled the mob but only for a heartbeat.

Then a woman released a scream—a scream louder than I believed any mortal could produce. Wild and barely human, it was like the cry of a she-wolf I'd once seen dogs tearing apart.

But this cry came from my mother.

"Stop! Stop the hanging! In the name of God stop the hanging!"

"Who dares to invoke the Lord's name in this manner?" Reverend Jewett thundered.

"There is a child!" came the scream again. "She is with child!"

Clawing her way forward, my mother was pointing frantically to my enlarged belly.

Soon *all* of the women were screaming. A chorus of men followed, shouting at a lower pitch but repeating the same demand as the women.

"Cut her down! Cut her down!"

After an eternity—no doubt it would have been only a blink in time had my feet been on solid ground, not my shaking coffin—I heard a voice above the rest. It was the same man who had betrayed me to the magistrates. The man who had called me a weed, a bramble, during my trial. And the one who had told me that he would rather cut my throat than baptize me.

Reverend Jewett, my fearful foe who had denied me eternal life and condemned me to hell for my sins, was shouting even louder than my mother. His bellowed command echoed from the stone ledges around us.

"Cut her down! Save her! We'll be murderers if we kill the child in her womb! God will punish all of us for this sin!"

Matthew, who'd been down on his knees weeping in front of everyone, sprang to his feet again like a warrior.

"You heard him! Cut her down or be damned to hell all of you!"

But it was too late. Sheriff Christophers had already raised his whip, determined to fulfill his duties as put forth in my official death warrant: to hang me by the neck between heaven and earth until dead.

"Stop, man! Stop the execution!" cried Matthew.

"What's the use? She can plead her belly now, but she'll have to stand trial for her crimes again as soon as the child is born," ranted the sheriff.

He brandished the whip over his head, ready to bring it down on the horses' flanks.

In the next instant, heaven itself exploded above me.

Although I didn't know it at that moment, it was a shot from a rifle. Nat Way had fired at the rope over my head and just missed severing it. His aim wasn't perfect—but his timing was.

With a cry of mad panic, Bryan's two mares bolted forward with the wagon, exactly as it had been planned for my hanging. Sparks flew as their iron horseshoes struck stones. Yet it wasn't their brute energy that seared the air around me like a lightning strike.

It was a far stronger power: my burning will to live.

Though some might have seen the hand of God at work that day, it was my own hands that pulled the giant noose straight up over my rain-soaked hair. Falling through billowing white smoke from Nat's shot, I tumbled off the back of the wagon and dropped onto the bodies of several spectators.

So many people rushed to my aid that the sheriff had to threaten them all with a fine if they didn't back away.

In spite of his injuries, Matthew was soon at my side. He grabbed my discarded cape, and with more loving care than shame, quickly covered my exposed breasts and belly. Before helping me back in the wagon, he even snatched up my copy of Cate's letter that had fallen into the mud.

Now the Reverend Jewett was shouting again.

"Go home, all of you, and think on your sins! Pray for mercy so no greater punishment will be levied upon this wretched town!" After pausing to compose his thoughts, he hurled a final command at the bystanders.

"Tell no one of what shameful actions came to pass this day, lest history record us all as murderers of infants. Innocent, unborn infants!"

"We'd be no better than criminals if we killed an innocent babe," a merchant's wife screamed in a magistrate's ear.

"That's English law, and we are all Englishmen, not savages," he shouted back at her.

As the crowd began to disperse, I saw that Nat was among the last to go. He had an air of defeat about him; even his horse had dropped his head low.

The rain was reduced to a gentle shower, but the storm hadn't passed. A strong gust of wind from the river lifted a dozen unsold copies of An Extraordinary Account of Several Occurrences and Remarks Concerning a Certain Mercy Bramble. I saw a second gust blow them in a devilish spiral before scattering them along the roadside.

Like schoolboys trying pick up their lost lessons, Timothy Greene and his apprentice were scrambling after them, but they couldn't grab all of their books. Many people had already stuffed them in their pockets without paying a penny for them. No doubt they would carry the booklets home and put them with their Bibles and important papers, the ones that they would hand down to the next generation.

Directed by God's hand, Nature herself hadn't finished her work that day. After the wagon had rolled back down the muddy slope, a bolt of lightning struck the hanging tree and set it aflame.

That was the last thing I saw, because that is when I finally fainted.

CHAPTER X
LIFE AFTER MY DEATH

*"Either write something worth reading or
do something worth writing."*

—BENJAMIN FRANKLIN

THEY TOLD ME later that I'd lain unconscious for two full days. When I awoke, I found myself in a small bedchamber no bigger than a closet. Joanna and Matthew Graves were bending over me, having kept me from harm under their roof.

I gave birth to a son a month later. He was a beautiful child with fair hair and blue eyes like his father's. When the midwife put my baby in my arms, I first felt his breath with my fingertips and then his heartbeat.

"You've done well," the midwife told me, beaming with pride as if she'd borne him herself. For a moment I felt sorry that my own mother hadn't been present, but then I swore that I'd never ask God for any greater joy in my life.

No one came to call on me at the Graves's, not even my mother. Neither of the Palmeses would have dared to be seen in town.

"Those two are outcasts now, shunned by all good men and women," Matthew had told me, with more pity than malice in his tone.

"Will they ever be punished or put on trial?" I asked.

"I cannot say. But no one will ever speak to them, nor buy any livestock or services from Master Palmes. Even the peddler Hugo Moreaux said he will steer his cart far around their farm, because it's cursed ground now."

As much as I hated to do so, I asked Matthew if he'd heard from Sheriff Christophers. I liked to think that Faith played a part in her husband's failure to perform his duties in a timely manner after my execution day.

But Matthew didn't want to take any chances; he feared that the sheriff might try to detain me again at the earliest opportunity. The night after I delivered, Matthew hired a wagon driver who brought the three of us to Lyme under cover of darkness. We were packed in with a load of potatoes, just as Coffey had once offered to carry me away.

A few days later, we crossed the river by rope ferry and took our marriage vows in Saybrook. After the same minister had christened our son—we named him John Bramble Graves—we headed west, following the coastline to New York.

From the doorstep of our new home, I could see many ships in the East River. The dwelling was a farmhouse that the Dutch had built years before on the upper end of Manhattan Island. Soon two pretty brown cows grazed in our small pasture, and I liked to think that they enjoyed the tranquil view as much as I did. The well was dug so deep I never had to worry that it would run dry as the Palmes' well had done years ago.

One night, when our baby was four months old and slept more hours without my nursing him, I woke to find myself alone in the bed that I usually shared with Matthew. Across the room,

I saw a figure hunched in darkness; it was my husband, peering into the cradle where his new son slept.

I lit a candle, and drawing near him, saw that Matthew was crying. His fist was pressed against his mouth so as not to make any sound and wake me or little John.

My heart sank, for I'd seen him weep that way after our first night together, when he was so overwhelmed with guilt and shame. I feared that he now saw our son as a reminder of our transgressions.

"Dear God, what is wrong, Matt?"

At last, he answered, although he was barely able to speak.

"I love him so much, yet he sprang from our sin." He caught his breath. "But our sin was *our salvation*."

I reached for his hand.

"If I was so wrong about that, what else could I be mistaken about?" he asked.

I led him back to bed but couldn't forget our unfinished conversation by the cradle. Our son was not here because of an accident; I'd known what I was doing when he was conceived, and I knew the truth now.

After a year, Matthew sent for his sister Joanna, and she came by coastal schooner to join our household. She brought all the news from New London. Pompey had run away one night, finally seizing the freedom he'd once been promised; no one ever captured him.

The Hawk had died in childbirth; some say that no midwife would go to the farm to assist her. I would wish that suffering on no one, not even someone who had wronged me in such a monstrous way. Bryan Palmes buried her alongside his first wife on the hill and went on living in abject poverty—alone.

Joanna never spoke ill of anyone, but she couldn't resist whispering as though telling a ghost story, "People talk about the

Curse of Bryan Palmes. They say his entire property is cursed. Chickens will not lay eggs there. Crops just sicken and die. The apple trees will not bear fruit, and they drip blood if someone cuts them!"

I didn't press Joanna any further, not wishing to discuss the affairs of my former master anymore.

Joanna worked hard in our home, but she said that work was a joy for her if it helped her loved ones. She wove fine cloth and made simple foods into a feast; we always had some left to share with the poor as well. As time passed, she became both my cherished companion and the sister I'd always wanted.

As for my own mother, I often thought how I wished to bring her to live with us should she be widowed, but she was elderly, and God may have had other plans.

Although Matthew still preached for the next five years, he spent more time sitting in coffeehouses—to discuss ideas and politics—than he did standing at the pulpit. Eventually he declared himself a freethinker and, after a long struggle with his conscience, parted ways with the clergy. Still, Matthew and I both worshipped the Lord our God, sometimes through the church, but just as often through helping others who were hungry or without a home.

I wasn't surprised when my husband found his true calling as a tutor of young children. Accustomed to schoolmasters who would beat the backs of their hands with a stick or apply a whip, his students responded to his kind manners and excelled at their studies. Matthew came to believe that all men and women should be free, and all children should be educated, including those of African slaves.

❧

Extraordinary events—marked by bloodshed and sacrifice—unfolded all around us in those years. Mr. Thomas Paine wrote so eloquently of the "times that try men's souls," but I saw how they tested women's souls as well. The struggle was so immense that it overshadowed the trials and suffering of my youth.

My husband was in the streets in New York when General Washington ordered the declaration of our independence to be read to the crowds: *We hold these truths to be self-evident, that all men are created equal, that they are endowed by their Creator with certain unalienable Rights, that among these are Life, Liberty and the pursuit of Happiness.*

John and his two brothers all fought in the war for independence. Our peaceful pastures became battlegrounds, and the East River a place of floating death below decks of the terrible prison ships anchored there. We gladly gave up our beds so that any sick or wounded could have sanctuary under our roof. Too often, ours was the last home that those boys knew, being called to the next life too soon.

One of our own was taken away also—my brave, sweet, charming Billy. The joy of my life was only sixteen when gave his life in battle at Saratoga, fighting under General Benedict Arnold. Three years later we all learned how Arnold, then turned a traitor, gave orders to burn New London to the ground. He watched the flames while sitting astride his horse in the burial ground on the hill, not far from my old prison.

I was told that Nat Way fought in a battle to hold Fort Griswold across the river from New London—he lost a leg to a cannonball. He spent his remaining years as a cripple, forever watching ships enter and depart from the harbor. He talked about places he had never been and a pretty girl named Bramble whom he'd almost married.

After New London's great fire, my old prison was probably

just a patch of ashes under a new cobblestone street. And yet, I believed that my treasures—a splinter from the lightning tree, a shell from the White Beach, and a wolf claw—were still buried safe beneath the earth.

Perhaps one of you would find these things one day.

Whenever the winds blew from the east, smelling of salt-water and bringing sea gulls that may had circled above New London's deep harbor, I couldn't help but think of my old home. I promised myself that someday I'd return to where my firstborn lay sleeping for eternity above the river. It would be a sad journey, but it would give me such peace; perhaps I could buy her a real gravestone at last.

I also longed to know that Cate and Coffey were alive and well. Just like my old friends had told me years ago, many Indian people, the last of their tribes, had gone to live among the Oneida Indians. They called their settlement of Christians, Brothertown. Although I sent several letters with travelers bound for northern New York, even old Hugo Moreaux, I never received any word from Cate and Coffey. Still, I always remained hopeful and did not stop trying. Perhaps one of my children or grandchildren will one day meet their children and carry on our friendship.

My new life as Mercy Graves was a good one, but I never told my children how it had all almost ended before it began or how I'd married their father in my heart before we'd said our legal vows.

No one was a better teacher than my Matthew, and no one more eager to learn than I was. He taught me how to write at last, and aside from our children, it was his greatest gift to me. Although I never would have boasted to anyone, my script was even finer than that of Bryan Palmes. Matthew said it had both elegance and *authority*.

Yet it is no use learning to write unless a person has something to say. At first, I described many scenes that I'd witnessed during the war; then I began writing about what I thought and what I believed. Finally, I started a journal in a little leather book, recording everything that happened before and after my so-called death.

If you are reading these words at some time in the future, you must be holding that same book or a faithful copy. You may have read all about a girl named Mercy Bramble: how fortunate she was to find a friend in Cate and to witness the love between Cate and Coffey. You may have been surprised that a brute of a young man with a hunting gun and a single shot could be a hero for an instant, for reasons only his Maker could understand. And you may have learned how Mercy found her true partner in life: a man who was neither handsome nor very courageous, but who loved her so deeply.

After all, sometimes salvation is right there in front of us, within our grasp. We have only to reach for it to save ourselves.

When I was a young woman, I believed that a person could find all the answers by studying a book, receiving a sacrament, or sitting in long services week after week. It took me many years to realize that I had to follow my own path, both inside and outside of a church, to find true faith. Words cannot express this, but I always felt closest to God when listening to silence under the stars at night or watching waves on the shore. I sensed an all-powerful hand behind the lightning bolt as well.

Every year, on the twenty-first of November, the anniversary of my intended death, I would lock myself in my bedchamber and remove a copy of Timothy Greene's pamphlet from the bottom of my linen chest. Once again, I would read the very brief account of my repentance and death. Not all of it was a lie, of course, but nor was it the whole truth.

With each passing year, the edges of those yellowing pages

began crumbling into a fine dust at the bottom of the chest. I would brush that dust into my hand, then send it out of our window for the wind to blow away. Once or twice, I'd made a move to put the remaining pages into our fireplace, but something always stayed my hand, and a familiar voice whispered, "Not yet."

As Matthew has said, not all history is knowable. Not every printed word is truth. I know that certain pathways through the past cannot be found on any map. Some old roads cannot be traced, yet they existed. I know this because I traveled one of them.

The world believed that my life ended on Gallows Road. But that is where my life—and this book—truly began. May all of you who come to read this find the courage to travel your own path and to find your own salvation.

ACKNOWLEDGMENTS

As Maya Angelou wrote, "There is no greater agony than bearing an untold story inside you." I wish to thank all of the people who helped me get past that agony by writing "Gallows Road."

I am most grateful to Ruth Crocker for championing this book and giving it the perfect home with Elm Grove Press.

The staff of the following organizations and libraries provided valuable access to materials and information that helped me to write this book: the Connecticut State Library, History and Genealogy Unit; the New London County Historical Society; the Linda Lear Center for Special Collections and Archives in the Charles E. Shain Library, Connecticut College; and the public libraries of Groton, Ledyard, New London, and Waterford, Connecticut. Libraries are true sanctuaries for a writer such as myself who loves to hear the sound of readers turning pages as I work. I am especially grateful to my friends and fellow authors, Susan B. Kietzman and Michael Sobol for reading drafts of "Gallows Road" and sharing their comments. Ginny Bitting, Maura Casey, Ruth W. Crocker, Bethe Dufresne, Carol McCarthy, and Jane H. Percy, all members of our Mystic Writers group, provided steadfast encouragement on this project and several others. Thank you to Georgiana Goodwin for her inspired cover design.

Above all, I am thankful for my family's support as I wrote—and rewrote—this novel. Steve and Tom, you inspire me every day. Special thanks to my sister, mother, and my late father and grandparents—all of you awakened the storyteller in me.

—Lisa Hall Brownell

AFTERWORD

When I began writing this novel, friends asked, "Is this a *true* story?" The book has a historical setting, and certain key events in the plot did, in fact, occur in New London, Connecticut during the early 1750s. Others, however, were products of my imagination.

My story was inspired by a young servant named Sarah Bramble who was imprisoned, put on trial twice, and condemned to death for a crime that she swore she didn't commit. Her newborn's mysterious death put the young woman's life in the hands of a jury while three ministers — and a group called the Children of God — all fought to save her soul.

As a New London native, I'd been haunted by this tale since I was a teenager, but I'm a storyteller, not a historian. I wanted freedom to explore circumstances and emotions that had gone unrecorded when these events took place; it was a time so unlike our era of constant sharing via social media. With notable exceptions, few people kept journals, and many women, like my protagonist, were not taught to read or write. New London did not even have a newspaper until 1758. Ultimately, can any of us truly know what happened one night, hundreds of years ago, in a remote farmhouse?

We do know that on November 21, 1753, Sarah Bramble was executed in New London, Connecticut, as thousands watched. Her grave was unmarked. It's also true that more than two hundred and fifty years later, I sat in the State Archives, held her death warrant in my hand, and saw the crooked X she used to sign her name. That's when I decided to write a story that would give her a voice. The rest, as they say, is history.

ABOUT THE AUTHOR

Lisa Hall Brownell, a fiction writer and editor, believes that stories have the power to connect one person to another, and past to present. A former journalist, media director for Mystic Seaport Museum, and director of publications for Connecticut College, Brownell edited and wrote for an award-winning magazine with 30,000 readers.

She graduated from Brown University, and earned an M.A. in English with a concentration in creative writing from San Francisco State University. Now a freelance writer, she lives in southeastern Connecticut. She has written two novels, screenplays, and short stories. A member of the Mystic Writers, she helped to launch a website and blog for the group. *https://mysticwriters.org*

CPSIA information can be obtained
at www.ICGtesting.com
Printed in the USA
LVHW091127030322
712402LV00005B/62